INTERNAL SECURITY

By

DAVID DARRACOTT

[signature: David Darracott]

LIGHTNING
ROD
BOOKS

Atlanta, Georgia

[handwritten: Decatur Book Festival 2015]

Lightning Rod Books
Atlanta, Georgia
Second Edition
First Electronic edition March 1, 2012
First Edition June 2012

ISBN-13:978-1475059007
Library of Congress PCN: 2012909544

Cover Photography by LyG-photo
Artwork, Cover, and Interior Design by Cyrus Wraith Walker
Author Photo by Michael Mollick.

For My Wife, Donna

ACKNOWLEDGMENTS

The author gratefully acknowledges the support of those who helped make this book possible. Several people read early versions of this work and provided invaluable suggestions for its improvement; among them, John Ross, Michael Murrell, Frances Clark, Larry Kahn, Michael Mollick, and of course, Donna. Thanks to everyone for your close attention, encouragement, and help in keeping my story on track, with details as accurate as fiction allows. I would also like to thank the Hambidge Center for the Fellowship that afforded an excellent writing studio and solitude in a quiet retreat where work and creativity reign supreme. Most of all, I want to thank my wife for her unending support and my never forgotten parents who allowed me to pursue a dream.

*He who commits injustice is ever made more wretched
than he who suffers it.*

—Plato

CHAPTER 1

Hector Mendez could hardly believe his good fortune, for on this lucky day he was being paid—well paid—simply to drive a truckload of furniture for a few hours. It was so much easier than picking green beans in Belle Glade, he thought he would ask for more work later, even though the man who hired him seemed to have *amenaza*, a menace, about him.

The truck was loud and the steering wheel vibrated nervously from every seam in the concrete interstate. Almost to his destination now according to the map, he took the next exit off I-95 and went east toward the ocean on Speedway Boulevard, felt the immense weight of the truck behind him as it leaned on the turn like an overloaded bus back home.

He checked his side view mirrors. The black pickup was still behind him, same speed, same distance. Everything the same.

Already the beach traffic was thick and slow, but he did not mind driving the truck into the clogged heart of Daytona Beach. He would get to see the *chicas* wearing their bikinis on the sidewalks outside the big hotels. The American *chicas* in heat, slim and sunburned, with their yellow hair.

Like the man in the pickup who hired him said, it's an easy job. Drive to the Tropical Fiesta Hotel, help unload the furniture, drive the truck back to Jacksonville, and he would be paid double to ensure the truck's return. Double! Two hundred dollars for such easy work. It was his luckiest day yet since he waded across the great river into America.

Yet the day had started out the same as so many others. Up at dawn, dressed and out the door in minutes. Hurrying to the front of the trailer park, he jumped over tire ruts in the muddy driveway near the main road where, beside the Laundromat, the gravel parking lot was already filled with young men. Then the waiting began, the milling about with other migrants in the gray light, sipping coffee from the convenience store, hoping for a *gringo* to drive by who needed workers.

Every day except Sunday it was the same way. Dozens of Mexicans, mostly new arrivals, gathered outside the Laundromat and store, waiting in the parking lot for hours, all wanting the same thing, all hoping for a job to appear. Some days, a few of them got work digging septic tanks or picking up trash, stacking lumber, perhaps working on a roof with a hammer.

Most days, nothing, but today was different.

The pickup had appeared a little after eight, a black Ford with dark tinted windows and big tires. Fortunately, it stopped alongside Hector when no one else was nearby. He had stopped near the road to tie his shoe when the driver's side window buzzed down a few inches, and Hector saw a man inside wearing a cowboy hat and sunglasses. The cowboy had reddish, freckled skin and old scars around his mouth.

Hector looked up and the man spoke first. "*Hola, amigo.*"

"*Hola.*"

"*Habla Ingles?*"

Hector said, "Yes."

"You got a driver's license?"

"Yes," Hector lied. "Here." He patted his hip pocket to make the point. Some of the other young men were already moving toward the truck.

"You want to make some easy money?"

"Yes."

"Then climb in."

Hector jumped into the bed of the pickup and sat down, his back against the cab, happy to beat the others to the job. Since he came up from Belle Glade to stay with his cousin in south Jacksonville, he'd had very little work, had no cash to send home to his mother in Coahuila. His cousin said he could get him a job busing tables in the restaurant where he worked, but before Hector even arrived his cousin had been fired for fighting. So far, all Hector had was a place to sleep, sharing the trailer with eight other men.

Twenty minutes later, the pickup pulled into a self storage center and rolled slowly past the long buildings of aluminum to the back where boats and RV's sat in rows, parked in an area surrounded by a high chain-link fence. The pickup stopped at a truck with huge letters on the side, which Hector could not understand completely because he did not know the word "Haul" but he knew it was a rental truck from the bright orange color of the body. The truck was about ten meters long with double wheels in the rear, built to carry a heavy load.

"Can you drive this truck, amigo?" The man spoke to him through the open sliding glass window at the back of the cab.

"Yes, I can drive."

"Okay, amigo." The voice was slow and calm, the way white men sounded near the border in Texas. Something about the man's authority made Hector wary of him, same as the bosses in the vegetable fields who cheated you at every opportunity, but to Hector's surprise the man passed him fifty dollars, keys to the truck, and a map through the tiny window in the rear of the cab. Hector took them and stood, looked inside the cab, but all he could see was the back of the man's hat.

"Just drive slow and steady to the hotel. It's all marked on the map. Don't stop or pull off the road. The gas tank's full and the back has a heavy duty lock on it, so you couldn't get in there even if you tried. I'll give you the key to open the back when we get there. Got all that?"

"Better if I follow you, then—"

The man's voice cut him off like a blade.

"We're going to do it just the way I said, amigo. I drive right behind you the whole way, make sure you do what you're supposed to. Stay on the route that's marked on the map. Any problem, just turn on the emergency flashers and we'll pull over together. Okay?"

"Okay."

Hector jumped to the ground, looked at the keys in his hand. The driver's window slid down a few inches and the big sunglasses moved closer to the gap.

"One last thing, amigo."

"Yes?"

"Don't let me down."

Hector understood his meaning. Do it right, and I'll give you the rest of your pay, maybe more work. Do it wrong, and there will be trouble. Something about the man's voice suggested trouble, but that was okay by Hector. He would do it right, would not give the man cause for anger, would not have to pull the knife he kept taped to his lower leg underneath his pants. He went to the orange and white truck and unlocked the door, started it with no problem and swung the rig in a big arc out of the storage yard.

Two hours later, Hector took a long bridge over the Intracoastal and found himself in the midst of the beach district. He turned left on A1A in front of a turquoise building with a roofline curved to look like ocean waves; palm trees grew close against the walls. In his mirrors the black pickup was still there, same speed as Hector, everything the same since they left Jacksonville.

He stopped at a red light and glanced at the map spread out on the seat beside him. Next, he would pass the signs for the pier, then take a right on Main. The light turned green, but the traffic barely moved. Everywhere he looked there were people clogging the streets, mainly students in their baggy shorts and caps, wearing sandals and tee shirts. They took their time in the crosswalks, ignoring the signals as if they were kings.

The young men mostly traveled in groups, paused at the bars and looked inside where music blared from the open doorways— the rap the black people made, with its thumping bass sounds and rhyming chants. He wished he could hear a Mariachi band at this moment, but he'd discovered the radio in the truck did not work.

The traffic inched forward and he watched the car ahead when it moved, but when the cars stopped, he turned his eyes back to the sidewalks. Oh, the *senoritas* were too much. Hundreds of them, on break from school. Young and smooth skinned, they wore tiny tops and showed all their bellies and legs, acting as if they didn't care, but oh, the strut they put on when they passed a gang of the young men told the truth. A few words and laughs passed between the groups, then the *muchachos* started to act up, make lewd moves with their bodies.

Hector oozed forward with the traffic and watched people go in and out of the beach shops, the shops with bathing suits and hats, sunglasses and plastic water toys. He wondered if he could make enough money to come back to this place later with his cousin. They could wander the streets, shoot pool and drink beer. Maybe some of the *gringas* would talk to them.

Then he saw it ahead to his right, saw the words Tropical Fiesta on the side of the hotel, then the parking lot entrance on Main appeared and he made a wide turn into the lot. The building was many stories tall, with glass walls and balconies. He had never stayed in such a place.

He drove down the rows of parked cars, looking for the loading dock, finally saw a sign that said "Trucks" and an arrow pointing toward a concrete ramp. Yes, the loading dock was over there, though it was mostly obscured by a wall of vegetation.

Beyond a row of palm trees and oleanders, he heard the sounds of a swimming pool, water splashing and loud music, hundreds of voices yelling and screaming their fun. An inflated balloon, shaped and painted like a giant can of Light beer floated over the area on a tether.

A deejay's voice boomed from speakers, "—wet T-shirt contest coming at ya' in a few—"

A quick blast from the horn of the pickup behind him broke his thoughts. He looked in the driver's side-view mirror and saw the man who hired him motioning him to stop. The man's hand extended through the open window to signal him—stop and come back here the hand waved.

Hector put the truck in park, left the engine running, opened the door and jumped to the asphalt. He hurried back to the pickup, looked into the opening at the driver's window. The dark sunglasses and black cowboy hat appeared.

"Good job, *amigo*." The man's voice was low and authoritative as before.

"Yes. And now?"

The man passed a sizable key on a big chrome ring to Hector. "This key unlocks the back. Drive down to the loading dock and wait on a man to open the hotel doors from the inside. He'll show you where to back up to the dock and he'll bring help to unload the furniture."

"Okay."

"And *amigo*, don't open the back of the truck till they come out. We don't want anybody stealing this furniture. You stay with the truck no matter what. You understand?"

"Yes."

"Okay, *amigo*, I'll be over there in a few minutes. Now get rolling."

Hector walked back to the cab and climbed up into the seat, put the truck in gear. He drove slowly up the ramp, decided to make the turn and back up to the dock himself. He knew how to do it. He swung the truck around, then backed up carefully to put the rear door square to the dock. He eased the truck into position using the side-view mirrors, got it good and close, then stopped and shifted into park. Good, he thought, better to get it done while the dock was clear.

Hector shut the truck down, looked over at the lot and saw that the black pickup was gone. He wondered if the cowboy had some drugs in the back with the furniture; the man was so careful about everything. No matter, the drive was over now. No police, no problems. The cowboy must have gone inside to get the help. Maybe Hector wouldn't have to wait long. After all, this was his lucky day.

Five minutes passed and Hector sat with the window down and watched the oleanders, their white blooms swaying, their thick leaves blocking his view of the pool. He smelled suntan oil on the breeze. The laughter and shouts enticed him and occasionally he caught a glimpse of bare flesh through the palm fronds. Oh, how he would like to be over there right now, with a beer in his hand, watching the *chicas* prance.

"Hey!" A voice shouted from behind the truck. Hector looked back, saw a man in a hotel uniform with a clipboard in his hand.

Hector pulled the door latch and climbed down. He left the door open, didn't notice the wind snatching the map and paperwork off the seat and carrying them away in the hot, steady sea breeze. "Hello," he said to the hotel man.

"What are you doing here?"

"Delivery. Furniture."

The hotel man looked at his clipboard. "I don't see that on the schedule. Who are you with?"

Hector did not understand. He climbed a set of concrete steps up to the dock, went to the back of the truck. "I have furniture."

The hotel man kept his eyes on the clipboard, riffled through the papers on it. "I don't get it. Where is it from?"

"Jacksonville."

"I'd better check inside, but for now, you've got to leave the dock."

"Wait." Hector dug into his pocket for the heavy key. "I show you." He inserted the chrome plated key into the lock on the back door. It opened easily. He removed the lock and grabbed the door handle, pulled up hard. The door flew upward on its rollers, and he heard a snap, an electrical sound.

For a split second, Hector's brain took a photo of the things inside the storage compartment. Huge plastic barrels stacked to the ceiling on metal racks—blue barrels with names of chemicals on them. Wires running between the barrels. Piles of nails. A row of batteries wired together.

"*Que es—*"

A groan, or perhaps a scream, came from the hotel man beside him.

Then Hector heard a sizzling sound, a small bang from the equipment. Next, he felt intense heat rush out in a blinding flame as it tore his molecules apart. He had no last thought as his brain and all of his body disappeared, incinerated to nothingness in a millisecond.

CHAPTER 2

Darden kept his eyes on the road as he turned on the radio, hit the seek button until he found a talk show. He hated the pseudo news of those shows, but considered it part of his job. A way to keep his ear tuned to the political fringes of the country, because there was always a story there.

Half the listeners were ignorant, the other half were true believers, all following the rants and insults of a fat guy making tens of millions of dollars a year, all because he was willing to say absolutely anything for ratings. Think of it, millions of dollars year and a worshipful following all for saying outrageous things, for repeating lies and rumors, the more outrageous and irresponsible the better.

Sometimes he wondered what his country was becoming. Had the populace always been so gullible, so unconcerned with facts, so unable to detect fabrication? Or did they even care?

He turned his mind away from those thoughts because they only made him feel helpless. He steered into the left lane and reset the cruise control, seeing a clear stretch ahead, most of the traffic staying to the right. That was a rare occurrence on I-95 southbound and he needed to make as much time as possible.

Work—real work—waited for him in Daytona. A major story was happening there, possibly a tragedy unfolding from what little he knew. Since he started working out of the Jacksonville office six months ago to be near his Dad, there had been little news to report and he was tired of doing small stories and covering non-events.

Jacksonville was a slow beat for sure, but things could be

worse. What if he was assigned to Iraq or Afghanistan, with somebody shooting at him every other day? A hot beat to be sure, but too hot for his liking. For the moment he was glad to be here, glad to get a real story to chase. As soon as the first call came across the police scanner in the office, his boss had told him to drive down and check it out.

From a career standpoint, he had to do a big story soon or he might not ever get a chance. His career would be over. The newspaper business was caving in on his head, crumbling within as electronic news destroyed circulation numbers. Salary cuts, firings, papers closing their doors; every day it got worse. Soon there would be no place left to work.

In the back of his mind, he'd always thought he would do an award-winning series then graduate from reporter to distinguished writer doing books about major stories. Hell, the way things were going, he wouldn't even have a job for long. What would he do then?

The radio voice rose to a new level of indignation and accused half the United State government of being cowards and appeasers. Darden caught the punched out words: "Security," "Weakness," and of course, "Failure." The fat host would ride this horse for weeks, months, even years. When he found a tragedy to ride, he would run it into the ground. Anything that stirred the public's emotions of fear and anger became a strong horse for a long ride.

The explosion had happened just after eleven-thirty and it was not yet one o'clock. Even the television crews couldn't set up that fast for a major incident. All the reporting so far came from the air by helicopter, but the police were keeping even them at a distant perimeter until it was clear what had happened. So far, all anyone could report was a beach hotel on fire, preceded by an enormous explosion. All the television helicopters could get were distant shots of black smoke mushrooming over the beach district.

If he could reach there by one-thirty, he might be among the first to get some of the early facts. Security would be intense around the entire area for a while yet, complete with roadblocks, a cordon of police detouring traffic, cleared airspace above. If he could penetrate the security bubble somehow, he might actually be able to get a significant story first, a rarity for him and his employer.

The radio host speculated wildly, calling it another nine-eleven, a U.S.S. Cole bombing, an Oklahoma City blast all rolled into one. "Unable to defend our soil," he said, "Or UNWILLING to defend our soil." Darden turned the volume up for the big punch line. "Yes, America. You heard it here. WASHINGTON is COWERING in the face of TERRORISM."

Darden grinned and turned the volume back down, tried to plan his next steps. He'd been driving south at about eighty since he first got on the interstate and now he was just past Palm Coast. The traffic in the oncoming northbound lane had slowed to a trickle. That meant the state highway patrol had already closed the interstate south of Daytona. Soon they'd do the same to the southbound lane and he'd be trapped in a massive traffic jam.

He took the next exit, 284, and decided he'd have to find a way to work across country on back roads. It would take longer for the police to close those. He could probably get closer to the city if he managed to find the smallest routes available. He decided to take county roads and surface streets and just aim southeast.

He knew this area fairly well, had driven it many years before when he was still seeing Jean Anne Colquitt. He'd hoped coming down here wouldn't make him think of her, but he couldn't help it. Too many memories unfolded on these back roads. The trips to the beach, many times after dark, where they ended up rolling naked in the waves. Wild, wonderful nights spent in worn-out motel rooms on A1A. But he'd also spent too many years wondering what happened to her after she got married—to a damned Aussie of all things. Just like her to fall for a smarmy accent.

Almost forty years old and still not married, he reflected, no need to wonder why with his thoughts still fixed on his girlfriend of fifteen years ago.

He made it to Ormond Beach before traffic really started to bog down. State Patrol cars took up position at every significant intersection, turning back most any vehicle that wasn't emergency related.

"Go back," the troopers said over and over again. "Go back."

They waved their flashlights in a loop at every inbound car and detoured them back in the direction they came from. Darden's press pass got him through the first two roadblocks, but he didn't think that would work for long.

He also noticed the state police stopping every car coming out of the Daytona area, with a routine quickly developing. License. Registration. Questions. Radio exchanges with headquarters. Finally, a car full of tourists with kids and suitcases might be waved through the intersection, but anything else, the police directed them back toward the city.

He had never seen such intense security around an incident. Why would the police direct outbound traffic back toward the scene? This was no ordinary fire. The rumors about a massive explosion might be true. Perhaps it had been a deliberate act, even a terrorist attack.

He crawled south on a county arterial until the flow stopped altogether, trapping him at least ten cars back from the intersection ahead. At the rate they were passing people through crossroads, he wouldn't get to the site for hours.

Change of plan.

He pulled over to the shoulder on the right and drove fifty yards on a tilt, his right wheels in the drainage ditch, but the maneuver got him to a residential street that allowed him to turn right. He took it for a block then turned again at the next left. It seemed that every neighborhood in Florida was a plain grid, so he worked his way south for a block, then found what he wanted, a convenience store and gas station on his left, facing a main east-west road.

He pulled into the parking lot and decided to abandon his car there. But what next? Check in with his boss, the news director, let him know where he was? Really not much point, he thought, but his boss was a fiend about checking in. He picked up his cell phone and dialed the office. Busy. The he dialed the headquarters of Southeastern Radio News in Atlanta. Busy. The switchboards must be melting down from all the calls.

He imagined every news service within hundreds of miles of Florida struggling to get through to any reporter, videographer, stringer, or old acquaintance who might be able to provide any solid information about the tragedy. About now, all the news services would be flying blind, desperate for anything to report. Somehow he had to break through the security bubble ahead of the crowd.

He thought about sending his boss an e-mail when a Volusia County Emergency ambulance careened into the parking lot and slid to a stop in front of the convenience store. Its lights still flashing, motor running, the driver jumped out and ran into the store.

Darden grabbed his laptop, Nikon, cell phone, and sunglasses. Hell, he didn't need instructions, he needed to act on his own. Following instructions had never gotten him anywhere in this business. That's why he was still reporting nursing home fraud and car accidents for a third-rate news organization. This might be his chance to cover a real story. He got out and jogged over to the ambulance, rapped on the window, passenger side.

A young woman with short, dark hair buzzed down the glass. Her face surprised him. It was open and unguarded, had few lines, not even a downward twist to the mouth. She was new. He noticed the front pockets of her uniform shirt bulging outward in a nice curve.

"Hey," Darden said. "You got anybody back there who's hurt?"

"No, we're heading in for our first pick up. We were off-duty, just now got rolling."

"So, you don't know anything yet?"

"Supposed to be hundreds of injuries."

He flashed his press pass at her and smiled. "How about if I ride in with you?"

"No way," she said, but she grinned at his bravado.

"Come on," he said. "I need a way in to the site."

"Sorry, we can't," she smiled. "Regulations." Her E.M.T.

uniform was crisp and professional, but he could see from her eyes that she was fresh on the job, excited, not yet jaded by the death and maiming that she would see eventually.

"Look," Darden said. "I'm a bit desperate. I need to cover this story, and I can't get past the roadblocks."

"Let me see that pass again." She tried to frown, as if she was accustomed to inspecting ID's, but she couldn't quite manage the drill and grinned again, perhaps toying with him a bit. "Who are you with?"

He showed her his card. "Southeastern Radio News."

She looked him up and down, squinted at the photo on the pass then at his face.

"Never heard of it."

"You're not the only one," he said.

"This says you're six-two and weigh one-ninety." She was definitely toying with him now. "You don't look that tall to me."

"The ID doesn't say that."

"What is your eye color?"

He took off his sunglasses and leaned closer. Good, he thought, she likes my looks.

"So, are you really a reporter?"

"Yes, and I need a break here."

"Ah, sorry, but we could get in a lot of trouble."

"Come on," he said. "This is not an ordinary day." He hooked his fingers on top of the window glass and smiled again at her.

"I don't know about this."

"I'll owe you a favor," Darden said.

She thought for a moment, took a second look at him and decided, then turned and flipped the lock on the side door. "Okay, but you can only stay if my partner agrees. He's got seniority."

Darden climbed into the back and squatted beside the gurney. "Thanks," he said. "My name is Tom. Tom Darden."

"I'm Linda."

"Lucky for me you stopped here."

"Special emergency," she said. "My partner had to take a leak."

CHAPTER 3

The ambulance stopped at a barricade just past Noble Street where most of the fire trucks and police cars had gathered. So much rubble lay ahead that everyone going any farther had to do it on foot.

"My, God," the driver said.

"We've got our work cut out for us," Linda replied.

Darden rolled back the side door, grabbed his gear, eager to get out and plunge ahead. "Thanks again," he said to the pair who had given him a ride. "You two are real champs." He meant it.

"Yeah, you too," Linda said, as she gave him a slight wave goodbye. "Good luck to you, Tom Darden."

He jumped out of the ambulance and started toward the hotel at a trot. Police and Emergency Services people seemed to be hurrying in every direction, with shouts and orders coming from most of them. Darden vaulted over a barricade and kept moving toward the hotel.

"Hey, you can't go in there," a fireman yelled at him. Darden ignored the command and continued forward through the barricade. The fireman shook his head and shrugged at the crazy ways of civilians as Darden slowed to a walk and began to take in details, making mental notes as he moved forward.

The destruction caused by the heat was extraordinary. Paint had peeled off cars in blackened strips and street signs melted like wax onto the concrete. Light poles and trash baskets had twisted away from the center of the blast as if alive, shedding their metal skin in liquid drops.

One look and he knew this was no hotel fire. Something very

big and powerful had exploded here.

The stumps of a few palms remained standing in spots, but everything else that had once been wood was now a charred heap of trash. Broken glass and burned debris were everywhere, blown from windows and stairwells, storefronts and cars. Specks of red that looked like bright paint had splashed across some of the scorched black surfaces. He saw a few burned bodies in contorted positions, the remains stiff and black, and he wondered how many more there were closer to the hotel. Surely dozens, perhaps hundreds.

He climbed onto the top of a blackened car a couple of blocks away from the fire and took careful shots of the destruction. Voices and radios of emergency personnel crackled across the obliterated space as the officers tried to organize a search and rescue operation, but the firemen hadn't yet been able to get water through their hoses. Hours after the event, it was still too hot to pick through wreckage for the injured.

Heat radiated off the walls of buildings and rose up out of the pavement. He could only imagine how hot it was at the base of the hotel where anything combustible still burned. Half of the first floor wall had been blown away and he pictured how the fire erupted there then quickly roared up the stairwells and elevators to successive floors. The hotel wasn't actually leaning, but it appeared unsteady like the husk of a tree where the inner structure was gone. Black smoke still poured through the openings of blown out windows. Where did the explosion actually originate? Not inside the hotel; the blast pattern and fire weren't right for that. He remembered seeing photos from the Oklahoma City federal building bombing and this was similar.

It seemed likely the bomb detonated just outside the wall which deflected much of the explosive force outward. That probably meant a car bomb. Otherwise, how could a device large enough to do all this damage have been placed and hidden in plain sight?

The only way he could figure it, this was some type of car bomb, terrorist attack or not.

Despite a strong breeze blowing in from the ocean, dark acrid smoke saturated the air. The smell was a mixture of burning plastic, wood, cloth, chemicals, and human hair. He fought a wave of nausea that seemed to start in his stomach and tremor through his lungs and up his throat.

God, it was hot.

He jumped off the car when the soles of his hiking shoes began to smoke against the metal roof. He stood for a moment and looked down to orient himself, saw a piece of fabric on the ground and picked it up. It was part of a bathing suit soaked in blood, red stains on yellow flowers, probably part of a woman's top. He turned it over and saw the smooth fabric liner inside a breast cup, stained with suntan oil, pieces of torn flesh embedded in the fabric.

His head reeled and he dropped the fabric as if it stung. A piece of paper blew against his leg and held there for a moment against his khakis. He snatched up the paper, wiped his hand with it to get the feel of the greasy flesh off his fingers.

His feet stumbled backwards involuntarily and he angled away from it all, found shade in the lee of a building. He stood for a moment, tried to cool off and calm his legs, which shook as if he'd run for an hour.

Still holding the scrap of paper, he wiped his hands again with it, noticed it was a piece of a map, singed and scorched by the fire. He wadded it up, threw it into the opening of a trash barrel standing against the concrete wall of the building.

His legs still trembling, he had to find a place to sit down, went inside a building which was damaged but not destroyed. He wasn't sure what the building had been used for, maybe offices, but there were a few signs of its hurried abandonment. A pocketbook lay on the floor, its contents strewn out as it was cast aside. A bottle of spring water still on a shelf. A computer monitor fallen on its side flickered hopelessly. Far back in a corner he found a desk that had not burned, had been protected by file cabinets.

He sat down and thought for a moment. This was far worse than anything he'd ever imagined, much less experienced. He thought all those wrecked cars and emergency rooms he had covered over the years would have conditioned him to withstand this, but it hadn't.

This was death on a massive scale and he didn't like being near it, wished he'd never come here. As much as he needed a big story, how could he possibly manage to report this, tell people what it was really like, much less investigate it? Who could have done such a thing? Even photos wouldn't do this destruction justice. How could he?

An old feeling welled up in him that he hated and had fought so many times in the past, a feeling of self-doubt that he knew was his worst enemy, a hesitancy he had never defeated. Faced with a task of this magnitude, he felt uncertain about his mettle, thought he simply wasn't up to the task; not a good enough reporter, not a strong enough man. Suspicion surfaced once again that he was still at the bottom of the heap because he lacked the courage and confidence to go out and seize a story like this one. He'd spent his lifetime going along and getting along. Why, he did not know. Perhaps it just wasn't in him to face such tragedy. The firefighters were out there doing their job. The emergency medical teams swallowed their disgust and bile and somehow did what they were trained to do. Why not him?

Get up, he told himself, get to it, but he could not move.

He sat for ten minutes, inert with uncertainty, finally managed to pick up the bottle of spring water. He opened it and drank the lukewarm water and it tasted like heaven going down his parched throat.

"Anybody in there?"

He heard voices out on the street, emergency personnel going door-to-door, one building at a time.

"Any hurt or injured around here?"

Three figures appeared on the front sidewalk, peered through the blasted out window front, searching the dim interior for any sign of life. One of them stepped inside and removed his sunglasses with his right hand. A uniform, maybe a cop.

"What are you doing in there?" he shouted to Darden.

"Resting."

"Are you hurt?"

"No."

"Well get out of there, now. These buildings are unsafe."

Darden picked up his stuff and walked toward the front.

The guy was a cop alright, his face flushed and belligerent. "Nobody's supposed to be in this area," he said. "What are you doing here?"

Darden approached him and held up his camera. "I'm a reporter."

The cop snorted in contempt, grabbed Darden by the arm and yanked him roughly toward the street. Darden snatched his arm free and glared at the cop as they stepped out to the sidewalk. He hated it when anyone grabbed him to make a point, took it as an insult.

"You got any ID?" the cop asked.

A retort popped out before he could stop it. "You got a badge?"

The two stared at each other hard for a moment.

Darden pulled out his press card and handed it over, decided he'd better say as little as possible. The other men were also cops, one very young, the other a bulked-up weightlifter. Darden was taller than all of them, and stronger he was sure, but they were cops and it was better if he could get them on his side. Nonetheless, he hated to shut up and back off when someone tried to muscle him around. Besides, what could you do against a badge and a gun?

The three of them huddled around Darden's card and scrutinized it front and back as if it were a forged passport.

"What the hell is Southeastern Radio News?"

"We sell stories to local stations and papers."

"Out of Atlanta?" the young cop asked.

"Yeah, but I'm based in Jacksonville right now"

"There's not supposed to be any press in this area," the weightlifter said.

"Why not?"

"Orders," the young one said.

"Whose orders?"

The first cop seemed to be the one in charge, had rank maybe. "We're asking the questions, not you."

"But I have a right to be here."

"Mr. Darden," the first cop said, "Do you have any knowledge of the explosion that occurred over at the hotel?"

"No, I was about to ask you the same thing."

The weightlifter pulled up his bulging shoulders and edged closer. "You trying to be smart with us?"

"I'm doing my job. It's my job to ask questions."

"I think we might just take you in because you're such a smart ass," the first cop said, waving the press card at Darden. "Check out the validity of this ID at the station."

Darden felt a string of obscenities welling up in his throat. He'd taken enough crap from these guys, taken too much crap from authority his whole life. His anger was going to get him into a lot of trouble if he didn't control it, so he tried to keep his mouth shut. He didn't want his temper to keep him from doing what he needed to do today.

"Hey, Tom!" A woman's voice. "Tom Darden."

They all turned as Linda, the E.M.T., pushed a gurney toward them. Her uniform was dirty now and her hair stringy with sweat, but she looked wonderful striding with youthful purpose among all the destruction and bad spirits. She steered past them and turned into an alley to their left.

"Hey, guys," she said, overloud. "Could you give me a hand? We have some injured over here who are trapped."

The cops moved toward her without hesitating and Darden exhaled in relief. A pretty woman in need of some muscle was all it took to draw the cops' attention away from him. They wanted someone to blame and harass, their emotions churned up by the bombing, same as his. Instead, she gave them someone to help.

He owed this young woman a favor, a couple of favors. Second time today she'd saved his butt.

CHAPTER 4

Dr. Josiah Baines loved his visits to the horse country of Virginia, so he was a very relaxed man as the limousine cruised the last few miles to the Marshall mansion. Despite the stressful task ahead, he found the ride calming as he buzzed his window down an inch to enjoy the sweet smell of spring grass rising from the fields. Outside the car, cross hatch fences stretched into the distance, dividing one pasture from another, one estate from the next.

This was rich countryside with the requisite tidiness and sense of order that came with great wealth, a rich land where horses lived better than half the world's population, well-watered and fed, groomed daily, and housed in secure, dry quarters. Of course, that was as it should be, in his way of thinking.

"Not far now, sir," the driver said, staring at him in the rear view mirror.

They passed a stone wall that reminded him of Ireland, the gray flat stones beautifully stacked and set, forming a true line that paralleled the curves of the terrain. With the stone surface absolutely uniform in pattern and line, the wall spoke volumes about the solidity of the people who owned these estates, people who believed in orderly, sturdy fences as a way to divide the world and its riches into rightful ownership.

To him, these people were the real thing, sound and sensible about managing their surroundings and their fortunes. These were the people who really ruled America, and in turn, the world. He envied them and mildly resented their ease, yet at the same time he yearned to become one of them quite soon.

Baines studied the notes resting on his lap and considered the importance of the meeting ahead. If he could convince the Wise Men waiting at the mansion, his plans would click into motion and money would flow forth.

He visualized the group of Wise Men in his mind, rehearsing how he would address them. They would meet in the old library, seated in spacious chairs of upholstered leather and silk. A group of six men, dressed in riding boots and caps as if they were country gentlemen, would listen patiently to his proposal as he stood before them, speaking in a low and moderate tone. They would pay attention very carefully because his words promised extraordinary profits to them and they were men who always put profit first.

The limousine slowed and turned between two enormous stone pillars at the entrance to the estate then accelerated up an oak-lined drive to a gentle rise capped by the mansion, a Jeffersonian edifice of old money and red brick. The mansion was quite far back from the road, perhaps a half mile, which spoke of the size of the estate.

"Shall I drop you at the front or the side entrance, sir?"

"The side," Baines said. "Same as always." Was the driver speaking to him simply to get a chance to stare at his face? He quickly dismissed the thought as old emotional baggage he should learn to do without.

Baines looked up from his notes and searched for the horses that usually grazed in the pastures on each side of the drive. Yes, there they were, six of them far to his left, near the old crooked oak. This level of wealth is so timeless, he thought, so replete with pleasure that I must have it. He resolved to sway every man at the meeting with his professionalism and bold planning.

Seventeen years of practicing medicine was enough, too much, he thought. Proctology was a depressing specialty and few people in medicine were drawn to it, so it fell to those who were in the bottom third of their class, like him, to fill its ranks. Probing the orifices of sick people was no way to live. It was time for him to make his move and become one of the gentry.

One hour later, the Wise Men met in the library just as the

doctor had imagined. Peyton Marshall, the host, greeted everyone with a handshake and exercised his patrician manners while serving them each two drinks of Lagavulin, then he gathered them to the seating area near the immense fireplace. The area was dim and felt old, smelled like wood smoke and old books, faintly of liquor. They sank into the deep leather chairs and settled themselves for comfort as the host gestured toward Baines, giving him the floor.

Baines stood up slowly and made eye contact with each of the men, making certain his face conveyed the seriousness of the occasion. A couple of them diverted their gaze to the floor when faced with his stare. Then he waited a full ten seconds before speaking.

"Gentlemen," he began. "We are here to change the direction of the nation."

They stared at him carefully, wondering about his broken face he suspected, but he put the old shame behind him and went ahead with his presentation.

"Just as you gather every four years and choose who you will fund to create the next president, you now have the opportunity to do much more, something much longer lasting. I am proposing to you a plan that will solidify the control of the wealthy in this country against the rising tide of the rabble. It will quell the noisy voices of those who wish to take away your rightful inheritance. With this Master Plan, if I may call it that, your future and that of your heirs will be assured indefinitely, shielded from the clamor of the masses. Allow me to explain in detail."

He held the floor for almost twenty minutes without interruption. As he spoke, they revealed nothing of their thoughts. Just as he'd predicted, they listened closely as he laid out his plan because it promised them still more wealth and power to use as they saw fit. These were men who turned away from no opportunity if it promised them gain.

Even when he finished, there was little indication of their thinking. He stood for a moment in silence and stared back at them as if they were the ones with disfigurement. He coughed gently and sipped at his unfinished drink. The faintly smoky taste of the scotch warmed his throat.

"Gentlemen?"

None of them seemed comfortable any longer and no one appeared willing to speak first. Perhaps he'd misjudged the Wise Men. Perhaps his proposal was too radical and too far-reaching to accept, even for them.

Finally, the Senator—of course—spoke up. "An observation," he said. The silver-haired politician shifted his bulk in the expansive leather chair and leaned forward, then for effect, took his time lighting a cigar. "You are proposing historic change in the United States government. Some people take civil liberties seriously. There will be strong opposition."

"Yes," Baines said. "There will." He stared at the senator in silence until the old man slid backward in the chair and cleared his throat uneasily. Few people wanted to lock eyes with Baines for very long.

Next, the tall oil man, Means, got right to the point. "How much?" he asked. "That's what I want to know. How much is it going to cost us?" His eyebrows rose in emphasis. "How much is it going to make us?"

"A good question," Baines said. "The prospectus, please, Mr. Marshall."

The host got up and distributed a thin, bound document to each of the guests. It contained the cost projections and a pro forma of the earnings expected for the new corporation. Three of the guests immediately flipped to the back page and saw the profit split due each participating shareholder.

No other words were necessary after they read and re-read the returns they would make. For the first time since the meeting began, their faces were absolutely transparent. Stunned is the word, Baines thought, or perhaps bliss. They are utterly speechless at the thought of so much money, possibly billions in profit for a handful of investors.

One of them, Stiles Hurst, a New York financier, put down the folder and rubbed his thin face roughly with the palms of his hands. Baines noticed that the man's hands shook and his face seemed drained of blood. Another tried to sip his drink but was unable to raise the trembling glass to his mouth.

Baines decided it was time to seal their support.

"Gentlemen," he said, "You are all extraordinary leaders in your respective worlds, powerful and wise. You understand politics, money, and the military. I, on the other hand, know one thing you do not. I understand humans and what they can tolerate. That is an asset you cannot buy on the open market, and it is essential to this operation. I, and I alone, have the Master Plan to test the limits of the people in this country, to find the level of subjugation they will accept. To extract such profits from them, you must know what they are willing to endure before they revolt."

He studied their faces and saw a war of emotions going on inside them. The Senator and the former Admiral, in particular, appeared conflicted. Despite their well known strong views about national security, they would be more difficult to persuade, perhaps they were too traditional to see a new way for the country.

"Further, gentlemen, I have the indestructible will to bring this plan to reality."

Peyton Marshall stood and straightened himself to his full height, addressed Baines with an enormous and warm smile. "Thank you, Josiah. Please feel free to stroll the grounds or visit the stables for an hour or so and let us discuss the proposal privately."

"Of course," he said. "The decision is yours, gentlemen." Baines nodded politely to the group and left the library with the lightest step he'd felt in years.

Later that night, Baines sat by the fire with Marshall as they enjoyed after-dinner brandies. Baines was quiet, subdued by the unexpected decision of the Wise Men. Considering their collective attraction to big money, he could not have been more surprised. These were men who never turned down an opportunity to increase their wealth, no matter how venal or repulsive the business might be, yet turn him down they had.

"Too bad," the host said again. "It would have been easier if they'd gone along."

"Yes, but we suspected as much." Baines swirled the brandy in his snifter, inhaled the sweet aroma. "We knew some might disapprove."

Marshall sipped from his glass and sighed. "They always decide together. If it isn't unanimous, they don't do it. The numbers staggered them, and the debate was the most heated I've ever seen, but in the end they couldn't convince the Senator or the Admiral."

"What a time for them to behave honorably."

"I know, Josiah. I know."

"I suppose we will have to develop another plan."

"Yes, I suppose so."

The following Monday, a two paragraph story appeared in the second section of the Washington Post. It reported that a former Admiral who had served at one time on the Joint Chiefs of Staff died of a heart attack in his sleep at the country estate of the well-known horseman and corporate head, Peyton Louis Marshall. The article provided few details about funeral arrangements or the death itself, except to note that the Admiral had suffered two mild heart attacks in recent years.

Though widely admired throughout the military community, the Admiral's obituary was completely overshadowed by the front page story of another death that was the subject of wild speculation in Washington circles. A powerful Senate Committee Chairman had also died over the same weekend in a car accident outside the beltway.

His Cadillac slammed into a bridge pylon on Interstate 95 at extremely high speed and struck the concrete support with such force it drove the steering column completely through the Senator's sizable torso and all the way into the back seat. The Medical Examiner noted in his report that the alcohol content in the Senator's blood was over twice the legal limit.

CHAPTER 5

A few minutes after midnight, Darden sat outside his father's hospital room while nurses changed the bed and replaced two empty IV containers. They removed the barely touched food tray, rigged the drip valves and finally covered the patient with fresh blankets. It was too crowded in the room while they did their routines, so Darden sat in the hall and waited for them to finish.

Darden felt tired after the long day in Daytona, and these daily visits to the Mayo Clinic in Jacksonville depressed him, but he felt even worse when he skipped them. His father would not live much longer and Darden knew that would be the worst feeling of all. Once his Dad was gone, would there be anything left that he truly cared about? He wanted to spend every possible minute with him, no matter how painful it was to watch him dying.

"You can go in now," a bored nurse said as she came out of the room. She wore a blue dress uniform over the regular blue pants and shirt. Perhaps that was protection against the aggressive air conditioning, perhaps against bodily stains; he didn't care to ask. Soiled sheets and towels loaded down her arms.

"Thanks."

He stood and looked at the linens she'd piled into a bulging laundry cart. He thought he smelled the reek of death on them, but it must have been the odor of the bombing site still holding in his olfactory nerves. It seemed that everywhere he looked lately, death waited in the shadows.

He stepped through the doorway and felt that familiar pang of dread inside, hoped it didn't show.

"Hi, Dad. How you feeling today?"

His father opened his eyes and turned his head very slightly toward the sound of his son's voice. Weaker than yesterday, much weaker than the day before, Darden observed.

"Sick," his father smiled.

"You're too tough to feel sick."

A weak laugh almost took shape on his father's face, then a disturbance erupted deep inside him—a cough—a punishing cough that seemed to say, stop that laughing old man, no mirth for you. It started as a strangled breath and climbed up his throat, gaining force, then finally came out as a rattling, wracking expulsion of air, an ugly punctuation mark at the end of a too familiar sentence.

"Don't try to talk if it hurts," Darden said.

His breath recovered, the old man managed a few normal respirations and nodded. "Might as well talk. It hurts either way."

Darden sat down by the bed and remained quiet a few minutes. Sometimes he wasn't sure if it was best to say nothing or try to act as if everything was normal. He hated the helplessness of it all, being unable to make his father better or even a bit more comfortable. Nothing seemed to be within his power any more, except to watch and wait.

"Not long now," his father said.

Darden couldn't reply to that, looked away, noticed the television hanging from the ceiling at the foot of the bed. The sound on mute, only images came out of it, images of smoke hanging over Daytona Beach, then the destruction on the ground followed by close-ups of emotional family members, crying and raging in front of the cameras.

"I saw some awful stuff today, Dad. A bombing in Daytona Beach that wiped out a hotel along with the whole block around it."

"Yeah, I wondered about that. Saw it on the news."

"It was terrible."

"Did you get your story?"

Darden didn't answer, didn't want to admit the truth. He still hadn't filed a report. Instead, after he left the scene, he drove straight here to the hospital in Jacksonville. Somehow, he just wanted to avoid thinking about his inadequacy, but he justified all that in his own mind by saying his father was more important.

"No story?" his father asked. "Why not?"

"It's too much to explain."

"Son," his father raised a finger. "Your life doesn't stop just because mine is ending."

"Dad." Darden hung his head a bit, couldn't look the old man in the eyes. "I'm not half the man you are."

"No, Tommy. You are me, and more."

Darden felt his eyes watering and he shut them quickly.

"I don't know about that."

His father sighed, but it came out as more of a wheeze. "You just don't know how strong you are yet, but I do. You are stronger and better than I ever was."

"Dad, I don't know if I can cover this story. The bodies were black and stiff, like burned wood. The smell—"

"Tommy, do you think it was a deliberate bombing?"

"Yes, I wish I could find out who murdered—"

"Then do it."

"How? The FBI doesn't even know anything yet."

"Find a way to do your job."

"Dad, I don't know how. I'm not much of a journalist. More of a low level hack, really."

"So you keep telling me, and your news service is not much better."

His father shut his eyes but he wasn't asleep. Darden reached for a water bottle on the bedside tray, held it up to his father's lips and the old man managed to sip some through the straw, seemed relieved. Darden sat and watched him for a while, wondering why it was so important to his father that he rise above his doubts and accept the challenge.

"There's something I never told you, Tommy." His father paused, gathering strength to talk, but he kept his eyes closed.

"When I was in Germany toward the end of the war, I saw things no one should ever see. My unit marched into a concentration camp near Munich two days after the front line liberated it. The memories of that place are still the darkest stain in my mind."

"You saw that?"

"Yes, a smaller camp near Dachau. It was pure butchery. Mass murder. Brutality just for the sake of brutality. I can still smell it, still see the walking skeletons who were unlucky enough to survive. You think any of them ever had a real night's sleep after living through that?"

"Dad, you don't have to—"

"I want you to hear this."

Another nurse came in the room and they both went quiet while she took his temperature and pulse, listened to his heart. She wrote the results down on a chart and left as quickly as she arrived.

"As painful as it was to see that stuff," his father said, "It was my finest hour too. Our best hour, yeah, I believe so. We stood guard while Patton made the local civilians march through those camps and see what their side had done."

"Sure, he wanted the world to know."

"What if we hadn't nailed the ones who ordered it?"

Darden shrugged, unsure if he was supposed to have an answer. He heard sirens outside, thought maybe it was more victims from Daytona arriving here for specialized treatment. He went to the window and looked out, saw trees whipping in the wind, low clouds blowing in from the west. A definite storm on the way.

"Somebody with authority ordered this bombing," his father continued. "Make it your job to find out who did it."

"Me? How?"

"Those villagers in Germany said,

'We didn't know; we were only following orders.' What if Patton hadn't made them face the truth?"

"I'm not the army, Dad, not the FBI."

"You can't let brutes win. Be the man I know you can be."

Darden still wasn't sure how to respond. In all their life

together, his father had never spoken to him this way. Were these his last words of wisdom or a deathbed recollection, or what? He went back and sat down beside the bed.

"Tommy, if nothing else, I die knowing that justice matters. I was a small part of it, just standing guard, but I was there."

"This is different."

"No, brutes are all the same. Brutes killed innocent people in the trade towers, to prove what? Germany or New York, it doesn't matter to the brutes, because they don't give a damn about life. Just do your part to keep them from winning."

All the talk had exhausted the old man. His head tilted sideways on the pillow and he breathed heavily through his mouth. He hadn't used up so many words and so much energy in days.

Darden sat quietly for a long time and watched his father sleep, held his hand, knowing this could well be the last conversation they would ever have together. He envisioned his father as a young man in an army uniform, a short unfiltered cigarette dangling from his lips. Had he been cocky or frightened, riding those olive green trucks through Europe? Did he go into the towns on leave, drink and chase the local girls or did he stay at camp and write letters home to his young wife? Whatever he had been like then, he eventually grew into a confident man who tried to do the right thing the rest of his life.

Darden wondered if he could do the same, wondered how he would respond to his father's entreaty. Could he also grow to match his father's standards?

He heard thunder outside, then heavy rain came hard against the window like a machine-gun firing drops into the glass.

A half hour later, his father soundly asleep, Darden got up and left the room, walked down to the lobby and left the hospital. Outside, the air was still warm and thick with humidity from the storm, the crickets noisy in the trees. The blue glow of fluorescents bathed the parking lot, reflected off the puddles of standing water, the parked cars mute reminders of the living. He walked to his own car and somehow felt the presence of others despite the stillness. At this late hour, the place seemed to be a waiting room for ghosts, his own life an empty space within it.

He decided to go home and write his story on the bombing. He did not know much more than anyone else, but he had been there, he had seen it. In just one day, his life was irrevocably different. There was something he needed to do, must do now. Perhaps standing guard was enough, simply because the dead could not do it for themselves.

The only question was if he could rise up and be the man his father thought he could be.

CHAPTER 6

After an hour of standing and watching the showy crowd, Dr. Baines wondered again what his friend, Marshall, had known about tonight's party, why he'd suggested the doctor attend this fund-raiser for the More Secure America Foundation. Nothing seemed out of the ordinary here, nothing that required his attention, but the always oblique Marshall must have had some reason to want him here.

Like most receptions in Washington, this one was held in a swanky ballroom, in this case at the Presidential L'Enfant Plaza Hotel where the chandeliers were enormous and the carpet and antiques a notch above hotel grade. The conservative contributors in attendance were dull and gossipy, self-important people who wanted to be stroked. If they weren't high enough up the pecking order to mandate stroking, they would at least gain attention by passing rumors or inventing stories of their connections to powerful people.

Flowers of red, white, and blue, and banners with patriotic slogans—Keep America Safe—decorated the banquet room. A stage at the front displayed yards of red, white, and blue bunting while the backdrop screen showed gigantic colorful waves of Old Glory receding into the distance. A band dressed in tuxedos played show tunes—he recognized Yankee Doodle Dandy and It's a Grand Old Flag—with an electronic flair.

To Baines these social receptions were all the same; they provided a time and place for the ego strutting that was the essence of Washington. Already several men with silver hair, dressed in formal tails and cumberbunds, had strutted to the stage to receive fund-raising awards. Their wives of social influence waltzed about in expensive jewelry and elaborate dresses, their hair piled high. All in all, much fussing about and maneuvering for access, for power, and most of all for the money that came with them. Yet these people paid so little consequential attention to the vital issues of the state, in his view.

This event was no exception. Sometimes the parade of status and hierarchy disgusted Dr. Baines, for he thought these people lacked purpose, but soon he planned to use their vanities to accomplish the most important task of his life. He depended on these preening peacocks to make his Master Plan work; they would be the ones who supported his remaking of the nation's homeland security.

Only two things distinguished tonight's reception; the first was a rumor going around that a very highly placed Administration official was in the hotel and might make an appearance. The other was the hot news item of the day, the topic of every conversation; that a city had been bombed on American soil.

"Those bastards ought to be hung," a heavy man with florid skin standing near Baines said loudly. His fellows, gathered in a rude circle, nodded and murmured in assent.

Baines turned toward them as if he intended to join their discussion. He took a step closer but one look at his face and the group shrank back involuntarily. One man with thinning hair averted his eyes immediately, rattled the ice in his empty glass and used it as an excuse to depart. The others tried to be more polite, but inevitably the conversation dissolved and they pulled away. Within seconds, all had left.

He felt no hurt or anguish at their reaction to his appearance. He had become accustomed to it and expected them to break off after a good look at his face. In fact, he had rather come to enjoy the power he had over others and to use it in a way that amused him. He joked to himself that he could intimidate and repel anyone, anywhere, anytime. Actually he had only turned toward the discussion in order to hear them better, to measure their attitudes against what he expected.

The doctor smiled at the righteous consensus of the group and viewed them with contempt. You could always expect an incident like the one in Florida to bring out the armchair hangmen. Somehow they always agreed who "the bastards" were without benefit of investigation or evidence, he reflected, because evidence did not matter to them. Their next stage of thought would be to urge the hanging of someone, anyone, who seemed a likely perpetrator. That vigilante reaction could well work to his advantage. The rush to punish someone—anyone—train of thought was especially prevalent in Washington, and it was so predictable it could be useful to clever people like him. Group reactions of fear followed by vengeance made it possible to manipulate people and policy, and that certainty pleased the doctor because it would help fuel support for his plan.

Men like them would talk about threats, but they would never take action, real action, against anyone. He would. That was what made him exceptional and of course the perfect man to execute the Master Plan. Others were afraid of what people thought and it caused paralysis within them. He had no such qualms. His grotesque face had long ago relieved him of that gentle concern. Children, and even some adults, had run away from him crying since he was four years old. His face had long ago erased the burden of worrying about what others thought.

He took a second glass of champagne from a passing server and maintained his position at the left rear wall of the banquet room. He stood at an angle to the wall, keeping the left side of his face turned to the ballroom curtains. It was a good spot to see who came and went, and more important, he was not highly visible so he could eavesdrop at will.

He'd accepted the invitation to the party only because Marshall suggested he attend, but again he wondered why. Marshall was his patron and the doctor would always oblige him in the name of business, but what did Marshall know that he didn't?

Despite his wish to accommodate the request, Dr. Baines soon became bored and just when he decided there was no reason to stay any longer, a man touched him on the arm and whispered in his ear, "Please come with me."

He followed the man without question, even though something about the man's bearing caused a snake of concern to coil in his lower abdomen. He assumed he was being summoned by someone at Marshall's bidding, but what if it was something else? What if his friend had told the wrong person too many details and he was being marched to an inquisition? Or worse? Many people would violently resist his plans if they knew of them. Was he under threat?

The escort walked him to the bank of elevators outside the banquet room and they stepped into the first one that opened. His heart jumped inside his chest and he felt sweat run down his ribs when the doors closed. He did not like being in such a small space.

His escort touched a tiny earphone mounted inside his right ear, listening to some unseen colleague, then he inserted a pass key into a slot on the elevator control panel and pushed a button. The elevator started to rise. The young man was undoubtedly Secret Service, crew cut and silent, who carried a lot of heavy muscle under his dark suit, moved with a faintly military bearing. The man's expression was so stoic, he seemed as if could kill without a second thought.

Baines fretted that he'd somehow led himself down a path of destruction. He did not like the young man leading the way because Baines wanted to be in control at all times. Following always made him uncomfortable, but he would go along for the moment.

The elevator stopped at the top floor and they moved out into a corridor that was heavily decorated with draperies and oil paintings. Two more Secret Service men stood at each end of the hallway. Dr. Baines took the escort's cue to the right and they went into an anteroom of a luxury suite where two additional agents stood guard.

They frisked Baines thoroughly, passed a wand over his entire body three times, required him to empty all his pockets, then asked him to sit and wait in an adjoining sitting room. He did as they directed and looked around. The room was very ornate. He checked his watch and tapped his feet impatiently. The room, the waiting, the guards, it all seemed theatrical. If they were going to murder him, why would they do it this way?

By his watch, exactly nine minutes passed before a door opened to his right and an aide turned the lights down low using a rheostat on the wall. The silhouette of a heavy, older man with hunched shoulders followed the aide into the dim room and sat down across from Dr. Baines in a deep club chair.

The light in the room was so dim it wasn't clear who the older man was, but judging from the number of security personnel on the floor, he must be the rumored, highly placed Administration official. The aide turned on a table lamp next to Dr. Baines and tilted the shade up so the glare of the light prevented him from seeing the shadowy face across the room.

It caused him great discomfort to have his face so well lit, and a familiar tic returned to his left eyelid. It twitched violently as his heart accelerated again.

"Leave us," the man said to the aide.

When the door closed behind the aide, the man sat back and loosened his formal bow tie. "Relax, doctor. We can talk freely here."

As soon as Dr. Baines heard the measured western drawl, he knew who was speaking, but since he could not see the man he would never be able to testify that he had actually talked to the Great Man. Therefore, he would never be able to say this meeting took place.

"I don't believe we've ever met," said Baines.

"No, and we won't."

"Why not?"

The Great Man cleared his throat as if to say, what a silly question. "We have a security problem in this country, and I understand you might have a solution."

A great wave of relief swept over him. No one but Marshall knew of Dr.Baines' Master Plan, so the meeting had certainly resulted from a direct communication between the two men.

Surely, Marshall would never have revealed such a dangerous piece of information to anyone other than the most like-minded man in the country. The doctor decided to talk openly. If he couldn't trust Marshall, he couldn't trust anyone.

"Our immediate problem," the Great Man said, "Is this business in Florida. These terrorist attacks must be stopped. Now they are on our own soil, but our hands are tied."

"Tied?"

"Yes, tied by all the legal crap. Congress. Lawyers. Bleeding hearts. How can we act swiftly and certainly under so many constraints?"

"So, you cannot weed out and crush these terrorists by the usual means."

"Exactly," the Great Man said. The pacing and volume of his words never varied, and to Baines, it was the most resolute voice he'd ever heard. He was Baines' kind of leader. Not really a politician, he didn't even care if he was popular, never wore a smile on his lips. He was a man of convictions and certainties; it never occurred to him that he might be wrong, that someone else might actually understand a situation better. Too bad so few Americans agreed with his concrete beliefs about national security. "Yet the country must be reassured, must know we can stop them."

"So you want the private sector to help out."

"You can act freely, without fear of restraint or oversight whereas we cannot. Private groups can do the job in ways that we can't."

"Are you offering me legal cover if something goes wrong?" Baines asked.

"Nothing must go wrong. I am offering you resources, in fact, the virtually unlimited resources of the American taxpayer."

"But no legal cover."

The Great Man remained silent and Baines realized he would never get a response to such a question, no confirmation of any sort.

"You must act on your own, Dr. Baines. In return you receive the full financial backing of this Administration. Funds to get the job done. Funds to do whatever it takes."

"That will cost a great deal."

"Money is not a problem. We spend hundreds of billions on internal security every year. Much of that can be channeled to private contractors."

"What about the uproar?"

"We can handle that reaction. When terrorists are brought to justice to prove our point, the American people will accept new realities."

Dr. Baines paused, sat quietly and thought of the implications of what he'd just been told. The light was green. The Administration would not only look the other way; they wanted him to proceed. This was a historical breakthrough. Never had any Administration dared to go so far in controlling the populace. Their willingness to do so now changed everything, and it would make him rich far beyond his grandest dreams.

He could barely control his elation. His eyelid jumped spasmodically, and he hoped it wasn't as obvious to the Great Man as it was to him.

"So, what do you say, Dr. Baines?"

"As soon as you direct the funds to our holding corporation, we will launch the Master Plan."

"Good." The Great Man rose and turned to leave the room. "Just one more thing." He stopped.

"Yes?"

"We're tired of being the good guys who won't fight dirty." He turned and looked back, and for the first time, Baines got a look at the heavy face behind the glasses, the unsmiling hawk that every American recognized. "It's time to take the gloves off."

Baines nodded, understood the latitude he'd been granted, understood that he'd just become the third most powerful man in the country.

CHAPTER 7

"I can't run this," his Editor said, throwing the story back across the desk to Darden. Weldon Keil eyed him over a tiny pair of half-lens reading glasses sitting on the end of his nose, his double chin shaking with every word. "You know we can't use it."

"Why not?"

"Because we don't run two thousand word stories speculating about who's responsible for a bombing we don't even know for sure was a bombing. Because we don't know shit yet, that's why. There's no meat to this. Why'd you even turn this crap in to me?"

Darden fumed even though he wasn't surprised. He'd worked all night on the story, and yes, it was a bit thin, but his current Editor was the most timid newsman in America. He wouldn't run anything that might possibly upset anybody. He was the King of Happy News.

"It's a perfectly valid story with possible scenarios."

"Forget it." The fat Editor put his feet up on the crowded desk, his chair creaking as it tilted back. Weldon grabbed the phone to resume his daily business. "Now, get out of here. Don't come back till you bring me a real story."

Dismissed again, Darden was sick of being treated like a third-rater. The biggest story to happen in the southeast since—since anything—and his Editor wanted to cover it like a local robbery. Business as usual. He couldn't resist a parting shot as he went out the door.

"Weldon, try doing a little news someday."

The newsroom outside Kiel's office was small and noisy, even though most of the desks were empty now. So many layoffs had them down to a skeleton crew, barely able to generate enough stories to keep the doors open, yet his chickenshit Editor turned away the biggest story ever to hit his desk.

Darden wanted a cigarette but knew he'd have to go outside to smoke it. He'd also have to go out and buy some since he didn't smoke anymore. He went to his crowded cubicle instead, slumped into his chair and kicked the bottom metal drawer of the desk, the one that always hung open beside him, the one with files spilling out of both sides.

After a moment of thought, he grabbed his stuff and headed for the back door. "The hell with you, Weldon," he said to himself. "I'm covering this story whether you like it or not."

After an hour of driving down I-95, he reached the Daytona Beach Police Headquarters on Valor Boulevard just east of the interstate. He locked his car and walked to the front door of the police station, remembered a tee shirt that was popular when he was a teenager, a souvenir kids brought home from vacation. It had black and white prisoner stripes on it and said: Property of Daytona Beach Jail. The joke wasn't funny now.

He asked questions in the lobby and found the office of the Communications Director on the second floor. Reporters and local citizens jammed the office, screaming for details. Most wanted to know about family and friends who might have died in the blast. No one seemed to get answers.

A harried desk clerk passed out photocopied handouts announcing a press conference at two o'clock. That was more than two hours away. The clerk ignored every shouted question and nobody else came out to answer them. He needed facts now. How many had died? How many wounded? Who were the suspects? What about a casualty list?

He decided to get away from the crowd and find somebody who would talk. He went back down to the lobby, located the Homicide Investigation Unit on the directory and walked back to their office upstairs. He asked the first person he saw for more information, and in return, got directions back to the Communication Director's office.

This wasn't working. The city was too overwhelmed to handle an event of this scale. Or was it something more? Not even the most basic facts were available yet. Why not? It wasn't normal for the local police to put a lid on information for a story as big as this one. Was the story being suppressed, and if so, why? He thought about raising hell all over the building, demanding answers, but decided against it. Something didn't feel right about this and he concluded someone higher up was indeed keeping the story from growing. If someone gave orders to clamp down to all these employees, they weren't about to loosen up for him just because he made a lot of noise.

There was only one person he knew in Daytona who might be willing to help him. It was a long shot, but he needed someone who knew cops and emergency responders and who might have some inside knowledge. He found a phone book on a counter and looked up local hospitals in the Yellow Pages. One nearby, Memorial, advertised a major Emergency Room. With luck, maybe he could find her there or at least figure out a way to find her.

Back in his Accord, he drove to the hospital, couldn't find a parking space within a half mile of the building. Finally he parked illegally on a construction site, hoped he wouldn't get towed, and set out on foot alongside the roadway. Within minutes his shirt was sopping wet and his shoes had sand in them.

The Emergency Room was so crowded there was a guard stationed outside the entrance to keep out non-essential visitors. Rather than argue with the guard, he stepped away and considered his next move. Two parked ambulances under the concrete awning had their doors open. He went up to the closest one, a Volusia County orange and white, and saw an E.M.T. working with oxygen equipment in the back.

"Hey, man."

The guy looked up but didn't stop working. "Yeah, what's up?"

"You know an E.M.T. named Linda? Cute girl. About twenty-five or thirty, dark hair?"

"Sure. Linda Ramsey."

"Know where I can find her?"

"She's probably inside the E.R. That's her unit parked over there."

"Thanks, bud."

Darden walked the perimeter of the building until he found a set of doors toward the rear. They were locked. He was about to start walking again when he heard the doors open from the inside with a metallic clank. Two nurses came out talking. He took a quick step behind them and caught one door before it slammed shut again.

Inside, he followed signs to the E.R. and found Linda within minutes. She sat slumped on a bench just outside the waiting area. Tired and dirty, she might have been asleep, but she looked up when Darden sat down beside her. She didn't appear to recognize him.

"Can I buy you a Coke?" he asked.

"Oh, yeah," she nodded, eyes half closed. "That'd be great."

He bought one from a machine down the hall, brought it back and sat down next to her again. "You look tired, Linda."

She looked over at him then, trying to place his face and voice.

"Tom Darden," he said. "You gave me the ride and talked the cops off me yesterday."

"Right." She tried to smile. "Now I remember."

"It was awful over there at the hotel."

She nodded. "The worst." Streaked with soot and sweat, her face seemed older in just one day.

"I wanted to say thanks."

"Sure. No problem."

"Those cops would've run me in if you hadn't intervened."

"Everybody was acting crazy out there."

"Not you. You stayed under control."

She shook her hair out of her face, gave him a tired grin. "Are you trying to butter me up?"

"Well, yes," he said. "You seem to enjoy helping me, and I

need help."

She took a sip of the Coke and stared at him, as if trying to understand, asking herself if this man was for real. "Okay, I'm listening."

"I want to find out who blew up the hotel."

She smiled at that, a quick laugh. "So do a lot of people."

"I haven't slept since I saw it."

"Same here."

He turned toward her and looked directly into her eyes. They were very blue for someone with dark hair. "Linda, listen to me. I want to investigate this. I want the truth, but the cops aren't talking. My Editor doesn't care. I don't know anybody here. I'm not even sure how to investigate something this big. I just know I need help."

She seemed to accept his sincerity, but there was doubt on her face, as if she had to know more to figure him out. "Why you, Tom? There are hundreds of reporters here now, big names, national television, the works."

He didn't have a ready answer, didn't really understand it himself. "It's hard to explain, but I know I have to do it."

She sat quietly and gave him a chance to say more. When nothing came, she stood up and he felt sure she was going to walk off, tell him to get lost, or worse, but then two horizontal lines appeared on her forehead as she seemed to wonder why he couldn't explain himself.

"You were there too, Linda. How can you see that mass murder and not want to do something? I just can't let it go, and I need help."

She seemed to think carefully before she answered. "I can't help you."

"Why not?"

"How can I? I'm not a cop. I don't know any more than you do."

"You can help just like you did yesterday, by getting me inside the security ring. I need access where nobody else is getting it. Help me get through to people, where I can find facts. I think somebody is trying to throw a blanket over this incident."

"Oh, come on. Who could do a thing like that?"

"I don't know, somebody powerful. But the press is certainly being held at bay. You don't want that, do you? Not after what we both saw yesterday."

"It's not my fight," she answered. "I'm a medic."

"The public and the victims deserve to know what happened here, and why."

"Man, you can put a serious guilt trip on a girl." She tucked in her shirt and picked up her jacket, smiled at him. She reached for his arm and pulled him up off the bench, her hand lingering for a second on his wrist. "Let's get something to eat while I think about it."

They elbowed their way through the Emergency Room and tried to get past the clamor and crying and chaos of it all. Gurneys carrying the unconscious lined the hallways and even strung out into the waiting area. The injured seemed to be everywhere, with too few medical personnel to tend them. Two men in bloody shirts and makeshift bandages leaned against the wall. A woman with burned hands sat on the floor, arms in her lap.

Darden wondered how many people had been injured. Certainly hundreds. For what? Why would someone cause all this misery and loss?

Linda seemed to read his thoughts. She leaned close to his ear to be heard above the din. "Awful, isn't it? A few are still coming in. Our last run, they were digging people out of the wreckage. We saw a lot of nail wounds."

"Nails?"

"Yeah, fragments of metal, looked like nails.

That added weight to his hunch. It had been a car bomb. He knew from tracking stories out of the Middle East that screws and nails were often used in car bombs. Added to inflict more casualties, the metal scraps made the explosion more deadly, every bit as effective as hot shrapnel.

He heard shouts coming from a treatment room and a pair of nurses at each end of a gurney hurried it out into the hallway.

Screams and crying followed them as a family rushed out to stay with the victim under the sheet. The blue uniforms wheeled the gurney down the hallway, deeper into the hospital, the grieving family in pursuit.

"Let's go this way," Linda said.

She steered him through a pair of doors, marked NO ENTRY, into a quieter area that ran perpendicular to the main emergency room layout. "There are exit doors at the end of this department and we can get out easier that way."

Fifty yards down the hallway, they walked past several large open rooms with four patients to each one. There was very little activity inside, curtains pulled around each bed. A whiteboard hung outside each room beside the doorway with the occupants' names written on it in capital letters. He stopped and read one of the boards: Johnson, Starnow, Haight, and a smudged out space. The attending nurse's name was also logged on the board for each shift.

"What is this place?" he asked.

"The burn unit," Linda replied. "These are the most serious cases. They're sedated. Some here will die."

He glanced into each of the rooms, thinking again how these people were leading ordinary lives just yesterday morning. Now bandages covered their faces and arms, their names written on a board to identify them as individuals who might not be recognizable otherwise, many never to have a normal day again.

They continued slowly down the corridor as he peered into each room, scanned the names on every whiteboard. It took real effort not to be overwhelmed by it. He imagined the emotional tides that must be pulling at their families, the lives turned to tragedy.

The last room on the left before the exit doors caught his eye. He had to look at the whiteboard for a moment before he made the connection. One of the patient names on the board jumped out at him and he felt his throat constrict: Jean Colquitt Hughes.

Jean.

His Jean. His old girlfriend Jean who married the Aussie, the great love of his life must have been at the hotel. The same Jean from years ago was now a burn victim, one of many from a deadly car bomb. Her once beautiful creamy skin was undoubtedly red and raw underneath the bandages, peeling away in layers from the top down, like dried paper. If she lived, Jean would never draw a man's eye again, except in sympathy.

CHAPTER 8

He was twenty-five when he fell in love with her. She was twenty-two. Of all unlikely places, they met on a golf course. He was on his first job, in St. Augustine, working for a small newspaper that sponsored an annual charity tournament for kids with cancer. He and the sportswriter were the only guys at the paper who could play, so they got the day off for the event.

Jean was part of the organizing committee for the charity, and she sat at a folding table near the clubhouse with another committee member where they registered the players and gave them their tee times. He noticed her all the way from the bag stand where he was putting on his shoes. One look at her and he knew he had to try.

He walked over to the table and made sure she was the one who checked him in.

She had the palest, smoothest skin he'd ever seen. It wasn't washed out looking; instead, it gleamed pearl-like on her slender arms and legs. Hardly a woman in Florida looked that way. Most had tanned, leathery skin he didn't like. Her hair and eyebrows were so light they seemed almost white rather than blond. Altogether, she was the most striking woman he'd seen in years, a vision of femininity that struck to his core.

She smiled up at him, took his name, and her light green eyes paused just long enough on his that he knew he might have a chance.

He couldn't stop thinking about her the whole round, started gripping the club too tightly with his right hand, and by the third hole he was hooking every drive into the trees. He shot twelve strokes over his usual score and the sportswriter never let him forget it. He didn't care. He only wanted to finish the round and get close enough to see her again before the event was over.

After the tournament he looked everywhere but couldn't find her until the awards ceremony where there was loud music and a lot of drinking. He saw her across the meeting room and she looked even better than before, so he went to her side immediately and refused to leave no matter who else came up to claim her attention.

"I thought you would do okay today," she said.

"Me, too."

"But you didn't win anything."

"Couldn't keep my mind on the game."

"You look strong enough to be a good player."

"Strength doesn't mean much in golf."

She leaned against him. "Did something distract you?"

"Yes," he smiled.

"Something I did?"

"Yes."

"What?"

"Being here."

They both had their share of alcohol and started dancing about seven. He remembered the sensation of holding her against his body and they seemed to fit together exactly right, her pelvis just below his, her face near his chest. He felt the charge running between them and it got stronger the more they danced.

Her dress was thin and cut low, an expensive dress with seashell designs on it. Every time he pulled her closer he could feel the sweat on the exposed part of her breasts against his polo shirt. She didn't resist him. Instead she seemed to melt into him more, with their bodies fitting better every minute.

It was a new thing for him to have a beautiful, mature woman accept his advances so willingly. In his experience they usually held back, being careful, not wanting to let things move too fast. With Jean, that didn't seem to matter. She gave in to the chemistry of the moment and seemed to revel in it.

By nine-thirty they were in a deep, full lip lock on the dance floor. No matter what song was playing, they just danced slowly right through it with his right thigh pushed between both of hers, their mouths working in a non-stop French kiss.

Finally, she pulled away. "Are you sure you want to get into this?"

"Are you kidding?" he laughed.

"Then let's get out of here, right now."

They stumbled outside and found a golf cart still parked out back from the tournament. They got in and started down a cart path, passed beneath trees out on the course, kept moving away from the lights of the clubhouse. She had her mouth on his neck and he put his right hand between her thighs.

He stopped the cart at a green with a huge live oak swaying alongside, Spanish moss hanging from its limbs, beards of parasitic life brushing the ground. They groped their way out of the cart and sprawled, laughing, on the short grass that was wet with dew. He had her dress off in seconds, tore his own shirt buttons loose pulling it over his head.

Later, the main thing he remembered was the smell and taste of her as he licked her breasts, so white in the moonlight they seemed otherworldly, her nipples full and soft as champagne grapes. He never before or since had felt such passion for anyone. He thought of the phrase soul mate over and over the next day, realized he had never understood what it meant before, the blend of genuine attraction and abandoned sex without having to go through the usual rituals. He wondered if it was possible for something this good to last.

For a few months it did. They spent every spare minute with each other, drove the roads between St. Augustine and Daytona again and again, always seemed to wind up at the beach. Late afternoons, they watched the sunlight fade from the waves until they looked dull gray turning over toward them. Later when the moon came up, the water took on a silver, shattered look as the curls broke apart on the sand. The sound of the water and wind was so rhythmic it felt as if they were making love every minute they spent beside the ocean.

Lunch in seafood cafes and long hours away from the heat in air-conditioned motel rooms, they couldn't get enough of it. She refused to come to his apartment for some reason she wouldn't reveal, and she wouldn't let him come to her place. He didn't care why; didn't think about it; all he wanted was the feel of her skin on his every day.

His job suffered, and he got a warning from his boss that he wasn't in the office enough. "Would it be too much to ask that you actually bring back a story when you're gone all afternoon?" Then, the city Editor grinned, as if he didn't know what was up. Still Darden pushed it, couldn't help himself. He was broke all the time because he spent so much of his pay on hotel rooms. Hell, he would have robbed a convenience store just to keep it going.

Then, disaster.

He saw her one night at the tourist strip downtown, her arm linked in a big guy's grasp. Standing inside a book store, Darden watched them through the front window. The guy was dressed-up and tanned, didn't seem like a brother. He was too young to be her father. He wore braided loafers with no socks, a silk shirt and linen pants.

She squeezed her torso up against the guy when they stopped to laugh at the plastic starfish and sharks in a beach shop window. He leaned and kissed her on the mouth, and they held it for a moment.

Darden felt all the blood in his body go to his feet. He wandered back to his apartment, stayed up all night smoking and thinking.

Next day, she didn't call him at work the way she usually did around ten. He tried her twice in the afternoon and couldn't reach her. That night, nothing.

Okay, he decided, I'll play it this way too. He wouldn't let himself call her for two more days. Figured she'd break down at some point and call him first, but she didn't. Finally, he went to her office and waited outside until quitting time. Her co-workers came out in an intermittent file over the next fifteen minutes;

she was one of the last. He followed her to her car, spoke as she fumbled with her keys.

"Hey," was all he managed to say, and that through tight lips.

"Tom!" she squealed. "You surprised me."

"Where have you been all week?"

She walked over and took his hand, kissed him on the cheek. Her green eyes never wavered from their open, sincere gaze.

"Oh, I just had some business to do."

Over the next few days and weeks, it was all breakdown. More missed calls. Less time together. Unkept dates. No lovemaking. Finally, there came a showdown one Sunday that left him hollow and feeling foolish. He found her at a shrimp house they both liked. Yes, she was seeing another man, she admitted, but it was nothing much, the two of them would still have their own relationship unchanged.

It took months for him to accept that nothing would ever be the same as it was before. She had gone through more men during that period; he didn't know how many. Eventually, his self respect became so battered, he had to stop calling her altogether. She never called him anymore. Communication between them eventually ceased and he knew it was pointless to try to renew anything with her.

Over time, he realized she was a rare woman, a woman who couldn't stay with one man. To him, it had always seemed most women wanted to settle down, but Jean was different. She felt stifled with just one man and had to move on to someone new as soon as a relationship started to deepen.

He had felt genuine love for her, the deepest he'd ever known, but for her, love didn't grow. It withered. So there it was, the only woman he'd ever wanted to marry and he knew it would never happen. He formed a hard coating over that feeling of irredeemable loss, made a decision he'd never let that happen to him again.

And his life went on.

Now, many years later, she lay a few feet from him on a curtained bed, struggling to stay alive. He found a nurse, asked about her condition, learned that Jean was badly burned on the upper torso and arms. No one could say if she would survive quite yet, but he could come back later.

Darden decided he would not go into the room and look at her, wouldn't come back later. He couldn't manage another deluge of feelings on top of what he already carried, but he would do his best to find out who had ruined her life.

CHAPTER 9

Before the afternoon press conference at police headquarters, they sat down for a hamburger at a Steak N' Shake, and Linda surprised him with her willingness to keep going even though she was exhausted. Now off duty, she shared what she knew with him. She'd picked up a few bits of information during her trips back to the bombing site. Firemen and police talked freely with the Emergency Medical teams and a few clues began to emerge; mainly, there was little doubt it was a bombing.

As it turned out, the press conference at the police station was a waste of time. The investigator in charge disclosed no information of substance as if nothing had been learned so far. The Police Chief only spoke of the incident as a hotel fire and anything else was speculative at this time. No, he couldn't discuss theories because of the active investigation. No, he wouldn't care to guess at the origin of the fire. No, he didn't know yet how many had died. And on it went.

Darden wondered why the police were so closed-mouthed about the incident. That was unusual. It was as if they were under an edict not to reveal a single fact.

Typically a higher-up would take to the cameras at a big press conference to grandstand before the public.

They left before the press conference was over and decided to drive back to the blast scene. Darden wanted a second look and knew he would never get through the police barricade without Linda's help. She knew some of the responders on sight and her dirty uniform was better than a press pass—which he no longer had anyway. Later, he'd have to get his boss to retrieve it from the police.

The scorched concrete and acrid smell had not gone away. Darden's mood fell as they picked their way across the site.

"Well, what now?" she said.

"Let's see what we can find out from the guys you know."

A lot of police and firemen were still on the scene, picking through rubble for anything unusual. A few men in plainclothes wandered about as well, taking photographs and making notes on pads. Darden wondered if they were federal agents or local detectives, perhaps some were reporters digging for a story just like him. He wondered whether the FBI or local police would actually handle the investigation, and he made a mental note to find out.

They walked over to the base of the hotel that now tilted inland—everyone already called it the leaning tower of Daytona. The burned area was cool now after constant soaking from fire hoses, but all that water had not washed away the stink. Black soot had turned to liquid and stood in every low spot, looking like puddles of oil.

An older fireman in an officer's uniform picked through a pile of debris, dropping occasional items into plastic bags. His concentration never wavered as he walked the site carefully, eyes down, searching for the history of the explosion in its aftermath. He carried a plastic hand shovel which he used to sift through any pile of wreckage that caught his attention.

Linda walked them toward the fireman, whispering to Darden, "He's the Chief Fire Inspector. Let me do the talking."

They stopped in front of him and he looked up.

"Hi, Chief."

He nodded in acknowledgment. "Miss Ramsey." Despite his formality, he seemed to know Linda well and almost smiled. The man's eyes had deep lines at the corners, his beard and hair mostly gray. He looked at Darden but said nothing.

"What do we know so far?" Darden asked.

Linda glared at him. The Chief glanced his way for a moment then turned to Linda. "Who's he?"

"My buddy, Tom. A reporter, but he's okay."

"Pretty damn impatient, if you ask me."

The Chief apparently liked Linda well enough to overlook Darden's bluntness. He addressed her and shook his head in a mixture of frustration and determination.

"So far, we don't know much. It was definitely a car bomb, detonated at the loading dock of the hotel. Most of the casualties occurred in the hotel and the swimming pool beside it. Used to be right over there."

He pointed to a spot that had been obliterated, then littered with black debris, mostly exploded car parts. Pieces of windshields, fenders, and tires were heaped and melted together in a giant tangle along with chain link fencing, concrete, and rebar.

"We've got all the bodies out, we think. These samples I'm collecting should tell us about the explosives used."

"There had to be a lot to do this much damage," Linda said.

"Right," the Chief said. "Most likely a truck was used to carry a big load of it."

Darden frowned. "A truck full of nails and explosives."

For the first time, the Chief deigned to speak to him. "They knew what they were doing, yes."

"So this was about producing maximum carnage."

"I'm afraid so, yes." He squinted at Darden. "But don't quote me on that in the paper tomorrow."

Darden glanced at Linda, saw annoyance on her face.

"Do you have any security video?" Linda asked.

"No, the explosion was too strong."

"Any witnesses?" Darden asked.

"Not that we know of." The Chief avoided their eyes for a moment, glanced at the ground.

"One more question," Darden said. "Any leads on who did it?"

"Not yet, no."

The Chief looked down again at the black crunchy detritus underfoot, ready to get back to work. His professionalism wouldn't allow him to show his emotions yet, but Darden suspected it would come later. The kind of guy who anguished in private.

"But we're collecting pieces of a rental truck over there." The Chief indicated an area that had been a parking lot. "Some of it we found two hundred yards away, mostly scraps of metal scattered in a fan shape from the blast zone."

"Can we take a look?" Linda asked.

He nodded. "But don't disturb the evidence."

They walked toward the pile of scrap the Chief had pointed out. An identifying sign had already been placed next to it with an evidence number written on it. The individual pieces of scrap were also tagged with identification numbers.

When they got close, one thing was obvious. If this was indeed the truck that carried the explosives, it had come from U-Haul. Even burned and shredded, pieces of the truck body bore the unmistakable orange color of U-Haul rentals. They looked over the wreckage for a moment and his eyes found a twisted piece of metal that still bore a small decal: WARNING! WATCH YOUR HEAD.

Darden assumed the decal must have come from one of the models with storage above the cab. The warning was placed over the doors at eye level to keep passengers from hitting their heads on the overhang when getting in and out.

Then it hit him. He had seen that logo, at least that distinctive color, somewhere else around here on the day of the blast.

"Linda!"

She looked up as he broke into a jog toward a row of buildings at the far edge of the destruction zone. He ran inland, ignoring puddles of black goop and piles of scrap. Linda caught up with him when he stopped at the blown-out storefront where the cops had threatened to take him in.

"What is it?" she asked.

He hurried around the corner of the building and there it was. An old trash can made from a metal barrel, shielded by the wall from most of the blast. He dug through the stuff inside it, wildly throwing scraps of paper, water bottles, styro containers, every predictable piece of trash from the barrel.

"What are you doing?"

"It's got to be in here."

"What?"

He yanked a softball-sized wad of paper from the can and took a closer look at it. Then unraveling the wad, he was sure he'd found it.

"This," he said. "I used it to wipe my hands."

He stretched it open, smoothed out the singed edges and wrinkled panels. There, on the top left panel, plain as day, they both saw the U-Haul logo.

"It's a company map of Florida," Darden said. "It came with the rental."

"But how do you know the bomber used it?"

"I don't, yet."

She stepped closer and they both examined it, but it didn't reveal anything of consequence. Only part of the map remained; a stretch of the east coast, from Melbourne south. Then he turned it over and they both inhaled audibly. The back side revealed the northern coast of Florida, complete with directional markings.

"I knew I remembered something unusual about it."

The map had a black line running north along I-95 from Ormond Beach, with instructions scribbled alongside the coastline. The felt tip markings were directions to a location in Daytona, although the city itself was missing, torn away by the blast presumably. They traced the black line up the coast where it ended with an asterisk somewhere in south Jacksonville.

"It doesn't seem possible," Linda said.

"What?"

"That they would have mapped a route and had it in the truck. They couldn't be that stupid."

Darden shook his head uncertainly. "Unless they felt sure the fire would destroy it."

"And it should have," she insisted. "How could a paper map survive that explosion?"

"I don't know."

She still didn't buy it. "We don't know for sure this means

anything. Maybe a tourist dropped it."

Darden nodded. "But tourists don't rent moving trucks."

"Maybe it has nothing to do with that orange debris over there."

"Maybe."

Her face changed, lost its doubtfulness when she realized he was going to follow his hunch no matter what she said. "Then again—"

"Then again," he interrupted. "This is the only lead I've got."

"Right."

He started walking, carefully folding the map along its original panel lines. She has to ask, he thought, even though she already knows.

"Jacksonville?"

He nodded. "Jacksonville."

"Now?"

"Right now."

"Wait. Can't I get some clean clothes first?"

"What do you mean?"

"I'm coming with you."

CHAPTER 10

Darden was surprised when she came back out to his car wearing a red sun dress and sandals. Two days he'd known her and only seen her in a dirty uniform stained with soot and sweat. Now she appeared completely feminine, bare shouldered and with a bit of make-up, and he realized how pretty she was. Best of all, she looked clean now, her hair washed and brushed back in short waves.

He realized he'd underestimated her in every way. She was tough enough to handle an emotionally demanding job and make her way among the macho world of cops and firemen, yet by her appearance it was clear she somehow remained and enjoyed being an attractive woman.

"Thanks," she said. "The shower worked wonders."

"Still tired?"

"Yeah, but coffee will take care of that. Let's roll."

Out on the interstate, he drove north while she sat slumped in the passenger seat. Her head began to sink after a quarter hour and he let her sleep until they got past St. Augustine. He liked the smell of her shampoo and soap in his car. It was an old Honda Accord, and he thought it looked shabby driving around town, wished for something better, but the smell of her closeness made it feel a bit better anyway.

He needed a shower and change of clothes himself, but he wasn't about to slow down for that. If this lead turned into something, he had a chance to be the first one to break a big part of the story. If the lead meant something, he thought again.

At four-thirty in the afternoon, traffic became heavy and he felt as if it was holding him back, keeping him from getting to the story ahead of everybody else. He fought for patience and told himself to stay clear-headed. Next, he needed two things, coffee and a phone book. He pulled off at the first populated exit on the southern edge of Jacksonville before they got to the 295 bypass.

The drive-through at Starbucks was five cars deep and the squawk of the speaker woke up Linda when the barista took his order. She stretched and sighed, but seemed to come awake quickly.

"Is a regular grande okay?" he asked. "Cream and sugar?"

She nodded, picked up the dirty, smoke-stained map and he could see her attention immediately turn to the problem at hand. Like him, she worked through fatigue and maybe even pain if there was a job to do. He respected that. She studied the spot where the route had terminated or more probably originated, the unknown place where the asterisk was drawn on the map.

After they got the coffee, he drove next door to a gas station and found a pay phone next to the air pump. Luckily there was a phone book chained to the kiosk, he thought, there were hardly any pay phones anymore, not to mention phone books. He climbed out and flipped to the yellow pages, found the section for truck rentals, two pages of them, and ripped the pages out of the book.

Back in the car, Linda stared at him with a mixture of amusement and mock disgust. "What are you doing?" she asked.

"I'm getting the locations of rental trucks."

"Out of a phone book?"

"So?"

"Quit thinking like a dinosaur."

She pulled out her phone and tapped the surface with her fingers to get the right app to appear on the screen. "This is the way to find stuff fast."

"But I don't like those phones. They're too complicated."

She laughed at him outright, her fingers darting over the screen. "Some reporter."

He stared lightning bolts at her, hunched his shoulders and

started the car. "Cell phones," he grumbled. "Okay, tell me the way to the closest U-Haul location in the south part of town."

A second later she held the screen toward his face to show him up, then called out a series of street names while he scanned a map of Jacksonville spread out on his lap.

"—one off of I-10, one near the beach, one—"

"None of those are close."

"One near Phillips Highway—"

"Okay, that's up near the river. We'll try that first."

He got back on ninety-five and they drove north again, got closer to the city then took an exit near Beach Boulevard. Finally, after twenty more minutes, they found the U-Haul location at a Food Mart station. It was small and had only a few trailers lined up out front. The woman inside said they never took reservations for big trucks at her location, because they didn't have enough space to park them.

By seven o'clock, they had tried three other locations and found nothing. Both of them were growing more tired and frustrated by the minute. Darden pulled off the road and shut the engine down. They were quiet for a few moments, both thinking.

"If you were going to rent a truck and blow it up," he said, "What would you do to cover your tracks?"

"Use a fake ID"

"Yeah, what else?"

"I'd get somebody else to drive it."

"Where would you load it with explosives and detonators?"

"Inside. Somewhere big, like a garage or warehouse."

"Yep, you'd also do it far away from the driver."

They sat quietly again, both trying to think it through the way the bomber or team of bombers would have thought.

"In fact," Darden said. "I'd rent it at one place, rig the explosives at another, and pass it off to the driver at a third place."

"That makes sense."

He picked up her cell phone. "Let's do this smarter, instead of driving all over town."

They took turns calling every rental truck listing and asked for the biggest trucks available. U-Haul's largest, they learned, was twenty-six feet, and the most likely location to handle those would be north of downtown near the 20th Street Expressway.

"Now we're getting somewhere," Linda said.

They drove to the location and immediately saw two twenty-six footers parked in the lot, but the office was closed. They sat, more annoyed than ever and feeling deflated by the dead end.

"Damn it," Darden said.

"No," Linda said. "We're not quitting, not yet." She fidgeted for a moment, said she didn't want their search to end that way, then got out of the Accord and looked around, saw a diner next door. "Come on, Tom. I've got an idea."

He climbed out and followed her across the shell and gravel lot to the diner. A forlorn palmetto drooped beside the entrance, the tips of its fronds dried to brown needlepoints. Inside, the restaurant was cold and brightly lit by fluorescents. They sat down on round chrome stools at the counter and waited for the waitress to make her way over to them. She was in no hurry, making a show of her weariness. She wore very heavy eye makeup and had tobacco stained teeth, her hair an indefinite shade of brown dye. They ordered coffee and two waffles, thanked the waitress when she came back with the hot coffee.

"You know what?" Linda said to her. "We really need to rent one of those big U-Haul's next door, but they've already closed down. Would you know who runs that place?"

"Yeah, I know him. Don't care for him, neither. Loud talker, that one. He's in here three times a day and never leaves a tip." She eyed Darden cautiously as if he too might be a non-tipper.

"Would you know how we might call him at home?" Linda asked. "We really need the truck tonight."

The waitress coughed deeply, looked as if she wanted a cigarette. "Well, he's got a card over there on that board." She tilted her piled up hair toward a cork bulletin board hanging on the wall beside the cash register. It was covered with bounced checks and business cards stuck on it with thumbtacks.

Darden went over and found an orange and white U-Haul

card, removed it and brought it back to the counter.

"This it?"

"That's him, the one and only king of truck rentals."

The cook slammed their plates on a chrome counter above the griddle. "Order up."

"Lemme getcha' waffles for you." The waitress took four slow steps to the food, brought it back to them and put syrup cartons beside each plate.

"Maybe we could look up his number and call him," Linda said.

"I wouldn't do that," the waitress replied.

"Why not?"

"He ain't a nice man."

"Oh," Darden said. "I see."

"Maybe, he wouldn't mind getting the extra business," Linda said.

"Hmpph! I ain't helping him any."

They started eating their food and the waitress continued to stand there, putting one forearm across her torso and resting the other elbow on it, hand up to her lips as if she were holding a cigarette. Linda looked at him, raised her eyebrows and urged him on; maybe the waitress wanted to say something else if they'd just give her a chance.

Tom cleared his throat and looked back at her, got out his wallet and put a twenty on the countertop.

"What's the matter with that man?" he said. "The service here is exceptional. Keep the change."

By then, the waitress looked as if she wanted to tell them something so badly she would pop. As she scooped up the twenty, he realized he could have held off with the money and she would've likely talked anyway. She must be the local fount of information and couldn't help but pass on what she knew.

"He wuz in here today, complainin' up a storm. Cussin' like a sailor. Said somebody didn't bring a truck back, who was supposed to. He's not a nice man, you know."

Darden leaned forward. "What exactly did he say about the

truck?"

"Said some Mexican boy rented it, but he didn't trust him. Had to rent it to him though, all his ID and cards was okay. Said he didn't think the boy'd bring it back when he rented it."

"Anything else?"

"Couldn't be important, might be something dirty." She looked as if she was dying to tell them this dark piece of gossip.

"Like what?"

She leaned a bit closer to them, lowered her voice. "Said a man in a black truck dropped the boy off. Expensive Ford truck. Said he wondered what a man like that had to do with a Mexican boy could hardly speak any English."

"Did he say what the man looked like?"

"Never got a good look at him." She tilted her head back and pinched up her face. "I ain't saying no more to help that s.o.b. find his truck."

Linda swallowed the last of her coffee, holding back a grin as she watched Tom work the waitress.

"Well, it's nothing to us. I was just curious, since those trucks are kind of scarce right now—"

"—cept he said the driver wuz wearin' a black cowboy hat."

"You mind if we keep this card."

"Ain't no hair offa' my head."

She walked away and retrieved a pack of cigarettes from her purse below the counter, headed for the back room.

They looked at each other between their final bites of waffle. Neither of them needed to say a word. When they walked back to his car, they high-fived each other and laughed with a huge sense of satisfaction.

Inside the car, Darden picked up his cell phone and speed dialed Weldon's home number. "News Editor," he said to Linda. "My finest boss ever."

Weldon answered after four rings, his voice sounded as if he'd started on his evening cocktails. "Darden, where the hell are you?"

"Listen, Weldon. I think I've found something."

"Since when do you leave the office without telling me?"

"Just listen. Has anything come across the scanner today, say down on the southside? Anything unusual?"

He could sense Weldon's temper building on the other end. "What are you into, Darden?"

"The bombing. I'm tracking a lead."

"Bombing? That's not your assignment anymore. What the—"

"Just answer me, Weldon. The police scanner. Anything today?"

"No. Not much happening."

"Nothing at all?"

Weldon paused. Darden could picture those huge jowls shaking as Weldon retraced the day in his mind.

"Some rental guy bitching about his truck being stolen."

"Anything else?"

"Not your kind of story. Had a missing person call at a trailer park off Phillips. The landlord called it in, said some Mexican claimed his cousin disappeared. Probably just an illegal decided to go back home."

"Where is the park?"

"Ah, off Phillips, down near Greenland somewhere."

"Go back to your gin, Weldon. I'm onto something."

Weldon bellowed into the phone, "Darden, get your ass into the office in the morning or you're going to be—"

Darden clicked the off button, laughed out loud, a tension-filled laugh, and once started he could hardly stop. Linda watched him with her mouth open, then she broke, had to laugh too. He laughed for a full minute and pounded the dashboard before he could get it under control, felt the tension releasing from his gut. When the laughter finally stopped, they both wiped their eyes.

"Oh," he said. "The guy is such a jerk."

CHAPTER 11

When they pulled into the trailer park, Linda saw that it was much worse than she had thought it would be. Trash, junk cars, and loose dogs covered the grounds of the trailer park, signs of too many people living too close together. Small children were still playing outside even though it was well after dark; a few men sat on their porch steps and smoked.

The front door of the single-wide stood open as they approached it in the dark, the blue interior light of a television shining through the rectangular doorway. She wondered if the occupants left it open all the time, oblivious to the mosquitoes that drifted in freely. They walked up and Tom rapped on the vinyl-covered wall outside, waited until an accented voice invited them in.

"Come."

Linda stood on the cinder block steps outside the door, watching while Darden went in to talk to the man about his missing cousin. There was not enough room inside for both of them.

She knew the migrants worked very hard on construction sites and landscaping crews, and she knew they sent most of their money back to Mexico, but she didn't know they lived so poorly. Everything about the place was worn and dirty. With no screens and no air-conditioners, most people would have abandoned the trailer years ago. She wondered how much rent they paid for it.

Bunk beds jammed the living room all the way to the ceiling, several of them occupied by young men at this very moment. But they really weren't men; teenagers was more accurate, teenagers already old beyond their years. Somewhere inside a television blared out a Spanish language station, the screen throwing blue light across the room that rose and fell on the impassive faces of the migrants. They sprawled on their beds and watched her intently as if she might be able to do them harm or perhaps wondering what they would like to do to her.

The furniture was a mixture of cheap castaway pieces that likely came from a charity store. Their clothes and shoes piled at the foot of each bed were a mismatch of cheap and durable garments that went unwashed, unkempt. The room was hot and smelled of too many bodies.

Sitting on a sofa, an outrageous plaid piece broken down in the middle, the cousin sat and heatedly told Darden about his callous treatment by the police. He said they ignored the complaint about his missing cousin, Hector, and instead questioned him, Jose, about his papers. He showed them his Social Security card and still they wouldn't talk about Hector. The others nodded and mumbled in agreement.

Once Darden had convinced them he wasn't from the police or the Immigration Service, he managed a conversation using a mix of English and stumbling Spanish that somehow worked. She watched their carefully controlled emotions trickling out, fearful of authority yet indignant that no one cared about the missing boy, despite his unimportance. They said the police assumed Hector had just left on his own, discouraged by so little work.

"Who did it?" Darden kept saying. It was obvious to Linda he didn't want to hear the police part; he wanted to know who hired Hector. "*Quien?*"

"Who?" Jose didn't understand.

"Who took him? Who did he leave with?"

"Don' know. A man in a truck."

"What did the police say?"

"They don' care."

Listening to the story, she suspected they were mostly angry about the risk they'd taken in talking to the police, only to have it come to nothing. From what she knew, they never would have dared complain to the police about anything in Mexico, and now, here, their first brush with American law enforcement had proved just as pointless.

Linda saw one of the teenagers on a lower bunk turn to them. He sat up and put his bare feet on the floor. "It was a black truck."

"You saw it?" Darden asked.

"*Si*. Was big and new."

"What else? *Mas*?"

"A Ford."

"What about the man inside it?"

"A, ah, *sombrero negro*."

"He wore a black hat?"

"*Si*."

"Anything else?"

"Was from Texas."

"Texas plates on the truck. You're sure?"

Several of the teenagers looked at each other and laughed softly. "Oh, yes. We cross Texas. We know the plates."

Darden questioned them a couple more minutes, but they didn't know much else. He looked about, almost shrugged, then Linda thought of something else.

"Tom, what about the truck that dropped the man off at the rental place? Sounds like the same one."

Darden asked them as best he could who among them rented a big truck a few days earlier. They conversed between themselves in rapid Spanish, low and serious. Finally, Hector's cousin answered, "Was Miguel. We did not know him. He did not return to the store at the highway."

"Did he live here?"

"No. We don' know where."

"Did you see him again?"

"No."

"Ever?"

"No."

"But it was the same man in the Ford pickup who hired him, right?"

"Maybe."

Linda took a half step forward into the cramped room. "Was it the same truck that picked up Hector?"

They all looked back at her with immobile faces until one of them in a corner spoke up. He was the youngest of the bunch, maybe fifteen, and seemed shy about talking to her. "Was the same truck."

"How do you know?"

"I saw it two times. Two days. He pick up one man only, then leave fast."

After a few more words back and forth, she and Darden looked at each other, both satisfied they'd learned all they could. They thanked the men and left the dim trailer, walked back to the Accord across the rutted parking area.

Back on ninety-five again, they were both quiet for a while, both thinking about a man in a black truck who'd almost certainly killed two migrants and masterminded the bombing of hundreds of innocent victims in Daytona.

Finally Darden spoke, "I have to think for a while, decide what to do next, but I'm dead tired."

"Me too. Crawling."

"Are you off tomorrow?"

"Thank God, after all that overtime."

"Do you want to stay up here tonight, instead of driving back to Daytona?"

"Stay with you?"

He grinned through his fatigue. "I didn't mean it that way. We could find you a motel room near my place. I'll pay, of course."

She stared straight ahead. "If you don't mind, I'd rather stay with you." It was out before she even knew she'd thought of it. What made her say that? She barely knew him, but she also quickly admitted that she loved being with this man, would much prefer his company to an empty hotel room.

"Okay, if that's what you want," he said.

"Then again, I don't want you to get the wrong idea."

"Like what?"

"Like I'm trying to jump your bones, first date, sort of."

"Okay," he said. "Is this a date?"

"You know what I mean." She punched him on the arm lightly and he grinned.

She felt better after saying it, didn't want to appear so forward to him, so eager. That was never good when you were just getting to know a man. "I mean, you have a couch or something, right?"

"Sure, and I'll crash there. You can take the bedroom where the bathroom is close."

"Okay," she said. "Could we get some food on the way?"

He turned into the first take-out restaurant they came to on the right-hand side of the street. "Is pizza okay with you?"

She nodded and he went in to get it while she waited in the car. Truth was, now that she'd composed herself, she would like to know him much better, was surprised how much she liked him, but she just couldn't let things move too fast. She really was dead tired and couldn't imagine staying up half the night, and, she just wasn't ready yet anyway. She didn't do that sort of thing, but gosh, he was good looking, she thought, a bit on the tall side with long, strong-looking legs, good shoulders, but none of those big pumped-up muscles she didn't like. His hair was light; a serious, almost sad face.

Best of all, he wasn't anything like the cops and firemen she worked with every day. He was more intelligent and thoughtful than most of them, less aggressive, or maybe just less certain about everything. They acted as if they were always absolutely right, too sure, never stopped to think about things. Worst of all, most of them assumed she'd go all rubbery over them, just because they wore a gun and a badge. She would never say it to the men in her job circles, but she actually hated guns. She hated them because she knew—had already seen on her job—too much of what guns could do to bodies and minds. Aside from horrible physical wounds, she didn't like the change that guns brought on some men who wore a weapon. They took on a personality of exaggerated power, of control.

After her experience with her ex-boyfriend, the last thing

she wanted was an overly controlling personality in her life. She wanted to make her own choices. Secretly, she felt any man who needed to wear a gun, or even enjoyed it, was a bit insecure and needed the illusion of power that guns gave him. Real strength didn't come from physical power over people; it came from compassion and—

The door opened abruptly, startling her. Boy, she'd been off on a real tangent there, her mind spinning out a whole argument in favor of this guy.

"I got pepperoni on one side and veggies on the other," he said. "That sound okay?"

"Yeah, great. You can eat the pepperoni side. It gives me indigestion." She made a face and touched her stomach.

They both laughed and then grew quiet while he drove to his place about twenty minutes east toward the ocean. His condo turned out to be a simple one floor unit near Ponte Vedre, not too far from the beach. Same as most men, it wasn't much on the decoration side, but it wasn't bad either. At least it didn't have those awful university mascot photos or any big recliner chairs. It was simple and comfortable, with beachy furniture and a lot of books.

They reheated the pizza in the oven and while it was warming up, he went and took a quick shower, came out in shorts and sandals, a faded tee shirt. He seemed relaxed and at home, pleased to have her there. That in itself was a huge relief. You never knew what men would be like when you went to their place because they were so territorial.

The two of them sat at the breakfast table in the kitchen, drank cold beer and enjoyed the greasy cheese taste of the pizza.

When they finished, they both sat back, sated, looked at each other.

"Let me ask you something," she said.

"Ask."

"When I saw you yesterday—the day of the bombing—I think it was yesterday, right? Seems a long time ago. Anyway, the cops were giving you a hard time. Why were they on you in the first place?"

"Thanks again, for pulling them away," he said.

"You're welcome," she said. "But tell me."

His face became serious. "I didn't ask for it, if that's what you think."

"I don't think anything. I just don't get it. I could see the anger on their faces and you were about to explode. Do you give cops a hard time, or what?"

"No, I just don't give in."

"To authority in general?"

"I suppose so, yes. I don't like people telling me what to do, that's all."

He paused for a moment, seemed to collect his thoughts. "Some people thrive on ordering others around. They have a thing about making people do things to suit them. To me, that's the ultimate insult. No one has the right to give me orders just because they're in a position to do so."

"Even a cop?"

"Especially a cop. There has to be a reason for it. Otherwise it's just a brute exercise of power for the sake of power. It's about their ego, their need to control, not about the reality of the moment."

She was taken by the strength of his conviction. He was more serious and far more cerebral than she had imagined. His was a considered approach to life, not just random reaction that determined the lives of so many others she knew.

He got up and led her into the living room, pointed to a book shelf. "That is my history section. Read any of them, and the same pattern emerges. If you cede control to unchecked authority, eventually you pay the price. People suffer when brutes are allowed to run things the way they want."

"You got all that moral foundation from history books?" she said doubtfully.

"No, of course not." He seemed to waver for a moment, unsure whether to be so open with her, wondering if he should share his innermost thoughts.

She moved closer to him, hoping, willing him to tell her what he was thinking. She wanted to know what was inside Tom Darden's heart and head.

"When I was in high school," he said. "There was a coach who wanted me to play football for him."

He sat down on the sofa and she eased into a chair flanking it.

"You didn't like football."

"Oh, I liked it okay. But I didn't want to do it anymore, gave it up in eighth grade because I liked golf more. Anyway, it turned into this thing with the coach. He started out harassing me, you know, insulting me in class, then it got worse. I tried to ignore it but he wouldn't let me. In those days, they kept a big paddle in their desk, with holes drilled in it."

"You've got to be kidding."

"No."

She watched him as he continued, his hands out on his knees, opening and closing the fingers, stretching them out. She curled her legs up under her, listening.

"I wish I was kidding. He started to invent infractions, rules I'd broken, rules I didn't even know existed, rules that didn't apply to anyone else. They were just excuses, of course. Ways for him to torment me. He beat me with that paddle every week for most of my junior year, and I wouldn't give in."

"But he couldn't get away with that."

"He could, and did."

"Why didn't anybody stop him?"

"Good question."

"Even though they knew he was beating you, no one stepped in?"

"I didn't tell any other teachers or my father. After a while, I don't think it was about football. He just wanted me to bend to his authority, just to prove he had it, and I didn't want to submit to his power over me."

"I can't say I blame you, but it must be hard fighting back against every bad ass you meet."

"Nothing that dramatic, but yeah, I've paid a price."

"So you've gone your whole life resisting people like that."

"Somebody has to do it. Otherwise, the brutes win and we—I—have a duty to keep them from winning."

"Why? Why you?"

"That's a story for another day."

CHAPTER 12

As usual Linda woke up a few minutes after five, her body locked into the internal rhythm of her regular shift hours. She lay in Darden's bed for a few minutes and stared at the ceiling, breathed in the smell of maleness coming from the pillows and sheets. The bed was firm and it felt good to lie there, but she had to go to the bathroom, tried to put it off, decided she couldn't and got up. Groping across the floor, she found the bathroom door, then the toilet.

Finished, she got up and went for the bed, glanced through the open doorway to the living room. In the half-light, she saw him stretched out on the couch, but his legs were too long and hung over the arm on one end, his feet sticking in the air. That couldn't be very comfortable but somehow he seemed to be sleeping okay.

She stretched out on the bed, knew she couldn't go back to sleep now, but made herself stay there anyway. She thought of him lying on the couch, just a few steps away. Enough of that, she told herself, but the more she tried not to think about him sleeping in the next room, the more the thought intruded on her mind.

Linda spent much of her time around men, a lot of different men, and every day she had them trying to make it with her. She had no trouble fending them off, but here, now, was a guy sleeping a few feet away from her, both of them undressed, and he hadn't tried anything all night. Maybe she didn't appeal to him. No, something told her that wasn't it. Well, what did she expect? She'd told him she didn't want to do anything tonight and he was respecting her wishes. That simple. Or was it?

Her mind ran on for some time, puzzling over the situation, most of all, trying to determine exactly what she did want. Did she want him or didn't she? Would he think less of her? Would it please him? Would she like it? She rolled around under the covers for a while, unable to decide.

Finally, she put her hand under the tee shirt she'd borrowed to sleep in. She found her left breast, stroked it gently, felt the heft of it, an almost swollen feeling. Her nipple was hard. She reached between her legs, felt herself. Wet. Something was happening here that was not normal for her. It took her time to warm up to a man, didn't it?

She got up, walked very quietly into the living room on her bare feet, the tee shirt covering half her thighs. She went to the couch, looked down at him. He was asleep, his feet still in the air, his chest uncovered, arms across it. She knelt down beside him, looked at his face closely, trying to discern its features in the dim light. Finally, she sighed in resignation, felt a tremor of excitement and nervousness run through her core. She could hardly believe she was doing this.

"Tom?"

He cleared his throat, rolled toward her. His breathing changed pace.

"Tom."

He opened his eyes, appeared to wonder at the voice.

"Linda? Is something wrong? "

"I … "

She wanted to say the right thing, something clever and romantic, at least something sexy, but words suddenly failed her. Her throat felt thick and dry; nothing at all came out of her mouth, and she found herself standing there in front of him, feeling a bit foolish, but not wanting to turn back now. Trembling with apprehension, there was only one thing left for her to do next.

She pulled the big tee shirt off slowly, tugging it over her head then dropping it beside her. She stood completely still to let him look at her nudity in the half-light of the room. It was the boldest and most exciting thing she'd ever done in front of a man. He said nothing, but his eyes snapped open at the sight of her and he turned to put his feet on the floor. At that point, words seemed unimportant. She shivered and took him by the hand then led him into the bedroom.

Next morning, they woke up and took their time, did it again, fell asleep, woke again, did it again. Linda hadn't felt so good in weeks. Maybe ever. She lay beside him, one leg draped over both of his, one breast resting on his chest, the other pressing against his ribs. She couldn't remember when it had been so satisfying just to lie next to a man with no clothes on, their skin warming each other. The sun grew bright through the blinds but neither of them wanted to get up.

Eventually his office called and he had to answer it. He flipped open the cell and she heard a voice on the other end talking loudly. Tom could hardly get a word in and the voice grew louder. Finally he got up and took the phone into the kitchen. From there, she heard him explain that he was working on the story and he'd have it in by the end of the day.

She got up, reached for the tee shirt, then decided to leave it off. She felt so good being nude in front of him she decided to prolong the sensation of having his eyes on her, taking in her fine legs and swaying breasts. Just the thought of his stare made her feel sexy. She went into the kitchen where he stood at the sink, after tossing the cell phone onto the counter.

"How about breakfast?" he asked.

"I'll make, you have work to do."

He smiled, pleased by her quick understanding of the situation. "Coffee first, please."

"Of course."

"You might try some clothes, too. Or I won't be able to write a thing."

"I thought you'd like to have me naked in your kitchen."

"I do, that's the problem." He pulled her close and squeezed her buttocks gently. "You can always take them back off, after I finish the story."

She kissed his chest. "Get to work."

He went to the breakfast table and opened his laptop while she started the coffee. She moved around the kitchen, collecting pans and ingredients, caught him twice watching her, noticed he didn't tap a single key until she went into the bedroom to dress.

After breakfast, she could tell he was at the point where he was ready to write the story. A serious frown descended on his face and a sort of focus on the keyboard began. She put the dishes in the washer and went to take a long shower. From the bedroom, she heard the keys clicking, fast and steady, sounding like sleet on a metal roof.

By three o'clock he told her he had finished about seven-hundred-fifty words and was ready to e-mail the story to the office. He asked her to look at it first and tell him what she thought. She sat down at the laptop and read it, then read it again.

Finished, she looked up. "This is pretty good."

"That's all? Pretty good?"

She didn't know what to say, thought perhaps she'd violated some sort of reporters' code. Maybe she was supposed to say it was fabulous. Maybe she was not supposed to say anything at all.

"What about the headline?" he asked. "Think it's strong enough?"

She read it out loud: "JAX MIGRANTS LINK TO BOMBING?"

He waited.

She wasn't going to make the same mistake twice. "Yeah, that's good. Real good. Very strong."

He waited. She wasn't going to get away with humoring him.

"Look," she said. "It is good, but why make it a question? You've found a real connection here, a definite link, so blare it out. What about the black truck and the missing U-Haul? Don't be so careful telling the story."

"Well, I have to be. My Editor is so cautious he won't accept a story like this unless it's written in very careful, qualified statements, triple-checked and triple-sourced."

"But that strips the guts out of it."

"I know," he said. "But it won't fly otherwise."

She thought a moment. "You mean it's that tough just to report what we found out yesterday?"

"In my organization, yes, I have to be cautious."

"Then, Tom, it's no wonder you are so unhappy with your job."

"I never said that."

"It's obvious."

He looked miserable. She got up and kissed him, but he wasn't into it. She could tell his mind was fixed on the story.

"Do you really want to know what I think?" she asked.

"Yes, I do."

"Okay, go back to the keyboard and write it again. Put all the passion and guts into it that you showed me out there yesterday. Then, if your Editor doesn't like it, at least you wrote the story you really wanted to write."

He kissed her back, this time with enthusiasm. "Thanks," he said.

She went outside and walked for an hour while he rewrote the story. When she came back he'd already e-mailed it to the office. She read it and thought it was great, not like the local watered-down news, but more like national investigative journalism. There was no hedging, no uncertainty, just hard reporting of facts that allowed the reader to conclude what they'd both already concluded. The two missing migrants were killed because the man behind the bombing had wanted them dead.

"That's wonderful," she told him.

They put their arms around each other and before long they were on the bed, lost in that world of touch once again. When he moved on top of her, she put her legs around him and locked her ankles behind his back, felt him racing inside her as she hung on, matching him stroke for stroke. Finally, they both accelerated together in a gasping, laughing collapse as their muscles let go.

Within a half hour, his boss called. By then, they were lying on their backs, breathing abated, hearts returned to normal, feeling the sweat evaporate in a chill on bare skin. The phone kept ringing until Darden had no choice but to answer.

Weldon immediately ripped into him, ruining the peace of the moment. His voice was so loud, she could hear every word. Darden put him on speakerphone since there was no privacy anyway.

"I'm not going with this story," Weldon fumed.

Darden answered in a monotone. "What's wrong with it this time?"

"This is hard news and you have no corroboration."

"Like what? Who could corroborate it?"

"The police, for one."

Darden breathed out slowly, trying to control his voice.

"I'm ahead of the police on this story, Weldon. They don't know any of this. That's what good reporting is."

"Well, if you're right about the migrants, why hasn't anybody else got the story yet? Five television networks—million dollar anchors—hundreds of reporters in Daytona and you're the only one who makes this connection?"

"Maybe I'm working harder than them." He pinched Linda's leg. "Maybe I've got some first-rate inside help."

She would have giggled, but this clash was becoming serious. His boss wouldn't be amused to know she was there. She put her head on his arm, listened closely.

"I've warned you before, Darden. Too many times. You need to stick with drunk driving arrests and house fires. That's your bread and butter. Not this heavyweight stuff."

"You've lost confidence in me, Weldon." Darden said. "If you won't let me report on this and won't run a great story when I get it, how can I do my job?"

"So you want to be a heavyweight, that it?"

"I think I am a heavyweight."

Weldon huffed on the other end of the call, his exasperation peaking. "Okay, you really want to know how it is?"

"Tell me, I can't wait."

"Word has come down from Atlanta to lay off this story. No way we're touching it."

Darden lurched upright, his face pale. "Why? Why would they do that? It's the story of the decade."

"You heard me. It ends now. Get back on track or I'm reassigning you, that is, if I can save your job."

Darden could hardly speak. "Weldon, you know why I transferred to Florida. My Dad is dying here, and I need the paycheck for the hospital bills."

Linda felt a throb of pain in her chest. She'd had no idea about his father.

"You don't have a choice, Darden."

"If you don't let me cover this story, I'll do it on my own."

Weldon's voice calmed, changed to a growl. "Where I'm sending you, you won't be able to cover it."

She heard the meanness under his words. Perhaps someone from headquarters really had decided to nix the story, but Tom's boss was taking too much delight in this, transferring him away from his sick father and taking him off the hot story. She guessed he had it all planned before he made the call.

"Well, how can you stop me from covering it?" Darden said.

"Easy. I'm giving you a real chance to be a heavyweight. As of now, your new beat is the war."

She looked at Tom in alarm as she mouthed the words, "The war?"

"We're sending you to Iraq."

"Iraq!" Tom looked incredulous. "I'm not an international guy. Why me?"

"Short staff situation. We need a new man over there."

"I won't go, Weldon. Not with this great story unwinding right here."

"Then, kiss your job goodbye."

The speakerphone went dead with a click, their good spirits and brief happiness turned off with it. Iraq. Or no job. Separation. The earth had collapsed beneath them.

CHAPTER 13

Darden's stomach felt so tight and raw inside, he had to admit such nausea could only be from fear. The Humvee bounced and heaved violently down the road, and he clenched the handholds on each side of the metal seat until his fingers ached. Holding your weight down tight against the seat was the only way to keep your head from slamming into the ceiling or against the side of the vehicle.

The soldiers wore helmets, so they didn't care, or maybe they were just used to it. They let their bodies rock and bounce wildly like marbles inside a can.

Driving through the northwest quadrant of Baghdad, miles from the safety of the Green Zone, he was as afraid as he could ever remember being. Sadr City was one of the most dangerous places on Earth after sundown and it was almost suicidal for a small unit to go in there this late in the day, yet here he was.

The Humvee blasted down the dirt road between rows of ugly buildings, jarring his teeth every mile they covered. He watched the decrepit buildings streak by, brown and worn, like everything else in this exhausted and ancient land. Open sewage ran in the gutters and collected in shallow pools on the roadway. Not a speck of green anywhere.

He still couldn't quite believe he'd asked to accompany the supply unit on a last minute delivery mission, but he'd never been in the Red Zone at night, and he told himself that he was here to report on the realities of the war. He couldn't allow himself to hide out in the command compound all day like the well-dressed television people who paid Iraqis to go out and ask questions for them. They were on a different journalistic plane from him. If he didn't get stories, he didn't get paid, and he needed a story badly.

Earlier that day at lunch he'd overheard a rumor there was a clandestine unit operating out here and something about the whispered tone of the voice that repeated the rumor got his attention. Sitting at a table in the giant mess hall, he heard the hushed voices behind him and the men spoke so low, Darden barely caught half the words but that was enough. Together with the men's tone, the few overheard phrases made him think there was something to it.

He dropped his fork on purpose and reached down to pick it up off the floor, twisting just enough to see the back of a man's head seated a few feet behind him. The man sat hunched forward, talking to an officer Darden could see fairly well, a colonel, he thought, but he didn't catch quite enough of the officer's insignia to be sure.

So he'd decided to follow it up and asked about a supply mission driving out to Sadr City late that afternoon. He squinted against the blinding sunlight as the Humvee took a right turn and headed west, accelerating down the narrow street and making the painful sound of metal grinding on metal. To him, every vehicle in Iraq sounded as if it were about to seize up and die from the effects of sand and dust. The airborne debris destroyed machines at an amazing rate as it clogged filters, shredded gears, and reduced engines to whining failures that defied repair.

The Humvee took another quick turn left, then slid to a stop in front of a plain brown block building. The sergeant in charge of the detail double-checked a map on his knees then put it aside. They sat for a moment as the dust swarmed around them and looked about to see if there was any threat in the vicinity, but Darden saw no movement in the street except three goats nosing through garbage farther up the road. The only sound was the slow idle of the engine.

"Okay," the sergeant said. He pointed out two positions with his right hand, front and rear. "Let's go."

Two of the soldiers immediately jumped out and took up guard as he'd directed, rifle butts poised on their hips, eyes looking outward. Two other men got out and went to the rear where they unloaded a metal crate with no markings on it. Darden didn't know any of the men, and they weren't wearing the usual name patches on their shirts. Nobody had said much of anything since they set out, so he kept his mouth shut.

"You," the sergeant pointed at Darden. "Stay put. No civilians allowed inside."

The sergeant led the troops to a heavy wooden door just a few yards from the Humvee, then pounded on it hard with his fist. They waited nearly a minute until the door cracked open and the sergeant exchanged a few words with whoever was inside. The door opened wider and the two soldiers carried the crate into the darkness of the building's interior. The door slammed shut behind them.

For a moment, even with the engine running, everything seemed very quiet to Darden. The low buildings cast long, dusty shadows across the roadway. A power line running alongside the road stretched into the distance, the poles looking crooked and not quite upright under the weight of sagging lines that rarely carried electricity. The soldiers on guard continued watching, said nothing.

Strange, he thought, looking about at the desolation, we just don't belong here.

After two or three minutes, the door to the building opened again and he watched the sergeant and two soldiers step back out into the low sunlight.

Then, he heard something that made his scalp prickle. His senses became acute and a tremor ran through him, his hearing straining toward the doorway. While the door was briefly open, he heard a cry—an elongated scream really—emerge from deep inside the building. Though it was muffled by walls and distance, the sound was unmistakable, a man in pain wailing from somewhere within.

It was the worst sound Darden had ever heard in his life.

CHAPTER 14

Hamed stood on a rooftop three blocks away and watched the Americans through a pair of stolen binoculars. If the soldiers stayed much longer, they might ruin his plans. Two on guard, one in the Humvee, three more who entered the building, but as he watched them and waited he began to reconsider. It would be so pleasing if he also killed them in the attack on the building. That would make the operation more damaging, but he wasn't sure if he had enough manpower with him to go up against a squad of American soldiers.

Then again, it was probably too late to stop his men from planting the bomb anyway. His men? Hah, he might as well say it, they were boys. Most were little more than children he was using for a purpose, as one would drive goats through a minefield before crossing it. That made them perfect for this job, because they were filled with *jihadist* ardor and too young to realize some of them would almost certainly die today.

He quickly came to a decision not to delay the attack. They would use the bomb as planned to blow open the exterior wall of the building. If the boys placed it exactly where he had instructed them, the blast would destroy the office located on the inward side of the wall. The target of their attack spent much of his time in that office, and Allah willing, that man would be killed in the blast.

His men called the building The Cave. They had been watching it for weeks and learned that only a few westerners spent much time in there, though exactly how many was not certain. Occasionally, a Humvee or local truck would deliver supplies or people under cover of darkness, but it was always a small group involved, with very little activity outside and never on a predictable schedule.

What fools they were to think we wouldn't notice, he told himself. His watchers had even managed to locate the office of the target by planting microphones around the perimeter of the building. Of course the microphones had been stolen from the Americans, then sold on the black market to one of Hamed's people.

The squad of American soldiers be damned, he vowed. If they stayed to fight, he would sacrifice his boys to kill the soldiers as well. He wanted to kill the target too much to worry about wasting resources.

Hamed did not know the target's real name, just as few knew his, but they all called the man Texas. It was said that the big American came from that place and his code name had become legendary among the insurgents as a hated figure.

They had to kill Texas because he defiled Muslim bodies inside that building. He used devices and methods on captives that not even the Iraqis themselves would use. He robbed Muslim men of their most precious possession, their dignity, by breaking their bodies and minds until they would say or do anything to stop the pain.

And Hamed wanted to kill him more than anyone, because Texas had destroyed his father in that way. Somewhere inside The Cave, the target had bent and crushed his aged father's body, then stolen his Godliness, and finally took the breath from the most important person in Hamed's life.

They learned of this from photographs that had been taken of his father's treatment and somehow smuggled out of The Cave. That the Americans could allow such a stupid thing to happen proved to Hamed that Texas was careless enough to be killed. He knew the photos were later seized from a kidnapped American who eventually died in one of the Iraqis' own interrogation centers, and the leadership decided to pass the photos among the members of the insurgency to rouse them to greater martyrdom.

The plan worked, because the fighters became enraged that such treatment would be used on followers of the true faith. That was the ultimate sin, an insult to Allah himself, to treat his followers in that way. It was not the same thing when they used such methods on the Americans, because Americans were infidels, and Allah would forgive or perhaps even reward them for mistreatment of infidels.

He moved the binoculars to his right and saw the car bomb exit the alley where it had been hidden, five blocks from The Cave. It turned and started to accelerate down the road. An instant later, he swung the binoculars back to the doorway and saw three American soldiers emerge from the building. One climbed back into the Humvee, but the two on guard did not move.

The car bomb gained more speed and drew within a block of The Cave. He heard the strain of its engine and saw the small figure of his man inside the cab, praying or arguing with himself in excitement. Dust swirled around the car as it reached the building then made a sliding turn toward the wall.

Good, he thought, the driver has the presence of mind to go for the precise spot that would make the mission a success. That spot was marked by two Arabic words he'd had a boy spray on the wall the previous night—*Budiya Uf"Uwan*—which meant "Desert Snake," the code name his men knew him by.

"Yes," he breathed. "There."

He watched the right front fender slam into the wall close to the spot where the words were painted, but the car was going too fast. It didn't penetrate the concrete surface as he'd hoped. The driver lost his nerve at the last second and swerved aside rather than angling directly into it. Instead of crashing through the blocks and lodging in the wall itself, the car caromed off and scraped down the wall several meters before it came to a complete stop.

Two of his men on the ground ran down an alleyway to avoid the blast. The driver—the martyr—remained behind to detonate the explosives. Hamed swung the binoculars to his left again and saw the Americans at the Humvee drop to one knee and raise their rifles.

CHAPTER 15

Feeling sicker by the moment, Darden sat in the idling Humvee and wondered exactly what he had just heard, that awful screaming. His nausea grew to the point he tried to get out of the vehicle in case he had to vomit, but the sergeant emerged from the building and waved him back to his seat.

The sergeant came straight to the Humvee and climbed into the driver's spot, picked up the radio and began calling signals to some distant point of contact, but he spoke mainly in code so Darden couldn't make any sense of the message. All four of the soldiers remained outside the Humvee on watch.

"Sergeant," one of the men called out. "Vehicle approaching."

The sergeant lowered the phone and twisted his head to look behind the Humvee where the soldier was positioned.

"Where?"

"On the cross street behind us," said a second soldier. "Coming fast down the southwest wall."

Darden saw the men drop to defensive positions, crouching on one knee, their weapons ready, pointing outward. The sergeant got out of the Humvee just as two of the soldiers jumped back from the corner of the building. An instant later he heard a racing engine, then a loud scraping sound, metal against stone.

The sergeant tried to give an order, but before the words came out a tremendous blast wave pushed its way down the cross street behind them. A hot sheet of flame followed and Darden felt the Humvee rock beneath him, then lift slightly. The deep sound of the explosion came next, just as he saw the sergeant fly backward.

God, it was loud, like thunder right on top of them.

Instinctively, he put his arms over his head and ducked. Then the blast fully enveloped them and it felt as if all the air had been sucked out of the area. He felt intense heat on his forearms and heard a soldier outside the Humvee scream.

Within seconds, the blast wave passed over them and Darden was able to sit up. He grabbed his Nikon, got out, saw dust and smoke everywhere. One of the soldiers sat against a fender, stunned, but the other three were all the way down, their faces blackened by the explosion. The sergeant got to his feet at the front of the Humvee; apparently its bulk had shielded him from the worst of the blast.

Darden ran to the side of the building and raised his camera. He peeked around the corner to get a look at the street that crossed behind them where the blast had occurred. He saw a lot of debris and a burning car about fifty yards away against the wall of the building which was heavily damaged.

Rubble and scraps of metal littered the street along the entire block. Two sheared-off electrical poles hung from the sagging wires like heavy laundry. Men with rifles spilled from alleyways and ran toward the epicenter of destruction, yelling in Arabic.

It seemed unreal to be in the midst of such destruction, reminded him of the sickening feeling he'd had at the Daytona explosion, but despite his trepidation the reporter in him took over. This was a real story, and he needed it. This was what he'd come to the Red Zone to get. He tried to focus his thoughts and lock his attention onto the specifics of the chaos in the street.

He took photographs as quickly as the camera could reset itself. He got shots of the running men in baggy clothes, shouting, firing their rifles into the air in excitement. The burning car, or what was left of it. Smoke and flames coursing from the side of the building. More shots, close ups of the men charging the wall, trying it seemed, to get past the flames and the burning wreck to get inside the building. Some of the men fired through the flames to spray bullets into the opening in the wall.

One of the attackers paused and shouted orders at the others. Then he turned around and faced the opposite side of the street and looked up into the distance.

Darden lowered the camera for a moment and followed the man's movements with his eyes, tried to determine where he was looking. Then the man signaled someone in the distance with a raised fist, and Darden scanned the rooftops until he spotted the silhouette of a tall figure in a robe staring at them through binoculars. The man appeared to be an observer, perhaps overseeing the attack.

Darden raised his camera, zoomed in and got two shaky frames of the robed figure on the roof.

Darden noticed his hands trembling, but he managed to keep the viewfinder on the rooftop and saw the man raise his left arm and sweep it toward him. Two more shots of the man, now with the binoculars lowered, his hand pointing emphatically in Darden's direction. Still more emphatically, gesturing. It took Darden a moment to realize, he is pointing here, directly at me.

He jumped back behind the corner of the building, now understanding the observer on the rooftop was indicating him, making him a target for the men on the ground. At that instant, someone grabbed his waistband from behind and yanked him backward. He whirled and almost fell trying to break free of the grasp on his belt.

"Get back here," the sergeant hissed. "I need your help."

Darden knocked the sergeant's hand away, glared at the young man's blackened face. "Let go of me."

"Give me a hand," the sergeant said. "We've got injuries, here."

Darden didn't like taking orders and his first thought was to ignore the sergeant, but he saw the soldiers who were down, two of them propped against the Humvee, still stunned but coming around. Another was flat on his back and appeared to be unconscious, his face and hands definitely burned, the skin black and blistering. The fourth soldier was already inside the Hummer, slumped against the side and not moving.

Darden took three quick shots of them before he put his camera on the Hummer's fender and helped the sergeant get one of the men to his feet. They used a canteen to wet down the soldier's head and face. He began to mutter and stamp his feet to shake off the numbness of his limbs.

The sergeant picked up the man's rifle and shoved it into his hands. "Get back on guard," he ordered. The soldier responded unthinkingly as his training kicked into gear, and he stumbled toward the front of the Humvee and got his rifle up into position.

They helped the second sitting soldier to his feet the same way, and the sergeant got him in place at the rear of the vehicle. Next they turned to the man who was flat on his back, doused water on his face and checked his heartbeat and respiration. He was certainly alive but not conscious.

"Let's get him in the truck," the sergeant said.

Darden thought the soldier needed a doctor immediately. "Why don't you get somebody inside the building to help him?"

"They don't help anybody," the sergeant replied. "I'm going to call for a medivac."

They lifted the soldier onto the front passenger seat then the sergeant got on the radio to raise headquarters. The soldier was completely out, possibly dying. To Darden, it seemed there was nothing they could do for him here.

Small arms fire continued in the street behind them, combined with a lot of voices shouting in Arabic. Darden hurried back to the end of the building and eased the lens of his Nikon around the corner to watch the men in the street through the viewfinder without exposing his body. The camera showed more attackers gathered at the blast hole in the building. The fire had died down and some of them jumped through the opening to get inside.

He snapped off a few more images, which he was sure would be better than the earlier ones because the smoke had thinned somewhat. He pointed the lens at the rooftop where he'd seen the tall observer with the binoculars, but the man was no longer there.

The soldier covering the rear of the Humvee had come to his senses, because Darden heard him giving the sergeant a running update on the situation down the street at the blast site. Then the soldier came up behind him and nudged Darden's arm with his rifle barrel. "Keep that up, shitbird, you're going to get your hands shot off."

Darden ignored him and continued to watch the attackers through the viewfinder, trying to imprint every detail on his memory. He knew he'd have to recall the sequence of events precisely to report about it later; every smell and image and sound would give him the foundation of the story he would have to re-create from memory.

The yelling increased at the opening in the wall and the insurgents jumped about in excitement as a cluster of their comrades emerged from the building carrying a man dressed in khaki fatigues. Darden got shots of them straining beneath the man's bulk as they passed him over their heads through the smoldering wreckage. He was a large man and they dropped him to the ground as soon as they were able to maneuver him to an open area.

The man was groggy but still alive, kicking and lashing out at his attackers with wild swings that missed; his face and hands were black with smoke but his bright red hair showed through the soot. He was definitely a westerner, probably an American, judging from his clothes.

Darden turned to tell the sergeant what he saw, but the squad leader was still inside the Humvee on the radio. When he returned his eyes to the viewfinder, Darden saw the tall rooftop observer emerge from an alley and step into the street near the cluster of fighters, his robe gathered about him in a regal pose. He stood as if he calculated every gesture to appear the dignified commander. Sure enough, the fighters fell quiet at the sight of him, though a few gunshots continued inside the building.

The robed man pointed at the redheaded American on the ground and gave orders to a subordinate. The fighters instantly swarmed the redhead and hammered him with rifle butts and kicks to the abdomen to subdue him. Now a writhing, helpless captive, they bound him with scarves and pieces of wire from the littered street then lifted him onto their shoulders and carried him out of sight down an alley.

Darden captured the whole scene in a sequence of photographs until the leader turned his attention toward the American squad. He pointed out Darden's position and spoke to the subordinate again. Several men looked straight into the lens of Darden's camera and raised their weapons.

He yanked his hands back behind the corner of the building an instant before bullets started zinging off the pavement out in the street.

Even though the Americans were shielded from view by the building, it wouldn't take the Iraqi fighters long to run down the street toward them and take up position where they could fire directly at them.

He turned, took two steps, and grabbed the closest soldier by the elbow and shoved him toward the Humvee. "We gotta go," he said. "Now!"

They yelled to the other soldier in front as they dove into the vehicle. The sergeant saw the look on their faces, dropped the radio hand piece and grabbed the steering wheel. The last soldier jumped on top of the man slumped in the front passenger seat and reached for the windshield frame to hang on.

"Go," Darden yelled. "They're coming!"

The sergeant threw the Hummer in gear and took off in a roar of exhaust and flying dust.

CHAPTER 16

Hamed looked at the devastation alongside The Cave and thought about the consequences of the attack. The target, Texas, had somehow survived the explosion of the car bomb so they had failed in their original objective to kill him, but they had succeeded in capturing him, which might even be better if he planned his next steps carefully.

The squad of American soldiers, though, had managed to escape because his lieutenant had been too excitable in battle, unable to take orders and act on them quickly and calmly. He would have to change that. The soldiers would have been a nice prize, but again, they were not part of the original mission, and the blast had harmed them enough that they were unable to interfere with the attack. So their escape caused him no real distress.

He watched as his men brought out the bodies of their fallen comrades. Perhaps a half dozen or more had died fighting inside the building. Their baggy shirts covered in blood, their arms hanging limply in the dust, they had sacrificed their lives for the good of the cause, he told himself. Still, a terrible thing for them to be martyred so young even though they would enjoy the delights of many virgins in paradise, if Allah willed it.

Now he must go into The Cave, the place of hell on earth, the place from which men did not return. He must go in and mourn the passing of his father there. He hated to go into that place more than anything he could imagine, but he must. His father's honor demanded it. The Cave must be dismantled and destroyed and all who were part of it, Iraqi and American, must be destroyed to avenge the souls lost in there. The defilement of true believers by infidels must end. He would see to it.

With the American torturer as his hostage, many choices lay open to him. He would carefully consider these avenues and decide his course, but first he must go into this place of screams and filth to remember his father.

He made his way slowly across the street, sidestepping shattered car parts and smoking debris. He avoided the small fires with long, heavy strides, the smell of burning tires filling his head, dread growing in his heart as he drew closer to the smoke-filled opening in the wall. With each step, the dark hole grew larger as if it might swallow him up as well, and the swirling smoke gave it a form and being until The Cave became a palpable presence, almost alive with the ghosts of those lost inside it.

CHAPTER 17

Back at the Green Zone, medics swarmed the Humvee within minutes and went to work on the injured men. Other soldiers rushed to the vehicle to welcome back their comrades and see for themselves the damage that had been done on the mission. For Darden, there was no welcome party. Two security men escorted him away from the motor pool and took him to an office in an unidentified building shielded from the compound by a block wall.

They called it a debriefing room, but it was most likely the office of the two men, or should he say goons, questioning him. It was drab in a way that only the military could enforce on its members and employees. Gray metal furniture, two desks, unpainted walls, a concrete floor, no windows and thus no outside light—this office had to be demoralizing to its occupant, Darden thought. Perhaps that explained the officer's terrible mood and obvious hostility.

Since the questioner wore no name patch or insignia of rank, Darden thought the man must be part of an intelligence unit, probably a captain or major. He had small dark eyes and a blunt face that twisted into a snarl with every question.

"What did he look like?" the officer demanded.

"I already told you," Darden said.

"Tell me again."

"Like I said, he was tall and thin. Wore robes. A *gallibayah*, maybe."

"What about his face?"

"Gray beard. Dark skin."

"That's it?" The Intel officer allowed his exasperation to show, leaned forward across the desk to make his point more emphatically. "A trained reporter, and all you remember is he looked like every other man out there?"

Darden became exasperated, himself. He'd told them the story three times, all about the abduction of the red-headed man, the explosion, the high speed drive back to the Green Zone, the whole thing, but they kept coming on like he was going to change the details or something.

"I told you, he was a long way off. There was a lot of smoke and dust in the air."

The other guy, the silent one with a buzz cut, sat and stared at him as if he wanted to drill a hole in Darden's forehead. He hadn't said a word so far, just stared, hardly blinking his gray eyes at all.

Darden slouched back in his chair, deliberately assuming a non-military posture, stretching his legs out and locking his fingers behind his head, elbows fanned out. He stared back at the silent guy as if to say, you can't control me because I'm a civilian, and I like the fact that it pisses you off.

No one said anything for a bit. All three just sat there in the debriefing room trying to out-stare one another. He heard the hum of air conditioning and smelled the stack of fresh paper beside the printer on the desktop.

The officer turned to his keyboard and tapped in a few sentences, then stopped and looked over at him very casually. He flipped his hands upward and almost smiled as if he too was glad this nonsense was about to be over. Darden did not trust the man's almost smile.

"One more thing," the officer said. "What about your camera?"

Darden tried to maintain his relaxed pose. He hoped his face didn't reveal any change as he tried to answer the question casually, just as he had the others. "I lost it."

"The sergeant said you had it in the Humvee on the way back."

"No, it's lost."

"At the ambush site or on the road?"

Darden shrugged in answer.

"Where exactly?"

"If I knew where I lost it, then it wouldn't be lost."

"What's on that camera?"

Darden said nothing.

The officer suddenly shoved his desk chair back, which made a hard, scraping sound on the cement floor. He stood abruptly, a purple rage building on his face. He leaned closer to Darden. "Godammit, this is no joke, mister. I ask you a plain question, I want a civil answer."

Darden didn't budge. He tried to stay calm as he looked up at the officer, "If I knew, I wouldn't tell you."

For the first time, the gray eyed man stirred. He didn't seem to be military; he was dressed in civilian clothes anyway, typical khakis and a tight polo shirt. He probably wanted to make the point that he was some sort of contractor for an Intel agency. He deliberately raised his right index finger and pointed it at Darden's face, the sleeve on his polo riding up so his heavy biceps were apparent. He held the fingertip on Darden and squeezed his thumb down like the hammer on a pistol, again without opening his mouth, but the threat was absolutely real, absolutely physical.

That pissed off Darden. He stood and kicked a trashcan against the wall, daring them to push him harder.

"Okay, I'm out of here," he said. "I've cooperated with you guys, and you haven't even identified yourselves. I'm a member of the press and I don't have to put up with this shit."

He went to the door and opened it, looked back to say one more thing. Neither of them tried to stop him from leaving, but now they were grinning, just sat there and grinned at him. All in a day's fun for them.

"Jerk wads," Darden said, as he slammed the door behind him.

Walking over to the mess hall, Darden cooled down a bit and felt as if the world was almost normal, but he knew it was an illusion to ever think of this place as real. Most of them called the zone "The Bubble" for good reason. It was an artificial bubble of America plunked down in the middle of Baghdad. With all the technology, cold beer, power point presentations, and other uniquely American traits inside The Bubble, it almost had an atmosphere of home, but it was not real. It only created a false sense of security and power in contrast to the disorder and misery outside in the city.

Though he'd had to sit through that debriefing with those edgy Intel goons, Darden was glad to be back in safe quarters where the food was good and the air conditioning worked. He knew he should feel more relieved, but the memories of the attack in Sadr City still had a powerful hold on his consciousness and he found himself thinking of little else.

Two of the injured soldiers had been carried from the Humvee on stretchers. Darden was the only one in the group who hadn't sustained any injuries at all, mainly because he'd been inside the vehicle and crouched down when the heat wave struck them.

He hated to admit it, but the sergeant who had ordered him to stay in the Humvee had actually saved his ass.

After he ate and rested in the infirmary, he wanted most of all to recover his camera, take it to his quarters and study the photos of the firefight, but he knew now he had to be very careful about that. Those goons wanted his photos, presumably to gather visual Intel on the attackers, but the shots were too valuable to him as ones he could sell to give them up to anyone, especially those goons. His agreement with Southeastern Radio News gave them first-use only, not exclusive rights to his work; he could re-sell original material to other news services. Since his outfit paid poorly and only for stories they accepted, they would never pay enough to acquire full rights from him or anyone else.

He also needed to go to his room and write notes on his laptop while his memory of the firefight was still fresh, but he found it hard to get away from his fellow reporters. They hounded him in the mess hall and the medical areas and even in the bathroom. With surprise, he found out how annoying it was to be surrounded by demanding members of the press.

It was bit ironic, actually. Among the dozens of reporters hanging around the Green Zone, he had been perhaps the lowest of the low. He worked for a low-status, low-profile news service out of Atlanta that supplied canned stories to local newspapers and radio networks, mostly radio, and he was an unknown reporter if ever there was one.

Now though, to all the lazy-ass national television people he was someone who was a must interview. They weren't about to go out to Sadr City and risk their hair-dos on the streets. Instead of running down facts and stories on their own, they paid Iraqis to do it for them and they were never sure if they were getting the straight picture.

Same thing with interviews of soldiers. It was rare to get a story directly from a combatant that was not sanitized first by the military, and everyone knew it. So, most members of the press were frustrated and felt guilty about their compliant coverage of the war. For the most part, they felt they were doing an inadequate job and were mad at themselves for letting the insurgents and the military keep them from doing it well.

Now, from Darden, they could get some authentic commentary and precise details about what it was like to be ambushed since he was one of the few American reporters who had actually witnessed a bombing and lived to tell about it. He fended off their questions with vague answers, but told them that he'd give a full account after he filed his own story, and they knew better than to push it beyond that point.

Most reporters cooperated on stories, but only to the extent that their own exclusives came first. When they finally accepted that he wasn't going to give anything away, they drifted off to the Sand Bar, acknowledging that they'd have to wait until he filed before they could get more from him.

By midnight, he managed to maneuver away from all of them and walked over to the maintenance garage to retrieve his camera from the damaged Humvee, careful to make sure no one followed him. Since those photos were gold to him, he'd hidden the camera underneath a back seat in the vehicle on the ride home to the base, wedging it between the bottom of the seat itself and the curved metal of a fender well.

He'd suspected that his camera would be confiscated if anyone with authority saw it. An unwritten rule in Iraq was that no photos or footage got back to America unless Washington approved it first. So much for the free press, he thought.

Fortunately the garage was empty of workers at this hour and he saw no guards. The garage was a big hangar-type building for ground vehicles where the mechanics tried to keep as many of them rolling as possible, despite the damage they suffered from combat and the harsh environment. He crossed the concrete floor, moving from one Humvee to the next, looking for the one that had been on the mission. They looked almost identical to him, lined up in rows, all painted in desert tan.

Many of the Humvees showed blast burns and torn metal and some had been cannibalized for replacement parts, allowing two or three unusable vehicles to be pieced together into a single working one. Several also showed black welding scars along the sides and lower fenders where jerry-rigged armor had been attached to make them less vulnerable to I.E.D.'s.

It was quiet in the cavernous space and his footsteps sounded distinct, each one echoing slightly off the walls and ceiling. He half expected someone to pop out from behind a truck and challenge him, but no one appeared. Suddenly, he felt extremely tired and knew the fear and excitement of the day was wearing off. He'd been running on adrenalin for hours and now exhaustion had set in.

The sixth Humvee he looked at closely was the one he wanted. He saw bloodstains on the rear passenger compartment where the soldier with the worst injuries had sat, slumped against the side wall all the way back. Darden remembered the man bleeding from his ears and he wondered how much brain damage the guy had suffered.

He opened the left rear door and reached under the seat, then felt a moment of alarm when his hand went to the right spot but did not locate the camera immediately.

"Damn it," he said to himself. "Don't tell me somebody got here first."

He crouched down and looked around the floorboard, still didn't see it, but it was dark in the interior of the Hummer. He swept his hand back and forth under both seats, brushed his fingers against something hard and round edged, grabbed it and knew by the weight and feel of it that he'd recovered his Nikon. As he pulled it out by the strap he felt relieved and realized how apprehensive he'd been about losing the shots.

He dropped the camera into a black plastic bag he'd brought from the mess hall then twisted the top of the bag and tied it off. He wanted to make it look like he was carrying garbage to a bin. Then he hurried out of the garage as quietly as he could, tried to look casual walking down the hallways of the compound.

Back in his quarters, Darden locked the door and barred it with a chair before he sat down on the cot with the Nikon. His heartbeat notched up a bit as he turned it on and hit the display mode button. After a moment, the display lit up to a gray tone but there was no image on it. Nothing there but a blank rectangle.

He used the toggle switch to advance to the next frame. Still nothing. He toggled forward several times, then backward, searching for the photographs. His hands shaking, he checked the read-out and it showed zero images out of zero in storage. He thumbed open the small lid covering the compartment that held the memory stick. Empty. The stick was gone.

"Those bastards," he whispered.

Someone, probably those two Intel guys, had stolen his photographs, possibly had someone take them while they questioned him. The questioning had most likely been an attempt to catch him in a lie. They'd guessed he would cover up the fact that he intended to smuggle out unauthorized photographs.

Now, he had no images to support the story. Instead of a few hundred extra dollars or more for a first-person internet and newspaper piece, all he would make was a couple of hundred for a second-rater's eyewitness account. Without photos, such a story likely wouldn't even get picked up by a larger news service.

He'd risked his neck for nothing. No money to send back home for hospital bills, no significant credit. His anger built and he considered for a moment just how he could best get revenge on the goons responsible for sabotaging his work.

CHAPTER 18

The butter knife bent slightly as Darden slipped it between the fire door and its metal jamb. Sliding the blade forward, he felt the bolt inside the lock mechanism then worked the knife up and down, pushing until it bit and slid down the curved side of the bolt, forcing the lock back into the door set. A bump with his shoulder and the door gave way with ease.

It seemed incredible to him that there were no additional locks on the door and no guard outside, but by all outward appearance this was only a nondescript office building and perhaps it had nothing to do with intelligence at all. If this was a classified area with high-risk materials, surely it would not be so easy to get inside. Maybe those goons were not Intel, but if they weren't, who were they and why did they steal his photographs?

The offices sat silent at three A.M. with a few lights left on and no apparent work in progress. He looked down the dim hallway and wondered if any roving guards made rounds through these buildings. Worse still, was anybody watching the video feed from the overhead cameras at each end of the hall? He pulled a towel over his head to shield his face from the camera lenses and stepped inside.

When he had first considered breaking into the goons' office to get back his memory stick, he doubted it would be possible. Lying on his bunk back in his quarters, it seemed like a crazy idea. Breaking into a secured military area during wartime had to be a serious Federal offense, so he had weighed the possibilities and risks and almost dismissed the idea, but if they were true Intel people, he reasoned, the office would be more heavily secured and he would be stopped immediately. Finally, he decided to try it anyway because there wasn't any unusual security when he was questioned in their office earlier.

Once he made up his mind, he got out his zoom lens, mounted it on the Nikon and went up to the roof of his building. There he watched the entrance to the goons' office for two hours. It took him a while to figure out how to get through the access gate in the fence surrounding the building. The gate was electronically controlled by a keypad mounted alongside it. He watched two men tap their codes into the keypad to open the gate and he saw one of them punch in all four numbers while he captured the entry code in his mind, 5-1-9-0.

Once past the gate late that night, he was surprised at just how easy it all had been. Perhaps that meant the most serious security was designed to keep people out of the Green Zone altogether, but once inside, security wasn't so heavy. Perhaps.

He avoided thinking too much about the consequences of what he was doing, though he knew the punishment would be dire if he got caught. He willed himself to keep his old hesitancy at bay, to prevent it from holding him back any longer. He was determined to change himself into a serious reporter who was willing to take more risks.

While deliberating the idea, it occurred to him that they could've simply deleted the photos stored in his camera, but instead they took the memory stick because they wanted his shots of the robed man who led the attack or perhaps their interest was the big American the insurgents kidnapped. Most likely, they had used his memory stick to download the pictures onto a hard drive, perhaps right here in this office. Why they didn't just take the camera, he couldn't even guess.

Now, he wanted his photos back. Maybe they were in the office, maybe not, but he would take the risk.

He walked quickly to the unmarked office where they'd questioned him, tried the door. It was locked and he used the butter knife again. It worked even faster than before.

Inside now, he pulled the office door shut. Darkness wrapped around him. Where would the photos be? Almost certainly, downloaded onto the computer, but it would be password protected. Or would it? Nothing so far suggested these characters were very smart about security.

He flipped on a desk lamp, went to the computer and pushed the start button. While Windows booted up he looked through the desk's drawers. Office supplies, a few printouts with numbered columns, notes, chewing gum and Tylenol. No memory stick; nothing of interest.

The PC flickered to life and he got to the familiar welcome screen. Only one user icon appeared. He clicked on it; the screen blinked then immediately advanced to the desktop and start screen. Incredible. These idiots didn't even have the system set up with any protection at all. If this was how our intelligence people work, he thought, little wonder the war kept dragging on for years.

He clicked on the start button, then My Pictures. The window opened and he stared at it dumbfounded. This was too easy, he laughed. Dozens of files appeared in rows with photo icons on each file folder symbol. His photos were not only there, stored in a single folder, but his name was right on the outside. The goons made no effort to hide them or even change the file name. How could they be so stupid?

He looked through the desk drawer of supplies for a flash drive or floppy to download the photos. Why hadn't he thought to bring one? He found a rewritable CD still wrapped in cellophane, retrieved it and tore off the wrapping. He highlighted his photo file and popped the CD in its tray on the tower, started the download.

After the photos copied onto the CD, he deleted the file on the hard drive and went back to My Pictures. Scanning the files quickly, he realized this computer contained much more than his own shots. There were hundreds of others as well; visual evidence of beatings, photo records of gross punishments and atrocities; much of the dirty laundry of the war was stored here in wide open, almost casual, fashion.

He clicked on one file and dozens of photos opened on the

display. What he saw sickened him. Row upon row of photographs detailed the chronology of an interrogation. Beginning with a hooded prisoner in a cell, then his naked body strapped to a table, even close-ups of alligator clips biting into the man's scrotum, with still more shots of an electrical apparatus wired to the prisoner's body; the sequence revealed the progressive torture of a man who appeared to be an Iraqi, first using electrical shock, then pliers, and finally a tilt board used to lower his head into a vat of water, all the torture performed by a white westerner in camo fatigues. Another shot further down the row confirmed the inquisitor was American. With the man's sleeves rolled up to tilt the prisoner's head into the water, Darden clearly saw a Marine Corp tattoo on the torturer's forearm.

This was much worse than Abu Ghraib; these photos were indisputable evidence of torture. These files made the hard drive a reporter's dream.

Still another photo taken a second later documented the prisoner's fear; his head rising out of the tub, his open mouth spewing water from his lungs and at the same time gasping for air; the horror on his face as he experienced drowning, struggling to suck life-giving oxygen back into his body, eyes wider than wide as he knew he was about to die.

Darden knew then what that scream meant that he had heard outside the building in Sadr City. The American military, or some of its contractors, were torturing Iraqi captives on a systematic basis. This wasn't a rogue outfit acting on its own initiative. The hundreds of photos here proved that military intelligence knew at minimum that it was happening and was perhaps involved even further.

This went far beyond interrogation; this was brutality exercised in the name of his country. He and his fellow citizens were now in league with the most extreme elements of governmental repression in the world, he thought. We are no better than the Soviets were, the Viet Cong, the dictators of banana republics we'd decried for decades for their brutal tactics. We were nothing but hypocrites when we criticized their inhumanity, their willingness to do anything to maintain power.

His own country, the country he loved, had descended into the blackest of black pits. In the name of security, we were now as depraved as our worst enemies, destroying lives simply because we had the power to do so.

With these realizations, he felt a psychic pain he'd never be able to erase. Like his father, the stain of these images would remain in his head forever. Americans were no longer the good guys bringing liberation. His own countrymen were behaving like Nazis.

He sat back and let out a long quavering sigh, tried to clear his thoughts. No matter what happened next, no matter what he thought about it personally, he had to get these photos home, had to show America what was being done here.

There was no telling what else might be on the hard drive, but he didn't have time to copy it all. He dropped to one knee and brought the desk lamp down to the floor where the computer tower sat. He turned it around, pulled the wires from the ports, unplugged the power supply. He had to figure out how to open the case, had to get inside. He knew he must remove the hard drive and somehow smuggle it back home.

By the time he found the release button and started to pry the case open with his fingertips, his concentration was totally fixed on the computer tower. He didn't notice the office door easing open, didn't consciously hear the light footsteps coming into the office. Only later, on an unconscious level, did these details come back to him. Only later would he picture the heavy flashlight swinging downward just as his eyes turned up, the weight of the goon's big shoulders behind it, the thought-shattering explosion of light in his head as the metal cylinder smashed into his skull, then a blinding darkness that engulfed his thoughts, carrying him to a place where the pain, and all else, stopped.

CHAPTER 19

Darden awoke in a cell with bright fluorescent lights overhead, the glass tubes shielded by wire mesh. The harsh light flooded into his pupils, setting his brain on fire. His head had never hurt so much in his entire life. He used a hand to cover his eyes and still the pain would not let up.

"Just stay down and it'll be easier," a man's voice said.

Darden rolled onto his side and felt nausea build in his stomach, the raw taste of bile in his mouth.

"Don't try to move." The voice again. "It'll hurt more."

"Where am I?"

"Military jail."

"Jail?"

Darden tried to get his thoughts in order, but the pounding fire in his head made it difficult to think. What had happened? How did he get here? A groan escaped his lips as he remembered the photos, his attempt to remove the hard drive, then the blow to his head.

"Somebody hit you with something hard," the voice said. "You have a huge bruise and open cut."

Darden reached up and touched his scalp, felt dried blood in his hair, stiff and clumped. His fingers found the wound where a rough scab had formed over it, the skin very tender to his touch. He needed to sit up, open his eyes and think straight.

Most of all, he had to get out of here, get back home and tell people what he'd seen.

Gradually he became aware of his surroundings. The sound of clanging doors against the walls. Loud voices far off, arguing, yelling. Metal doors slamming again. So this was jail. He hated it already.

"Are we still in Baghdad?" he asked.

"Hell, we're still in the Green Zone."

Well, that was good news anyway. Darden got his hands underneath his body and pushed himself off the concrete floor. His head and stomach tumbled with waves of pain, but he managed to get upright, opened his eyes.

The cell was tiny, perhaps six by five, with heavy wire walls made of chain-link fencing that formed a box over and around him. Five feet of space separated him from a series of identical adjacent cells. The one to his left was empty. To his right, he saw a man in thick gray pajamas sitting against the wall of his own cell, staring at him without interest. The man had a few weeks' beard on his face, brown hair, a wary look. His hair was filthy.

"Who are you?" Darden asked.

"You go first."

"I'm Tom Darden, a reporter."

"You can call me Beckwith." He pointed to a dark area behind Darden's cell. "That guy over there is Fariq. He doesn't say much."

Darden turned his head painfully to the rear and he could just make out a darkened cell, covered with black plastic. "Who is he?"

"An Iraqi national. They keep his cell covered to drive him crazy. Never knows if it's day or night."

"How long has he been in here?"

"Damned if I know. He was here when I arrived. He speaks English, but their plan is working. Whenever he talks, it's nothing but gibberish. He's half crazy."

Darden rubbed his arms and legs to ease the stiffness in them. His head still pounded but he could open his eyes all the way now. If he kept his head quiet, as better golfers would say, the pain was less severe. Golf. The idea of a green fairway seemed a million miles away. He resolved to start moving around the cell as soon as possible, try to get himself back to normal.

"So, Darden, why'd they throw you in here?"

"You go first."

Beckwith stalled, obviously did not want to discuss his crime. "I'll tell you later."

For the next two hours, they remained quiet, except for an occasional babble from the man inside the plastic tent. Darden concentrated on regaining range of movement in his limbs. He raised his arms overhead, increasing the number of repetitions until the dull stiffness left them. Then he started on his legs, lifting each one slowly, increasing the speed and height of the lift. After forty-five minutes, he was ready to stand.

"Better not try it yet," Beckwith warned him.

He went very slowly, pushing his back upward against the wall, using his hands to help support his weight. He managed to get his legs underneath him, pushed until he was on his knees. His head started to whirl and a black wave of dizziness overcame him. He fought to stay conscious but slid back down the wall, his whole body turning to rubber. Then, onto his side, and sleep.

When he awoke, he wondered how long he'd been out. His head felt better this time; his body did, too. He sat up, discovered a half bucket of water in his cell and a pan with a bit of food, though he couldn't identify what it was, some sort of brown mush.

Beckwith was still in the same position, still staring at him. Only this time, he seemed more curious than wary. "I told you to stay down," he said. "Concussion takes a good twenty-four hours to shake off. Try to stand before you sleep and you'll fall again."

A clue, Darden thought. "Are you a physician?"

"No, a medic. Army."

"How long have I been out?"

"I don't know exactly. Long enough. Time plays tricks on you in here. They never turn the lights off; serve the food on irregular cycles. Keeps you off center, intended to soften you up."

Darden pulled the bucket toward him and drank water in big swallows.

"I could tell you to slow down with the water, but I don't think you'd listen."

Sure enough, Darden's stomach began to heave, and a

minute later, half the water spewed out of his mouth in a burst of vomiting. His head reeled again. He sat back and tried to calm his restless gut.

"Go slow," Beckwith said. "But try to eat and drink everything. If you don't, they'll take it away and it could be a long time before you get any more."

This time, Darden took the medic's advice. He drank the water in sips and ate the mush in tiny bites over the next hour. As his body absorbed the liquid and nutrients, his head cleared and he felt better, but before long he had a desperate urge to relieve himself.

"Do they let us out to use the toilet?"

"They never let us out of here. Use the empty bucket."

It was awkward, but Darden managed it. He pushed the stinking bucket to the far end of the cell, looked at Beckwith. For the first time the man had changed position. He was lying in a fetal curl on the concrete floor, hands flat under his head for a pillow, sound asleep.

Darden sat for a while and thought about his situation, realized it didn't look good. He wondered if anyone even knew he was here. The last communication he'd had with home was an e-mail to his office, telling Weldon he was about to go out to the Red Zone to follow a lead.

Who would even care he was here? His Dad was practically comatose, at least he was the last time Linda sent a message about him. She visited or called the hospital every day to find out how his Dad was doing, then wrote Darden the news. Linda was the only one who would miss him. He wrote her a letter every day, sometimes two, e-mailed them before he went to bed at night. She would try to find out what had happened to him.

But even with her help, how would he ever get out? He had been caught spying in a war zone. No, things didn't look good at all. That was his last thought before he stretched out on the floor and let sleep come to him.

CHAPTER 20

Hoyt Bellows searched his memory and tried to recall the lessons of his childhood, because he desperately needed to remember those lessons under the present circumstances. Soon, the guards would be back and he suspected things would get much worse for him when they came. If the Iraqis followed doctrine, the earlier beatings had only been to take the fight out of him.

Now they were using sleep deprivation. Based on the level of fatigue he felt, they had kept him awake for at least forty-eight hours, but he couldn't be sure of the exact length of time. His eyelids were taped open, hands and feet shackled to the floor. He was unable to see anything beyond the plywood walls of his cell, didn't even know where he was. The guards played Islamic prayers very loudly on speakers just outside the cell and kept a naked light bulb burning constantly overhead.

The next step would be serious pain. For that, he tried to prepare himself using childhood memories.

He recalled his past for the lessons that Jim Ed, his father, had burned into him long ago. Lesson number one—never cry or show emotion. That lesson had come when he was five years old. He cried over a calf, and for those tears, his father showed no tolerance.

The calf was a weaned yearling and the care of it had been Hoyt's first assigned chore. It was his job to take milk, water and feed to the calf's stall twice a day even though he could barely manage the heavy buckets. He remembered his tiny cowboy boots squishing through wet manure on the floor of the barn, carrying one bucket at a time to the calf which grew larger every day.

When the calf stood still, swinging its snout from side to side in a bucket, Hoyt stroked the smooth patches of black and white hair on its back. He grew to enjoy the feeling of its short summer coat, the hair soft as his mother's fur collar. The calf's wet, dark eyes rolled up at him as its long rough tongue swept up every drop of fresh milk Hoyt brought.

Then the weather turned in October and Hoyt had to wear a denim jacket when he went to the barn. The fattened calf's breath plumed out like smoke from its flaring nostrils in the morning air. One Saturday, a cold wind pushed down from the northern plains and changed everything.

His father tied a rope around the calf's neck and told Hoyt to lead it out to the huge oak standing alone in the pasture, the gray limbs stripped of leaves, the branches looking like huge fingers against the blue sky. There his father moved close to the calf and pulled out a pistol, put Hoyt's finger on the trigger and held the barrel to the animal's forehead, tilted down at an angle. He squeezed Hoyt's finger, then a single loud crack of the pistol made Hoyt jump and the calf went to its knees, then down on its side.

Hoyt cried as his father hung the calf up by its hind legs on a post oak limb, then gutted it, dressed it down before Hoyt's eyes, tossing the undesirable parts aside. Jim Ed placed the good cuts on sheets of waxed paper, wrapped them tightly, then used tape to secure the seams. Those cuts would make good eating on cold winter nights, he told Hoyt.

Later, after the meat went into the freezer, his father walked him back out to the oak in the accumulating darkness, showed him the scraps from the slaughter left on the bloody soil. The hide lay like a discarded rug, thrown out because of indelible stains that showed like rust on the pure black and white coat.

"Some have to die," he explained, "That others might live."

Hoyt did not understand and continued to sob.

"That is the law of life," he said to the boy. "To cry over death is foolishness. You won't ever do it again."

He opened an empty feed sack and had Hoyt fill it with the discarded scraps of guts, hooves, skull, and skin. The smell made Hoyt throw up, but his father stood and waited until the boy recovered then finished filling the sack. Walking behind his father, Hoyt dragged it across the pasture, crying the whole way as his father led him to the far end of the fence-line, through head-high brush and rocks, down into a gully of mesquite and thorns. It was dark down there and the gully seemed a threatening place, full of ugly crawling things.

"Now, empty out that sack."

Hoyt did as he was told. Jim Ed took the sack from him.

"Find your own way back to the house, now. I won't have no cryin' son."

His father climbed quickly out of the gully and vanished over the rim at the top. Hoyt's legs were too short and weak to keep up. By the time he made it out, his father was nowhere in sight. Hoyt exploded into loud, terrified wails, but it did no good. No one came.

Hours later he appeared on the back porch, bleeding and cold, his clothes ripped. Underneath the single porch light, he took off his boots, left them beside his father's just outside the door. He had stopped crying, even though a heavy lump of something seemed to have settled just below his throat. The lump became hard and never left him. Lesson learned.

Now, Hoyt knew he needed to hold onto that lesson with all his might. Whatever they did to him next, he would only make it worse by showing emotion. It would give his captors great pleasure to see him cry, begging for mercy, and that was a joy he would deny them, no matter what came.

Ever since they dragged him from the detention center in Sadr City, he knew what was coming and knew how he would respond. He had tortured many men, even women, and understood how the mind and body reacted to each stage of pain, and because of that knowledge he could do something none of them could ever do. He could remain silent. He would give them nothing.

He believed it was true, as many said, that torture was useless. Every man would break eventually and say or do anything to make it stop. Torture provided information, but it was useless information, so confused and invented, so random that he rarely got enough worthwhile intelligence to even pass it on to his superiors. He made much of it up himself to justify the act.

The command structure said harsh interrogation was acceptable to acquire intelligence, but anybody involved could see it did not do that well. Instead, he believed it was actually used to punish. Torture humiliated a recalcitrant foe, exerted ultimate power over the conquered.

Hoyt didn't care what command's reasons were anyway. He tortured not for purpose, but for pleasure. He, and every person he knew who committed torture did it for the same reason. It provided sublime pleasure to the omnipotent torturer. To hold the ultimate in power over other human beings and to gut them of everything they valued was to be supreme.

He knew this was true because he had stolen many souls, many times.

He could make men curse their mothers. Deny their God. Make them promise to slaughter their children. He had even made men plead for him to rape their wives. He could make them do anything, because he was so skilled at inflicting pain.

He had cut the core out of the hardest of men, robbed them of their beliefs, their dignity, their humanity; he had destroyed their very souls, leaving nothing but burned out husks behind. That was why he did it, and that was why his captors would do it to him. For every man he had tortured, they would punish him three times over. Punishment. Retribution. Revenge. No matter what you called it, torture was a soulless act by soulless men, and he was one of them.

Now, it was Judgment Day. But he would give them nothing, say nothing.

The light and noise and sleeplessness continued for a long time, how long he did not know. He was aware that his senses changed, became distorted as the hours went on, and his mind too. Thoughts became more fluid, bending and flowing through his mind in a disorganized pattern that was not familiar to him.

Jim Ed taught him to think on one thing at a time, to separate thought from emotion, both from action. Many more of his father's lessons followed, all harsh, until eventually he found he was unable to forget them. The lessons became part of him—no— the lessons were him. What he became, he knew with certainty, was a result of Jim Ed's lessons. They made him a perfect vessel for the training that came later.

In high school, the other students steered clear of him. Not even the toughest boys would fight him. He won a reputation as a vicious and merciless combatant who never quit and never lost. Girls shunned him and Hoyt spent most of his time alone, out on the open range with a rifle, shooting any animal that crossed his path.

Later, the Marines honed his skills and instilled pride and patriotism in his ferocious nature. The corps trained him as a sniper and eventually he became an interrogator in the first Gulf War. His superiors noticed that he got results, mostly because he was so intimidating and so coldly threatening that most prisoners believed he would truly tear them to pieces if they didn't talk.

After the war, Hoyt knew where his future lay. He signed on with a murky intelligence unit without ever really knowing who he worked for, only that he was a member of America's security team, reporting to a man known simply as the Major. The less he knew about the organization's command structure, the better, they said. Command transferred him many times. He worked in dark sites from Egypt to Bosnia, following orders, doing what he was told, usually underground in prisons where captives rarely walked out.

When his immediate superior, the Major, joined a private contractor after nine-eleven, Hoyt signed on too, because he was tired of restrictions on his work, thought he would have more freedom to interrogate in his own way if he worked outside the military. He knew so much about illegal interrogation by then, he figured the Major would have to cover him if anything ever went wrong. He could take the Major down, and others too, so everyone involved eventually joined together in a bond of silence. The bond existed throughout the clandestine services, as much for self protection as national secrecy.

He never expected to be captured. To him, the rag heads weren't competent enough to pull it off. Even now, he figured someone else had to be behind his abduction, because the Iraqis just didn't have the savvy to knock out the dark site where he was taken prison—

Suddenly, the loudspeakers went dead, left his ears ringing in the unexpected silence. That meant they were coming. He steeled himself against what was to happen next, knowing that anticipation and fear were valuable tools for a torturer and he resolved not to give in to those emotions.

Jim Ed, he thought. Remember, Jim Ed. Show no emotion. Show no fear. Do not cry. Remember, Jim Ed.

He, and perhaps he alone, was equipped to withstand the pain. He knew the pattern they would use, the techniques, all the methods. Still he would not talk. He would give them nothing. He would not flinch.

He heard a door slam open. Two guards in baggy pants kicked their way through the plywood walls and screamed at him in Arabic. "Down! Down!" He glared at them and one guard rammed his head with a rifle butt. "Down!" Hoyt lowered his head while they unlocked his shackles from a metal ring in the floor.

They dragged him across the concrete by the chains on his hands. Out a doorway and down a dim hallway they continued to drag him, then through another doorway into a large room. His eyes were half blind from the days of constant light and he could barely make out troughs of some sort along a wall.

They dragged him into an open area and two additional guards joined them in lifting him upright into the air where they looped his shackled hands over some sort of hanging metal fixture. They let go and his dead weight hung by the chains, setting off slashes of pain through his wrists and arms.

They left him to hang there and when he was able to make out his surroundings he realized he was hanging from a meat hook mounted in the ceiling. Other meat hooks snaked down from the ceiling alongside him. Below were drains in the concrete floor. Finally, he knew where he was. A slaughterhouse.

CHAPTER 21

Darden felt much better after sleeping. He sat up and stretched, looked around the large room that contained the cells. It was old and had a high ceiling, its concrete block walls covered with decades of dirt. At least his vision was better and his head did not ache even though the wound on his scalp was still sore. He wondered how long he had been in the cell because he noticed his clothes had begun to stink.

Beckwith sat in his usual position in the adjacent cage, staring at Darden again, but now with genuine curiosity. He seemed to have grown used to his fellow prisoner, perhaps welcomed the chance for conversation. Already, Darden could see that boredom was the greatest enemy in jail.

"Okay, what?" Darden asked.

"How you feelin' today?"

"Like new. How does my head look?"

Beckwith got up on his hands and knees and came closer. Darden did the same.

"Lower your head and hold the hair back."

Darden did as he was told, felt the crusty remains of blood breaking away from his hair. "It's not as tender as before."

"Yeah, it looks better. The swelling is down and there's no obvious infection. You might actually survive, but I'd wash it the next time they give us water. God gave you a hard head, Darden. Do you know who hit you?"

They sat back down. The cells were not tall enough to stand up straight.

"No, he blindsided me."

"Why?"

"Caught me breaking into a computer. I don't know if the area was classified, but the contents of the hard drive surely must have been."

Beckwith whistled. "If that's true, you're in for it. Anybody know you're here?"

"I don't know."

They paused while Khalid babbled inside his plastic tent, releasing a string of obscenities in Arabic and English. They looked at each other and almost laughed. If the mad Iraqi wasn't so pitiful it would be funny.

"What about you?" Darden asked. "Anybody going to come and get you out?"

"No." Beckwith frowned. "I'm military and when it's a military matter you can wait a long time for justice. Maybe forever."

Darden had to ask again. "What did you do?"

Beckwith shook his head with regret. "I reported something to my unit commander when I should have kept quiet."

"What?"

Beckwith closed up as if he didn't dare trust anyone with his secret, but Darden could see it was more than simple distrust. There was fear in the medic's brown eyes.

"Nobody's listening in here," Darden said. "What happened?"

Beckwith sighed, then seemed to accept that he must trust someone with his story. He lowered his voice and whispered, "I treated an Iraqi whose injuries were not normal. He was a prisoner, not a combatant. His body had electrical burns and dog bites on it. Other things, too. Damage to his genitals. He showed strong signs of post traumatic shock."

"You were supposed to report it, right? That stuff is against the book."

"My commander said I needed to adjust my attitude and get with the program. I disagreed. Next thing I know, I'm arrested and tossed in here."

"On what charge?"

"They don't need a charge."

They stopped talking when a metal door clanged open. Two M.P.'s brought water buckets into the area.

"Hello, pigs," one of them said. The guards laughed and kicked Beckwith's cage.

Darden started to say something to return the insult, but Beckwith shook his head no, signaling him to stay quiet. They remained silent while the guards unlocked the small pass-through doors to their cells and shoved water buckets inside.

After they left and locked the metal door behind them, both the prisoners went for the water and drank until their bellies were full, though Darden saved enough to wash his head wound. They grinned at the pleasure of having enough to drink, indulging in the momentary relief of the parched feeling in their throats. Then they sat back and felt briefly contented.

"What assholes," Darden said. "You have to put up with that every day?"

"That's nothing. You gotta learn to take it. You say anything back, they'll come over and piss on you."

Darden made a long face, doubtful they'd do that to fellow Americans.

"I've seen it," Beckwith said.

They were quiet for a few minutes while they reflected on their situation. Apparently it was a real mistake to land in jail over here where no rules seemed to apply.

"What's going on in this country?" Darden asked. "You report a case of abuse and you get locked up. The guards treat people like animals. You wouldn't believe the things I saw on that computer."

"Like what?"

"Like outright torture."

"Military or private contractors?"

"I don't know, but certainly Americans. Why doesn't somebody stop it?"

"Well, you see what happened to me when I tried."

"That means it's got to be coming from the top."

Beckwith lowered his voice again, leaned closer. "Sure it is. Abu Ghraib was just the tip of the iceberg. A lot of people know this stuff is going on, but nobody cares, or they're too afraid to speak out against it. Officially, we treat prisoners by the rules. Unofficially, anything goes. I keep hearing this thing, "Take the gloves off. Take the gloves off."

Darden felt the same disgust he'd experienced when he saw the photographs in the goons' office. He couldn't understand why Americans would do these things. It didn't make sense.

"What's the point?" he asked Beckwith. "Why resort to such crap?"

"Intimidation. Somebody at the top wants it done. That's the only possible answer. According to military doctrine, skilled interrogation gets you better results than abuse or even torture, but here, everything is upside down. Half the people we arrest are just bystanders. They're not even criminals, much less Insurgents. They couldn't tell you anything useful if they wanted to."

"So who is ordering this?"

"You tell me, man. I just work here."

More than ever, Darden wanted proof that he could take back home—if and when he got back home. This insane policy was much more damaging and widespread than the public knew. Somebody had to break this story to the American people. Most were decent and law-abiding, and if they knew the truth, they would demand that torture stop.

"Beckwith, if we get out of here, could you find me proof?

"Man, I can't do shit while I'm in here."

"I mean eventually. They've got to let you out at some point. You didn't break the law."

Beckwith laughed. "You just don't get it. This is a war zone, and the military is a different world. They can do whatever they want with me."

"I've got to tell the people back home about this."

Beckwith laughed again, harder. "Nobody'll believe you. Not without absolute proof. They still think we're the good guys saving Europe from the Nazis."

"In this war, I'm not sure there are any good guys."

The next day, at least Darden guessed it was the next day,

the guards came to remove Khalid from his plastic-covered cell. Behind the guards the two goons appeared, presumably to take custody of the Iraqi prisoner.

They looked down at Darden and hooted in derision at his dirty squatting form.

The first one spoke to him. "Not so smart-assed now, huh? Are you, reporter?"

Then the other one with the pumped-up shoulders came closer. "How'd you like that goose egg I gave you, Darden? That was sweet, cracking your skull like a watermelon."

"You?"

"Damn right, and that was just the beginning. Fell for our little trap like the rat you are."

"A set up."

They just stood and grinned at him, the same ugly grin they'd given him during the office interview. Darden felt he'd been a chump for falling into their scheme. He'd behaved like an amateur and now he was under their control because of it.

The big one sneered, pointed the finger-pistol at him again. "Later, alligator."

Then the goons turned their attention to Kalid, directed the guards to take him outside, but he was so weak and emaciated, he could barely stand. All he wore was a pair of underwear, his beard and hair grown to a bushy mane, his skin filthy and covered with sores. The man was clearly paranoid, half out of his mind with fear and disorientation. He tried to cover his eyes against the light and cringed when the guards took him by the arms and dragged him toward the door. He glanced at Darden and Beckwith, but quickly averted his eyes, afraid to look at them directly. He babbled under his breath, sobbing as they carried him through the door.

Darden stared in shock, dismayed by the man's condition. He wondered if the same thing was going to happen to the two of them eventually. They were quiet for a long time after that. He imagined himself after years of captivity in a place like this. Would he become a zombie like Kahlid? Would he even survive?

When the metal door slammed open three hours later,

Darden didn't know what to expect. The same two M.P.'s marched in quickly, came straight to his cell and unlocked it. The one with the keys beckoned him out.

"Let's go, Darden."

"Where are you taking me?"

"Don't make us come in there."

Darden didn't move. "I demand to know where you're taking me."

"Let's go, damn it."

Darden refused to move.

The second guard went outside and brought a short, well-dressed man back to the cells with him. He wore a suit and had a good haircut. Nothing about his bearing seemed military, but he projected command and self-confidence. The visitor looked at the conditions in the cells and frowned at the guards, a look of threat in his eyes, but the jailers maintained their composure and said nothing.

"Mr. Darden," the man said. "I am Harrison Yates with the United States Embassy. Please come with me."

"Where?"

"To the airport. You are going home."

CHAPTER 22

Hoyt hung from the meat hook for hours. Despite the pain in his arms and back, a sort of half sleep descended on him, a dream-filled state where his mind flashed with images and blips of thoughts, most of them from victims he had damaged. He knew deranged thinking came from sleep deprivation, nonetheless he found himself unable to manage his thoughts and stop the deluge of memories.

This state of mind made him vulnerable, just as he had seen in so many other victims before. That concerned Hoyt, but those victims had not been hardened, did not have the steel nerves inside that Jim Ed had created in him.

He heard the slap of sandals on stone, low voices approaching from the shadows. Several men in *galabiyyas* surrounded him. One, a giant stripped to the waist, wearing a black hood, poked him with a tool or blade of some sort. Hoyt tried to raise his head.

"Up, now," the giant said. "You are in the presence of superiors."

A tall man stepped forward, one who held himself with great dignity. His eyes ran over Hoyt's body as if he were about to bargain over an animal.

"Hello, Tex-as." The man came closer. "I have wanted to meet you for a long time. Now, I do, you are not so big as they say. You are red and freckled, covered with scars."

The other men snickered. Hoyt tried to kick and heave his body in defiance, but his limbs had no power in them anymore.

"My name is *Budiya Uf"Uwan*. We shall learn to know each other well."

He signaled to the others with a slight wave of the hand. "Begin."

One of the men retreated to the shadows and returned with a tripod, topped by a digital video recorder. He spent a couple of minutes setting it up, fiddling with the adjustments to get the best light level on Hoyt's body. When he nodded that he was ready, the recording light on the camera turned red.

One of the other men stepped in front of the camera, his face covered from the nose up by a head scarf. He spoke in defiant tones to the lens, only his mouth and beard moving. "The man you see here is American. A jackal. An enemy of Islam and the Iraqi people. His confession shows to the world what the invaders do. Watch and learn the truth."

The spokesman moved away as the giant stepped forward. He gave Hoyt's body a slight push, causing it to swing a bit from the hook, taking his time.

"Tell me everything," the torturer said, touching Hoyt on the genitals with the tip of a blade. "We both know you will, in time. Why not now? Perhaps then we allow you to die sooner."

Hoyt mustered up what saliva he had in his mouth and spat on the giant's torso. The man roared with laughter and the others joined in on the fun. They all moved forward with mocking laughs and each in turn spat on Hoyt's face.

The giant continued to laugh with genuine pleasure. "This is so much better than the timid rabbits I usually have to skin."

The men stepped back and the giant moved closer to Hoyt's ear. "We start with your name. Tell the people who you are, Texas."

Hoyt said nothing.

The torturer sighed as if genuinely sorry for what he had to do, then bent over and went to work with the knife. In seconds, Hoyt heard screams reverberating off the walls of the slaughterhouse. He wondered where they came from, then realized they were his own screams. The blade prodded and sliced at sensitive spots and he felt a very intense, hot sensation everywhere it touched. Despite his iron control, he screamed every time the blade moved.

"Your name?"

Hoyt mumbled a lie, and the knife returned, this time working its way deeper and more slowly. Hoyt screamed as it penetrated his scrotum and found the *vas deferens* attached to his testicles. He felt pain within pain, a searing wire of it that found the most vulnerable of nerves and drew them out into stretched rubber bands of tissue, racing with brain signals that he could not stop. He continued screaming as the pain heightened even more and the hot wire snapped. The giant pulled and twisted and tore something away from him, then held it up to Hoyt's eyes.

"Look at yourself, Texas."

Hoyt opened his eyes and saw a pink, egg shaped organ in the giant's bloody hand. It had been wrenched from him and the ducts dangled from it obscenely.

"Bellows," he groaned. "Hoyt Bellows."

"Yes," the giant replied. "You will tell us all."

"No."

They let him hang for a while to allow his nerves to recover and he wished he could die. Victims had tried that with him before. Holding their breath or trying to will their hearts to stop, but it did not work. Always the involuntary nervous system took over and forced them back toward life.

With his strength and health, this could go on for days. Was there no way to make it stop? Jim Ed had taught him never to show mercy. Was it possible these men were different? If he said or did something to please them, perhaps they would be merciful even if he would not. Was it possible?

His mind seemed to flip flop inside his skull. He saw Jim Ed's stark, weathered face swimming before him. Saw the expanse of Texas sky. Green fields. The old white frame house under a stand of oaks. Bloody soil. A black and white calf. A dark gulley that tumbled away into an abyss of darkness, like a river rushing toward a black canyon at night.

One of the men came forward and poured water over his head to revive him. He opened his eyes and saw outlines of the men shimmering in his field of view. His eyes played tricks; the men, the camera, all appeared as if underwater, unclear and blurry in his vision. They encircled him, their faces hard and immobile, their eyes cruel.

"Mercy," he said. "Please."

The very tall one came forward and stood close, gazing into Hoyt's contorted features. "Did you show my father mercy?"

"What?"

"When he was under your control in The Cave, did mercy enter your heart or mind then? He was an old man. He knew nothing. Yet you twisted the life out of him. Now you ask us to be merciful?"

"Who? Who was he?"

"He was everyone you harmed."

"I only did my job."

"As we are."

"But I'm not guilty of anything."

"If you are innocent, you will remain silent. If you confess, you are guilty."

The tall man stepped back into the shadows and the giant in the hood came forward again. In a moment of clarity, Hoyt saw that coarse, dark hair covered the man's body; sweat ran down his massive torso and soaked the waistband of his trousers.

"Tell more, Bellows. Who do you work for?"

Hoyt looked into the camera lens and thought of the people who would see this afterward. He did not want to be known as a man who broke. He turned his head away and said nothing.

"Look at this," the giant said. He held a pair of shears before Hoyt's eyes, snapped the blades shut twice. "You will talk."

The tall man spoke from the shadows. "Again."

As the giant worked on his toes with the shears, Hoyt felt the screams building. He could not prevent them from rising in his throat and voicing the pain inside. His agony reverberated off the walls of the room. He screamed and pled as the giant slowly removed the toes, joint by joint. Between screams Hoyt tried to talk.

"The Major was—"

"Who?"

"I work—"

The shears stopped for a moment and he got his breath.

"—for the Major."

"Oh, you lie, Bellows."

"It's true!"

"Liar!"

The shears moved to his left thumb, squeezed and reached bone just behind the nail.

"Don't! Jim Ed!"

Some time after they put away the shears, Hoyt felt water poured over his head and it revived him enough that he opened his eyes. Again, they'd let his nerves recover long enough to re-establish a lower pain threshold. Now, they would begin again and increase the pain until his body reached the point of shutting down. He knew the cycle well. Allow recovery, then reintroduce and intensify pain. Over time, the victim developed anticipatory fear that made the wait worse and the pain worse when it came again.

By the time they employed electric shock, many hours after the first round of exploration with the knife, he'd been through hot irons, twisting of the joints until his bones broke, and the fracturing of his teeth by pliers. He had told them everything he knew. Every name. Every place. Every victim he could remember. He also told them much that was not true. If he thought they wanted to hear something, he said it—made it up. In the midst of the worst of it, he gave them names and organizations that he invented or plucked randomly from his memory, no matter how unrelated to his work. For the tiniest sliver of relief, for just an instant of cessation, he said and did anything they asked. He even tried to imagine what they might want, and gave them that too.

When they applied electric shock to his tongue and eyelids, he repeatedly confessed to the world who he was, named everyone he had worked for, told what he did to his victims, and revealed who gave orders to do it. He also gave them the names of his school teachers; accused fellow Marines from boot camp of treason; he offered up Jim Ed as an agent for Israel; the Major as a spy inside Iran; all the women he had slept with who hated Islam and corrupted *Jihadists* with their western depravity. He imagined and revealed in great detail the American military plot to destroy faith in Islam by introducing cocaine and nudity to Iraqi culture. He told them the private contractor who employed him had embedded electronic devices in the brains of thousands of Iraqi prisoners to control their actions, coercing them to become assassins for America. These inventions of his mind spilled out for hours on end. The confession was so rambling, distorted, expansive and disjointed it was well beyond the realm of belief or interpretation; but he did not know this. He was unable to know because his mind was beyond thought, beyond any understanding. By that point, only incoherent passages of words and ragged fragments of memory came from his mouth.

By the time Hoyt Bellows confessed all his crimes and more, he was little more than an uncomprehending, terrified animal who had been led to slaughter.

CHAPTER 23

On the way to the airport, Darden tried to thank Harrison Yates for freeing him from the jail. He also explained that he was only trying to recover photographs that belonged to him, but the embassy employee seemed uninterested. Instead, he told Darden to get his clothes and other gear from a bag behind the car seat.

"I had an associate collect personal items from your quarters," Yates said. "It's better if you not go back there. Get dressed." He had an abrupt northern accent and a business-like manner, seemed to Darden as if he must be very good at his job.

Darden turned and hauled the bag to the front, looked through the contents and everything seemed to be in it. He tore off his stinking prison clothes and threw them out the window of the speeding black Suburban, put on clean pants and a shirt.

"The highway was swept this morning for I.E.D.'s," Yates said. "That's why I'm personally able to drive you without an armed escort. It's better if your exit is low key."

Yates said nothing about how or why he'd managed to get Darden's release. When Darden fumed about his imprisonment, demanded to know more, the man turned and looked at him coldly. "You can return to jail if you want to fight them, but don't forget you were caught breaking into an office at a U.S. military installation. Only because you are ostensibly a member of the Press are you now free.

Your colleagues, and the State Department, do not take the jailing of a reporter lightly."

Darden started to say something else, but Yates cut him off. "Without our influence, you might have remained in jail for months simply awaiting a hearing."

"Of course, you're right. I should thank you."

"Don't thank me," Yates said. "Just don't come back. You have enough trouble at home."

"What trouble?"

"Your father. I got your release on humanitarian grounds."

"What happened to him?"

Yates did not answer and Darden felt a wave of unpleasant heat rush through his body. His father. It couldn't be good.

Dropping him off at the airport, Yates stopped at the curb and gave him his identification, passport, and airline tickets all the way through to Orlando. Darden almost said thanks again, but caught himself in time. Yates put the big SUV in park and waited for Darden to collect his camera, shoulder bag and laptop. Darden opened the passenger door but Yates held up his hand, gesturing for him to wait a moment.

"A final word of advice, Mr. Darden. Anything you found in that office, anything you learned in that jail, anything you heard over here," Yates paused and looked directly into his eyes, "You would be wise to forget it."

Darden nodded, got out.

The next evening, his flight landed in Florida and Linda met him at the airport. He had called her from Atlanta during a connection and asked if she could pick him up. Her voice sounded thrilled, so eager he found it difficult to ask about his father, but when he did, she just told him to hurry.

She was waiting for him outside baggage claim in the pick-up lane. No one had ever looked better to him in his life. She threw her arms around his neck and kissed him hard on the mouth. He squeezed her with his arms and held her that way for several minutes, soaking in the heat of her body.

"Welcome back," she whispered.

"I missed you."

She backed away and looked at him, saw the heavy beard, the bloody scab under his reddish blond hair, the dirty skin. "What happened? You're hurt."

"I'll tell you about it on the way."

"Where?"

"To Jacksonville. I've got to see my Dad."

She agreed without hesitation, took the Turnpike over to I-75 and made good time in the northbound lanes. Two hours to Jacksonville; he hoped his Dad had at least two hours left in him.

"How is he?" Darden asked.

She dodged the question, taking the conversation back to him. "First, I want to know about that cut on your head and why you smell like you haven't had a shower in a month."

"How is he?"

She paused, searching for the best words. "Getting weaker. I called about him last night and the nurse was vague on the phone."

"That's not good."

"One other thing, I hate to tell you, but they're making noise about the bills. They want to move him to hospice."

"I was afraid of that."

He needed to think, so many problems descending at once. The decisions he made in the next few hours would be life changing and he hoped he would make the right choices. He looked out the window at retirement developments and cattle farms while she drove.

Thankfully Linda stayed quiet, letting her own questions wait.

At the hospital, his worries only grew. His father was unable to speak or eat, though he could move a finger occasionally and open his eyes at times. He was visibly smaller since the last time Darden saw him. Darden took his hand and spoke to him for a half hour, describing what had happened to him in Iraq. He wasn't sure if his Dad understood or not, but it made him feel better to think that he did.

It also helped that Linda sat across the bed from him and listened to the whole story. He decided not to keep any of it back, no matter how fearful it made her. The path he was taking required that he be totally honest with her. He did not want to involve her further in his life without being open about the risks ahead.

His mother had died when he was a four years old, and he
had no brothers or sisters. Once his Dad was gone, he would
truly be alone except for Linda. He hoped he could hold on to her
through the coming storm.

The nurses came in on rounds and asked them to leave the
room for a few minutes. They went out to the hallway, but before
they could sit down and talk, hospital employee showed up and
requested a meeting with him. While Linda waited outside the
room, he went down to the hospital's administrative offices and
listened while the employee explained the corporation's policy on
terminal cases and prolonged care.

He wasn't even sure if he heard her words. So many things
circled in his mind, mostly his Dad's deterioration, and that the
details of patient transfer and payments seemed insignificant.
Part of his mind recognized the bills would loom very large
eventually, but for now, all he wanted was comfort and dignity for
his father's last days. The employee pushed papers in front of him
and asked him to sign in several places. He signed without truly
understanding the meaning of the documents; he only wanted to
get back to his Dad.

In the elevator, he became light-headed, felt as if he might
keel over at any moment. He was on emotional overload, knew
that if he had one more brick of bad news to carry, he might not
be able to move ahead. He stepped out on the fourth floor and
passed the nurse's station, turned a corner and saw Linda sitting
outside his Dad's room, elbows on her knees, face in her hands.

His legs and arms grew heavy, his head felt dizzy and rising.
When he got to her, she looked up and her face was wet, her eyes
red and brimming. She didn't say a word, just stood and hugged
him, and he knew what her manner meant.

She held his arm and walked with him into the room. His
Dad was still hooked up to the machines, but everything else
was different. The main thing Darden noticed was the absolute
stillness of the body, the slight rise and fall of the chest gone, the
twitch of the eyelids missing. Already, his skin lacked color.

Darden sat on the edge of the bed and took it all in. After a few moments, he bent and kissed his Dad on the forehead, stood and went back out to the hallway. There was nothing left to do. The giant wheel had turned another revolution in its endless cycle of life and death. Oblivious to observer or participant, the great wheel moved at its own pace, of its own volition, all humans subject to its ceaseless momentum.

CHAPTER 24

On her way home from work, Linda—who now thought of Tom's place as home—worried about his state of mind. A full two weeks after the funeral he was still numb with grief, drained of feeling and energy. She watched him push his Iraq experience and the Daytona bombing investigation further away from his minds, he seemed to think of little except the loss of his father and the many details in settling the estate.

Mostly she worried about his lethargy and wondered how she could get him going again.

Since his father's death he had done very little work even though his jerk of a boss, Weldon, called him every day saying it was time for him to get back to the office. It was apparent Southeastern Radio News was out of patience with him. After his jailing and removal from Iraq, only the seriousness of a family death and fear of a wrongful termination suit had kept them from firing him.

Weldon claimed he had personally worked with the Embassy to get his release and never failed to mention how grateful Tom should be, but at the same time, he berated Tom for the actions that got him thrown into jail in the first place. Weldon also claimed the company had absorbed serious fees in getting legal advice prior to Darden's release.

Family crisis or not, Tom told her they would soon demand his return to work or his resignation, for they needed little excuse to unload reporters in such lean times. Like most traditional news organizations their revenues continued to decline monthly. Further, Tom was sure they would not support him in what he intended to report about his brief duty in Iraq.

The only good thing about his current state was that she was able to provide the small pleasures in his days. They spent every minute together when she was off work, often doing little more than talking, but it was obviously a balm for his soul. Grocery shopping, walking, even washing the car took on new meaning with the two of them together.

She caught him watching her movements during even the most mundane tasks as he took pleasure in the subtle motions of her body. With a taut muscle here, a sway of the breasts there, she held his attention as she had never done with any man before. Both of them reveled in the mystery and joy of sexual attraction, marveling at its power even in the midst of grief.

She got home about seven-thirty, coming off a twelve hour shift. Despite her fatigue, she sat down on the couch with him and coaxed the thoughts from his mind, asked about his feelings, asked if the days were getting better. He opened up and told her everything while he rubbed her tired back and shoulders.

"Let me get this uniform off," she said. "Then you can rub me all you want."

When she got out of the shower, he was in the kitchen. He'd made up a salad with grilled chicken on it and poured them a glass of wine. She wore a thin nightgown that clung to her shape and allowed a good view of her swaying breasts when she bent forward. Since their first night of intimacy when she sensed how much he liked her body, she made a point of wearing little or nothing when they were alone together.

They sat down to eat and halfway through the salad she noticed a plain, brown package on the kitchen counter.

"What's that?"

"I don't know. It came in the mail today."

"Who from?"

"I don't know."

"And you haven't even opened it?

He shrugged in reply.

Her curiosity was up, and there was no way to turn it off.

She got up and brought the package to the table. It had no return address or other evidence of its source except the postmark which read Washington, D.C. She opened it with a steak knife, removed the contents wrapped in layers of newspaper. Inside the folds, she found three digital video discs, their shiny silver surfaces trembling in the overhead lights, but there were no labels or identifying marks on them.

She looked at him and made a puzzled face.

"I don't get it either," he said.

"What do you suppose is on them?"

"Let's find out." He took the shiny discs into the living room and loaded one into the DVD player connected to the television.

He tinkered with the remote for a minute trying to switch over to the player, finally got it powered up and selected PLAY on the menu. They sat down on the couch and within a few seconds a recording came on the screen. The lighting was dark, the video plainly the work of an amateur. A blank wall of dirty concrete blocks appeared, then a bearded man stared into the lens, his face mostly covered by an Arabic scarf, his *keffiyeh* pulled down over the nose.

"What is this?" Darden said. "A joke?"

"Looks like the Arab from hell."

The man spoke in slow, awkward English to the lens, only his eyes, mouth and beard exposed. "The man you see here is American." The shot widened and they saw a naked torso hanging by the arms. The man was white with red hair; he looked bruised and semi-conscious. "A jackal. An enemy of Islam and the Iraqi people. His confession shows to the world what the invaders do. Watch and learn the truth."

"Oh, my Lord," she said. "What is this?"

"You don't have to watch, Linda. You want me to turn it off?"

But she was as transfixed as Tom, didn't move until the hooded torturer entered the frame and toyed with the victim using a knife. As the camera moved down the victim's torso she cringed and started to squirm then grabbed Darden's arm when the knife reached the man's genitals.

"This is horrible!" She buried her face in his shoulder. "Why would anyone do such a thing?"

He turned the video off and they locked eyes, both rattled by the rawness of what they'd seen.

"Who sent this to me?"

"Yes, who?"

"Beckwith, maybe."

"I can't watch it."

He took one of the other discs and swapped it for the one in the player. She didn't know what to expect next; she was afraid to look. He started the player again and this time photographs appeared on the screen in rows of thumbnails. He selected one at random and she saw a burning car surrounded by insurgents on a Sadr City back street.

"That's my shot!"

"Yours?"

It occurred to her that he hadn't told her all the details of his Iraq experience, nothing about the fighters in the photo with automatic weapons; nothing about an exploding car. "You were in the middle of that battle?"

"I was just an observer."

He paged through several other photographs, all of them his, he said. All of them from the insurgent attack on the building. "These are shots I took of a car bomb in Baghdad, some of the ones the Intel guys stole from me."

She sank deeper into the couch as she saw how close he'd come to serious danger while he was over there. Little wonder he had become so lethargic. His mind had absorbed a lot of trauma in a short period of time. For someone not conditioned to such violence, then jail, then the death of his father added on to that, it was a measure of his strength that he wasn't seriously ill at this point.

He went to the player and put in the third compact disc. On it, they found more still photographs, this time of various forms of torture and abuse of naked Arabic men. She thought they were as horrible as the first disc, just not as hard core since there was no motion or sound.

"Is that Abu Ghraib?" she asked.

"No, these are the ones I found on the computer in the Intel office."

"Before you were smashed on the head."

"Yeah."

She felt tears and knew her voice had quavered. He took his eyes off the screen, looked at her and turned the player off. "I'll look at all this later." He took her in his arms and stroked her hair, trying to calm her worries.

"I'm afraid, Tom."

"I know. It's ugly as it gets, but this is real world stuff. Real victims who suffered. Most people want to be shielded from it, don't want to know what's going on over there."

"Who sent this to you? What do they want?"

He thought for a moment before he answered. She wondered if he was thinking of a way to cushion his answer, to make it more palatable to her.

"This is proof. It's evidence of what we're doing over there. Somebody wants me to break this story wide open."

"But, why you?"

"I'm not sure."

"Tom, just holding onto this stuff could get you killed."

He said nothing, had no soft answer for that, because it was plain truth. She knew it and he knew it. The minute he exposed the proof of torture contained on these discs, he would become a target.

"Many people from different camps have kept a lid on the brutality over there," he said. "There is a secret war of torture underway, committed by both sides, and it has essentially gone unreported."

She thought of the implications of what he said. The press had failed. The government had failed. Those who had kept it secret so far would most likely do anything to prevent him from baring these crimes to the world. If he reported this, their safety would go out the window.

They went to bed and clung to each other, each of them carrying fear into their dreams.

The next morning, she was off work and managed to sleep late. When she woke up, he wasn't in bed next to her. She got up and went into the kitchen where he was clicking away on the keyboard of his laptop. She didn't say anything, just made coffee and kissed him on the head.

She went out for a run, and later shopping, didn't return until late afternoon. He still sat at the table, re-reading his story. She put away groceries, waiting until he finally looked up at her and said, "It's done."

She didn't ask to read it, didn't want to read it yet. After seeing the photos and video the previous night, she knew the story would be explosive and she wondered if either of them was prepared to face the repercussions. She just hoped it didn't ruin things for them, because she'd never been so happy before.

He e-mailed the story to Weldon and they waited for the call. It came an hour later. Tom put the conversation on speakerphone to let her listen. For once, his boss didn't sound angry at Tom. His tone was more serious—more like resolved.

He asked, "Do you have proof?"

"Yes, incontrovertible proof."

"How did you come by it?"

"I can't answer that."

Weldon sighed. "I already told you the parent company would not touch such sensitive material, yet you went ahead and covered it anyway. Didn't clear any of it with me in advance. What do you expect me to do?"

"I expect you to show some spine, Weldon. Are we in the news business or not?"

"Well, we're not *The New York Times*. We don't have the financial or legal resources to handle the fallout from a story like this."

Tom looked at her and shook his head in dismay.

"Then, what's the point, Weldon? No wonder newspapers are dying like flies. Radio news is nothing but ranting showmen.

Television is three-fourths opinion. If we don't have the guts to cover hard stories, to tell the truth, why should we deserve to stay in business?"

There was a long pause at the other end of the line. "Well, you are not in this business anymore, Darden. Not with us. We'll send your final paycheck in the mail. Don't bother to come back to the office."

She watched Tom's face as he accepted the inevitable. Before he could say anything else, the phone clicked dead at the other end. Tom's course was set, and despite her fears, her course was the same. She would back him all the way.

CHAPTER 25

After he got the green light from the Administration, Dr. Baines had moved with all possible speed to initiate the Master Plan he and Peyton Marshall devised for their new holding corporation. So far, most of the billing went through the governmental maze as consultation and planning fees with the invoices directed to an assortment of obscure Federal Agencies, most of those dummy organizations run by the intelligence community and funded through the Department of Agriculture. He set up dozens of corporate bank accounts, all under the umbrella of the holding corporation, to park and dispense the funds when needed.

The billing and authorization paperwork moved with speed unknown in government circles. Invoices in the millions circulated across various departmental desks with barely a pause. The Great Man proved true to his word. Funding on this scale would have been impossible without his approval and muscle behind it. Without him, the funds surely would have been blocked by oversight committees and budget watchers throughout the federal watchdog agencies. The Great Man's power inside the beltway was far greater than perceived by those outside. Somehow, through his years in Congress and as a cabinet member, he'd developed pathways to move money when and where he wanted it.

Baines could scarcely believe such money was available to him to use as he saw fit. All those years he'd spent building a practice, grinding through the daily ritual of appointments and pharmaceutical reps and collections. It seemed so far away now. Already, he and Peyton had each peeled off more money than he could have made working an entire lifetime, and there was still plenty of cash to keep the gears of the Master Plan turning.

Perhaps for the first time ever, Baines felt he was really living. Without children or personal attachments—his face had made all that impossible—life had always been a solitary existence for him. His few pleasures were rooted in possessing things; in his previous life he'd often spent weeks selecting something as simple as a new watch. He savored the process of choosing exactly the right object for a certain occasion or mood, be it a watch, a car, or a suit.

Now, though, he exercised that pleasure without restraint. Already he had placed a contract on an estate in Virginia with hardly a thought for the multi-million dollar price tag. Now, he was able to live as he wished. All he had to do was keep the wheels of the corporation in motion and generate results for the Great Man, and he had all the confidence in the world that he could accomplish that.

He ran the corporation from his own desk in a rented office suite in Alexandria. He kept no staff, because he wanted no prying eyes near the operation. Instead, the Great Man had provided a list of freelancers and individual contractors who could be engaged secretly and who would remain discreet as they bought land and equipment, purchased electronic records, and subcontracted surveillance to the necessary telecommunications and data mining companies.

It worked smoother than he and Peyton had ever imagined it would. As it turned out, by having the Great Man on their side, they could have done it without involving the Wise Men at all. With the enormous amount of money at their disposal, he found he could hire almost any service or individual he needed and maintain a hard wall of separation for secrecy. Many organizations were willing to bend laws and adjust to his requirements if they were paid well enough.

He started operations by acquiring old facilities in remote places, mostly abandoned barracks and hangars, concrete installations, much of it on former military bases.

On a beautiful April morning, with trimmers and leaf

blowers scouring the grounds outside his office, he spent several million dollars hiring a firm composed of former military and intelligence officers which specialized in boots-on-the-ground services. They called themselves Security Consultation Providers, but they were essentially mercenaries, men who knew how to use weapons and had the willingness to take orders from anyone who paid them. Soon, they would start recruiting foot soldiers among the radical militia groups gaining strength across the country.

He felt it had been a successful morning until Peyton reached him by phone a bit after eleven. There was no greeting or small talk.

"Have you seen the news services on the internet today?" Peyton asked.

"No, I have been busy."

"Go online and look at the *Washingtonian Update*."

Baines did as he was told. While the site downloaded, he wondered what could have upset Peyton, because the man was normally reserved to the point of stoniness, yet this morning his voice conveyed urgency that was rare for him. Then the site came up and the doctor felt his own heartbeat rise as he saw the headline on the screen.

"The top story on the left."

"Yes, I am reading it now." Then the photographs came into view and he understood Peyton's alarm. An array of torture photos accompanied the story, all of them graphic and inflammatory. "Damn it, who did this?"

Peyton answered uncertainly, "I'm not sure. That's the question. I checked a few sources in the news community and nobody has ever heard of the reporter. They don't even know where he works."

"The byline says, Thomas Darden, with an e-mail address. Somebody has to know him."

"That's why I am calling you. We don't need the media stirred up any further attention on this torture issue, and we can't have Congress grandstanding just as we're getting underway."

"No, of course not."

"I want to keep to our original deadline and be operational by June first."

"As I do."

"Since he's a nobody, he'll have trouble getting traction for follow-up pieces. Before this grows, we need to take care of it."

"How exactly?"

"Put out this fire, Josiah."

"With all possible finality?"

"This is no time to be timid."

As he hung up the phone, Baines thought about the best way to solve the problem. He could simply use the new individual locator data system they were building to find him, then send an operative to remove the man, but would that really resolve the threat? If it weren't for those damned photos, he could easily plant disinformation among favorable news organizations and dismiss the piece as speculation by an unknown opinion writer. But since the guy had photographic proof the story had instant credibility.

What about discrediting the photos themselves? He could have a few paid experts doctor them and claim they were all fakes, but that would simply draw more attention to the original photos and bring additional scrutiny to any tampering. No, without finding the source of the evidence, the threat would likely reappear in the form of more stories and new photos professionally authenticated before they even appeared. Simply claiming they were fake wouldn't quite end it. Other reporters might surface with more evidence and the story would gain strength.

Okay, he thought, first step is to stanch immediate bleeding, the second is to find the primary source of the blood and repair the damage. His mind moved along familiar pathways as he approached the problem, much as he would a medical case. Gather information, diagnose, then treat. So when he considered the situation within that clearly defined and time-tested process, the solution became apparent to him within minutes. The treatment must be two pronged—first, get a team moving to find the source of those damnable photographs and cut them off at the source, and second, remove Thomas Darden. Since no one knew the guy, Baines reasoned, his removal would draw less attention that a second story coming out of his loose mouth.

He picked up the phone again and felt a distinct thrill, one unfamiliar to him. He was about to order his first assassination.

CHAPTER 26

Darden's cell phone had not stopped ringing since the story first appeared on the *Washingtonian Update*, a minor political news website. He wasn't sure how people found his number, but they had. Perhaps it was impossible to stay hidden in the electronic age. Anybody could find you anywhere.

Hundreds of e-mails bloomed in the inbox of the e-mail address he'd posted with his byline at the end of the story. Some of it was hate mail, but a lot of it came from supporters who applauded his revelation of the facts. Most amazing, a number of them were inquiries from television producers and magazine editors wanting to speak with him about future projects. Most of the phone calls were from other reporters and bloggers trying to get more details on the story, trying to squeeze leads and quotes from him that they could use on their own sites in follow-up pieces. A few calls came from federal employees; one from the FBI, one from the Department of Justice, others from congressional staffers. Finally he turned the phone off and let the voice mailbox fill up with messages.

Even Linda's cell phone rang from local people trying to find him. How had they known she might be a connection to him? They had only been together a few weeks. The answer, he supposed, was people talk, so word gets around.

Any way he looked at it though, he was a hot item for the first time in his career. Through luck and moxie, he had re-vitalized a story originally broken by *Sixty Minutes* and *The New York Times* years earlier, but their expose' of Abu Ghraib did not accomplish much more than generating dismay among the

American people. Rather than provoking widespread outrage and demands to end to prisoner abuse, the story dissolved mostly into a series of internal investigations and official denials. From his own experiences, Darden knew the story had just been driven deeper underground. It was much larger than Abu Ghraib and whether through negligence or misguided patriotism the press let the rattlesnake go free.

He quickly went to work on his next piece. He wanted to write a story about his brief imprisonment in the military jail and explain why he'd been detained and what he'd seen on the computer. He envisioned it as a springboard story to expand on the cover-up of the underground torture network, and yes, it would be an indictment of the tacit approval that he and Beckwith agreed had filtered down from the very top in Washington. At least some unknown officials had sanctioned the use of torture by the United States government and he wanted to shine light on that fact even though it might bring a thunderstorm of trouble down on his head.

But no matter what it cost, he intended to live up to his father's belief in him.

Linda interrupted his work at midday and held up her cell phone for him to hear a message she'd received that morning. It was from the Volusia County Chief Fire Inspector, the official they had seen at the Daytona bombing site.

"I called him a couple of times while you were out of town," she explained. "I asked him to call me if he learned anything significant about the explosion."

She pushed two buttons on the phone and the message played back on the tiny speaker. "Miss Ramsey," the Inspector said, his voice flattened and thinned by electronic processing. "You asked me to call with any new developments. I'm not sure what your personal interest is in this case, but I think it is important that I keep you and Mr. Darden up to date. We have found the remains of a video recording made near the site prior to the explosion. It is a partial recording and it is in bad shape, but there are a couple of things on it that I'd like to ask you about. Please give me a call back."

Darden looked up at her in surprise, then smiled, pleased that she had kept at the hotel bombing story while he was away.

"What do you want to do?" she asked.

"Drive to Daytona this afternoon."

"Well, okay, but you might be too big for this story now," she grinned. "After all, it was only a terrorist attack right down the highway, and you're practically a celebrity now, doing international intrigue, that sort of thing."

He pinched her on the butt and she ran for the bedroom.

"Get dressed," he said. "We've got another story to work."

While they took her Jeep south, she called the Inspector back and asked if they could drop by his office that afternoon. He agreed and they drove straight to the Fire Services Administration Building, pulling into the parking lot a few minutes before three.

She eyed Darden as they entered the front door. "This time, let me do the talking. I know the man and we'll get better results if you don't sound so much like a hot-shot reporter."

"Oh, he just has a crush on you."

She punched him on the arm. "You."

When they entered the Inspector's office, he stood up and shook hands with them, always the serious professional. To Darden's eyes, the man looked even more tired than before, the weight of responsibility pulling at the corners of his eyes and mouth. He walked them down the hall to an open work area with pieces of charred evidence arranged on table tops, white boards on the walls covered with charts and lists. This looked like the war room where they reconstructed evidence from fires and disasters, forever digging for truth among ruins.

"Thanks for calling, Chief," Linda said.

Darden lagged behind them, letting her do her thing. The Inspector glanced at her but said nothing when she gave him a huge smile. He was a man of few words, but he seemed to like her youthful energy and wanted to help; maybe she reminded him of a daughter or his wife at a younger age.

"This is all evidence," he said. "It is now under the jurisdiction of a Joint Counter-Terrorism Investigation Task Force comprised of the FBI and local and state law enforcement. Our job is to investigate the bombing."

They stopped at a tall table with various burned objects scattered across it, most of them damaged components from electronic devices.

"The only reason you're getting a look at this is because I think you can help our investigation," the Chief said, eyeing Darden. "So think twice before you write or speak about anything you learn here today."

He picked up a Compact Disc that looked a bit scorched, but it was still flat and whole. He put it into a player, started it, and they saw broken images come and go on the display, small rectangular segments breaking up and reforming in an array of colors.

"We think this was part of a security system aimed at the parking lot of a store down the street from the hotel," the Chief said. "There's not much left on it, except some traffic on the street, but at this stage, you know almost as much about this case as we do and I want your thoughts. Tell me if anything catches your eye." He pushed the fast forward button and the scene jerked along, sometimes with a relatively clear image of the parking lot and street, at other times, with nothing but broken pixilations. "Here it is, coming up now."

He slowed the video back to normal and they watched for a moment, seeing nothing but a string of cars moving toward the ocean. Then a U-Haul truck lurched into the frame, though not much of the driver was visible except an impression. He was short and had black hair, perhaps dark skin.

"I've studied this for hours," the Chief said. "This is one of only four trucks large enough to have carried the bomb, in my opinion, that got close to the hotel that morning. According to the date and time stamp, it passed down the street shortly before the explosion."

The truck jerked across the display, followed by a large black pickup, one with huge tires and a lot of chrome.

"Stop there!" Linda said. She grabbed Darden's arm in excitement. "That might be him."

The Chief put the player on pause, and they studied the image that held on the screen. "What is it?" the Chief asked.

"That's him, I'd bet anything," Darden said.

"Who?"

The dark tinted windows of the pickup obscured the driver, but the truck was exactly as described by Hector's companions at the trailer park. Darden did not think it likely this was a coincidence.

"Chief," Linda said. "Do you think the state crime lab could enhance the image of that pickup truck, get some identifying marks from it, maybe even the license?"

"That depends," he answered. "I was certainly going to send the disc to them to study the rental. What do you know about the black pickup?"

She looked at Darden, waited for him to answer.

"If we can trace that pickup, I think it will lead us to the man who planned the bombing," Darden said.

The Chief whistled with satisfaction, the first sign of emotion Darden had seen from him. "How can you be so sure?" the Chief asked.

"If that truck has Texas license plates, I think the man inside it hired two Mexican illegals in Jacksonville—one to rent the truck, another to drive it—and now both of them are dead. They had no other links to him; he's the one responsible."

"How soon can they study the disc?" Linda asked.

"Normally, the lab has a backlog of weeks or months."

"Months?"

"Of course, with the high priority of this case, we've been moved to the head of the line. The FBI lab in Washington is examining some evidence right now."

"Will you call me as soon as you know something?" she asked.

"Sure, Miss Ramsey." He looked at Darden. "But try to keep your reporter buddy here reigned in until we know something definite. Remember, we're sharing vital evidence with you. Don't compromise the case for an easy story."

"I'll put a leash on him if I have to."

At that, even the Inspector had to smile. "I'm sure you will."

"Thanks," Darden said with sincerity. They turned and left the investigator to his work, his eyes and concentration already back on the worktable.

Outside, the afternoon sun was strong and presaged the heat of summer. They walked toward Linda's car and he took her hand, feeling the hint of progress ahead. It was such a high moment, Darden couldn't resist a small jab. "I knew he had a crush on you."

CHAPTER 27

"Damn, I hate that son of a bitch."

Arvin sat in front of the television, frowning at every applause line in the speech, a worried expression on his face.

"Well, that's two of us, anyway," the Under Secretary said.

They watched the War Hawk giving a speech to a gathering of campaign contributors on the west coast, many of them defense contractor lobbyists. It was eight o'clock in the evening in Washington and two of the twenty-four hour news networks were broadcasting the speech live to the nation. It was standard red meat fare for the Hawk's crowd, row upon row of American flags arranged precisely as the backdrop, a room full of cheering business suits in front of him.

"—past time to take off the gloves!" the Hawk declared, followed by his familiar smirk as if he and his followers alone understood national security, as if the gloves had ever been on. The crowd erupted in yet another explosion of applause and cheers.

"Nothing like him since McCarthy," the Under Secretary said.

Never in Arvin's years in Washington had he seen a politician so blatantly exploit fear and hatred for his own ends. Speech after speech he announced the imminent destruction of America by its enemies, and more often than not, his version of the enemy sounded more like the opposition party than foreign terrorists. Be afraid, he said to every audience, because we are too careful of individual rights and too weak-willed to make total war on that enemy.

The Under Secretary looked at Arvin. "Apparently we don't spend enough on bombs to suit him."

"Two wars at a time are not enough," Arvin said.

"A hundred wars would not be enough. If we are not waging perpetual warfare on someone, he thinks the country is cowering before the world."

"Terrorists are everywhere," Arvin mocked. "Perhaps we should attack France too."

They both sighed in resignation.

"Let's talk seriously, my friend," the Under Secretary said.

He loosened his silk tie and turned down the volume on the television set. "The man is a loose cannon and the President will not rein him in because that drumbeating keeps their base excited."

"But the damage he does is real. The more he talks, the more we lose allies and gain enemies."

"That's why I called you in here. I have a special favor to ask."

Arvin put down his drink and looked at the man's heavy, lined face when he detected a subtle change in the Under Secretary's tone. What exactly did the old fox mean by a favor? What could he, Arvin Webber, do for the most respected foreign affairs specialist in the United States? He'd never seen the Under Secretary more solemn than now.

"We are facing an emergency." The old man tapped his fingers on his desk and locked his eyes on Arvin. "I, and others I respect, have good reason to believe that the War Hawk is setting up a hidden government within the Administration."

"Whoa!" Arvin's mind went dizzy at the thought. With his own private governmental apparatus, that man could bring the country to the brink of destruction. He already wielded far too much power because of the President's weakness. Given more influence and resources, the Hawk could destroy the checks and balances of the Constitution.

"I don't have to tell you what a radical agenda he would impose on the American nation."

"But what about Congress and—"

"Hell, Congress means nothing to him. He'll override everybody, every law, and go ahead and do whatever he wants. He must be stopped by other means."

Arvin thought for a moment before he spoke, wondered if there could be a mistake. "How reliable is your information?"

"One hundred percent. My sources tell me massive amounts of military funding are being diverted. He is bypassing the usual channels through the Pentagon, OMB, everyone. God only knows what he intends to do with that money. I have suspicions, but I don't know with certainty where it's going."

"But, the Department of Justice could threaten to prosecute and drive him out of office. Congress could cut off the funding."

"In the middle of two wars? They'd be crucified. By the time Congress or Justice acts, the damage will already be done. He might be removed from office eventually, but we need to act before then."

Arvin could see the usual precision in the Under Secretary's reasoning. The War Hawk was the most dangerous public official since Nixon. He simply did not believe in legal processes or the Constitutional system.

"What do you want me to do?"

The Under Secretary leaned forward and rapped the table with his knuckles. "I want you to find where that money is going."

"Do you have any idea where to start?"

"Yes, start in Iraq."

"What the—"

"I had a disturbing conversation yesterday with an old friend at the embassy over there. If I hadn't heard the story straight from him, I never would have believed a word of it. Damndest thing. An army unit threw a reporter in jail without charge or trial for days. Apparently they laid some sort of trap for him."

"What did he do?"

"Broke into an office, snooping around, trying to recover his own property apparently. Never actually took anything—he couldn't because they knocked him out. Some idiot major had stored classified material on his own computer in an unsecured office. The reporter tried to take it. The Major wanted to jail the reporter for espionage."

Webber laughed. "The major screws up, so it's blame the reporter."

"Sure. Someone else is always to blame."

"Why didn't they just call his employer and kick him out of the country or charge him officially?"

"My question exactly. You and I know there are some strange jails over there, and too many would-be decision-makers think they can throw anybody into one of them on a whim."

"What happened to him, the reporter?"

"My friend gave me a call. I made a few calls. He was released. Crisis averted."

"Good. All we need is a First Amendment clash in a war zone."

"It may come to that eventually. He's still not in the clear, but there are too many cowboys running loose in Iraq, most of them working for private firms that are accountable to no one. My friend thinks this business with the reporter might be tied to a rogue intelligence unit."

The Under Secretary spun his chair to a credenza behind him. He opened the top drawer and removed a file with an elaborate cover, handed it over to Webber. The file had an official Classified stamp on it, the top sealed. It wasn't very heavy.

"What we know so far is in this file. We'll know a lot more when you get back from Baghdad."

"Baghdad," Arvin said under his breath. "I have two children, sir. What about my duties here?"

The Under Secretary shook his head from side to side. The bald skull looked heavy on top of his shoulders, as if he'd acquired so many years of knowledge, been involved in so much intrigue, that his head was stuffed full of weighty details. All those facts and responsibilities seemed to weigh his brain down, making his head sag forward in a constant droop.

"I am sorry to pull you away from your family, Arvin, but I have to send someone I can trust. I'll take care of things here."

"Okay then, Iraq it is."

Arvin's stomach tumbled as he thought about it. The thing he disliked most about his job was going to war zones and foreign disasters. Early in his career he'd spent a year in Beirut, trying to patch together a framework of agreement among dozens of bloodthirsty militia factions. All his effort had been for nothing; the factions would settle for no less than mutual destruction. He hated the meaningless violence, the consequent starvation, the sheer irresponsibility of the warring militias. Mostly he remembered the hungry children, the blasted buildings, all that history and culture tumbled to fragments in the streets. Nothing had been solved by a decade and a half of warfare in Beirut. Nothing.

And now, another war zone.

"Well sir, who do I see there?"

"My old friend, Harrison Yates.

"What am I looking for?"

"Crooked war contractors, mainly. You saw the stuff in the news about Blackwater, right? There are too many private companies getting rich off the misery of people over there—all at the expense of the American taxpayer. That has the War Hawk's fingerprints on it, and it always goes back to the money. The Great Patriot has two gods, profit and power. I want you to assess the scale of funding these corporations receive and find out what they're doing with it."

"But that's huge, more of an accounting or espionage role."

"I am not talking about auditing the contractors who provide Pepsi and bed sheets to soldiers. I want to know where the hidden money is flowing, the stuff that never shows up on appropriation bills or budget reports. I need to know about the secret ops, the pay-offs, the bribes. Look beneath the surface. Harrison will point you in the right direction; he has his own local sources."

"You want the real dirt."

"Exactly. I must have it if we're going to stop that war hungry lunatic."

They turned their eyes to the television where the speech concluded and the businessmen swarmed around the War Hawk to shake his hand. Despite the applause and smiles, their faces appeared more rapacious to Arvin than anything else. For them, war was good business and profits trumped patriotism every time.

CHAPTER 28

Linda marveled at Tom's concentration. When he was into a story mentally, nothing could distract him, except her, of course. Stretched out on the couch, reading a magazine, she listened to the steady clicking of keys on his laptop in the breakfast room. With his work discipline and focus, his passion for righting wrongs, she couldn't understand how he'd ever been anything other than a giant success in the news business.

He had been working almost non-stop for several days. He spent hours and hours researching names and leads on the internet, compiling notes and writing fresh stories for the internet news sites that were now after him day and night for new revelations. The more research he did, the more ideas and connections he found. His files on the subject grew daily, then grew even more. He discovered there were actually many untold stories about government excesses since nine-eleven. In his view, the press had utterly failed to keep up.

She watched as he cleverly doled the stories out one-by-one to a variety of sites with only a few photos at a time. That way they always wanted more, and for the first time ever, he told her, he could collect a decent dollar for his work. His only disappointment was that the stories always took a back seat to the photos. To Tom, journalism had fallen into a pit of sensationalism. Any image or opinion that was shocking took precedence over solid, fact-based writing. Television and the internet had infected all forms of news reporting with a slant toward the emotional, the obscene, the momentary jolt.

Despite the deterioration of the news business in general, it was apparent he reveled in his newfound success. Most gratifying of all, a friend from Southeastern Radio News called from Atlanta and offered him his job back. The friend said Weldon had been demoted and transferred for letting Darden and his investigative work get away. It seemed that the parent company had changed its tune about covering big events. Tom merely laughed at the notion of returning to SRN. He felt vindicated, but he had moved on to bigger things and had no intention of going back.

She was glad for him, but all the attention wasn't necessarily a plus for them. For one thing, he had far less time to spend with her.

Another downside of his new notoriety was that other reporters and curiosity hounds pestered them around the clock. The volume of calls and e-mails actually increased, and some people had even come to the door looking for him. He refused to do local television and newspaper interviews, because he did not want to lose the writing time he needed to keep churning out fresh stories.

He's on a mission now, she thought, as she sipped her iced tea and watched him from the sofa. That's the difference. Before this, he didn't like his job because he wasn't interested in the assignments. Accidental fatalities and local event stories had little impact, and he just didn't care enough to do them well. But the torture story and the Daytona bombing, those lit a fire inside him.

She got up and made a pot of coffee. He looked up once without saying anything, but went right back to the keyboard. She placed a cup of fresh brew on the table beside his laptop and kissed him on the ear.

"I'm going out for a run. Back soon."

He nodded and mumbled in reply, but kept on typing.

She changed clothes, went outside to stretch. She loved the feeling of stretching her legs, feeling the strength and flexibility in them before the run turned those muscles to jelly. Secretly, she also loved the feeling of showing off her body to the world.

Her legs had a good shape to them, strong and lightly tanned with trim ankles, and her breasts had a pleasant bounce and roll even under a firm sports bra.

Men usually turned when she ran past them and that was always a good thing, to know she still had it. Thing was, now she knew she had a lot more of it, whatever you called it. Sexiness, confidence, self esteem, maybe a combination of things—whatever it was, she had more of it. What was more, she knew the reason why. She was totally in love with Tom Darden. His fire had flowed into her, and it showed.

Further, she knew she did the same thing for him. Somehow, her being behind him gave him enough internal security to make the transition to a serious reporter. She doubted if he'd have been able to do it without her. Other than his father, no one had ever been as close to him as her; she was sure of that. Though he hadn't said it yet, like most men, she was sure he loved her too.

The spring afternoon was luxurious. Only a few clouds; the humidity not so bad this time of year. She took her time warming up, pulled her hair back off her neck and tied it with a rubber band. The golf course, she thought, I'll take the route around the perimeter of the course. Palms and elephant ears lined much of the way and traffic was light there. It was a good way to run on a day like this.

When she really got up to speed, she ran for thirty-five minutes then walked thirty more, the rest of the way home to the condo. Sweating and loose, she arrived back at the condo parking lot after a full hour of exercise. Next to her car, she stretched again to cool down slowly before going inside. Heavy sweat and air-conditioning did not match. Hand on the fender of her Jeep, she put one leg out and let the thigh muscles straighten into a hamstring stretch. Then the other leg, then turning side to side with her arms extended to rotate the torso. She felt good.

Keys out, she headed for the walkway and wondered what they'd do for dinner. Pick up a pizza? Maybe grill a salmon steak out back?

The roving security guard for the complex had left his golf cart at the end of the walk and she had to step around it onto the lawn to get by. Wet grass clippings stuck to her feet. She'd have to remember to take off her running shoes before—

Twenty feet up the walk, blue pants and black shoes jutted from beneath the stairs. A man's legs. She walked carefully to the spot and saw the guard stretched out, motionless, his body in an awkward position where he had fallen. His hat was off to one side. Then, she saw blood on the back of his head.

Oh, Lord!

She ran for their unit, around to the backside of the building. There, she saw the door standing wide open, late afternoon sunshine filling the living room. She went in and found Tom on his knees, his hands clenching the inside of a wire looped around his neck, struggling to keep the wire away, but it had already cut something because blood poured through his fingers.

Behind him, a stocky man clenched handles at each end of the wire. He looked up in a rush, seemed astonished to see her appear suddenly in the room. His arm muscles bulged with strain against the wire handles as he pulled at the loop. For a moment the man seemed unsure what to do about her, but he kept tension on the wire. He didn't dare ease up with Tom fighting against the tightening noose.

Tom struggled more violently when he saw her there, and the man pulled harder, dragging Tom deeper into the room.

"Get back!" the man grunted.

She opened her mouth. Yell for help, she thought, but no sound came from her clenched throat, suddenly dry as dust.

"Get the hell out!" he said.

Without a thought, she snatched the heavy ceramic lamp off the end table next to the sofa, tearing the cord from the wall.

"Don't do it," the man warned, his voice punctuated by heavy breathing. "Go!"

She took a step closer, holding the lamp by the brass neck.

He turned, facing her, pulling Tom another half step backward. He looked as if he wanted to let go of the wire, but didn't. Tom's legs were thrashing, his face violently red, almost purple.

"Don't!"

She rushed him and swung the lamp with all her strength at the man's crew cut head. The ceramic base shattered on his skull and he stumbled backward, went to one knee and lost control of the wire. Tom continued to clutch at his throat, coughing and gasping for air.

She went closer and swung again. This time a jagged piece of the lamp's base caught him in front, drew a deep cut down his forehead and nose.

"Shit!" he blurted, straining to breathe. He reached up, felt the gash on his face.

"You, bitch!" He stumbled toward her, but somehow Tom was aware enough to grab one leg. The man went down hard.

She hit him again with the brass stem of the lamp, what was left of it. More blood appeared on the back of his head and he struggled to cover up with his hands. She kept hitting him with the length of brass until the man stopped fighting it. He still moved, so she knew he wasn't dead, but he wasn't getting up either.

After a minute, Tom got to his feet, and came to her. He had a thin red line ringing his neck and hands, blood dripping from the cuts. She erupted in tears, crying and raging at the man on the floor.

"Tom! That man! What the—"

Tom managed to stop coughing, gasped for breath and put his arms around her as they both trembled from adrenaline.

The man moved and moaned something, tried to crawl forward. Tom went into the kitchen, snatched a heavy frying pan off the stove. He came back and hit the man hard on the head, twice. Finally, the man went limp.

When the police arrived, she and Tom were sitting on the couch, the frying pan still in Tom's right hand. The door stood open and the man lay on the floor, bleeding slowly from the cuts on his head. Their guns drawn, it took the police a couple of confused minutes to sort out who they should cuff, until one of them recognized Linda.

They holstered their guns and one of them checked the man's pulse. "He's alive."

"Who is he?" Linda asked.

No one answered.

The E.M.T.'s who showed up minutes later knew Linda and took their time checking them out, giving Tom a careful field examination without any of the usual banter. One told them the security guard outside was dead.

They dressed Tom's neck and wanted to take him to the hospital but he refused. The wire had broken the skin, but the bleeding had stopped because there was no major blood vessel damage. Both assured the E.M.T.'s they would drive themselves to the emergency room later, just to be sure.

While they rolled the unconscious attacker away, Linda and Tom answered questions for the police and tried to explain what happened. Slowly, the story came together. Apparently, the security guard surprised the man snooping around the condo which led to a struggle and ultimately the guard's skull being crushed against the metal stairwell.

When Tom heard the commotion outside, he opened the door to check it out, he moved toward the noise, and the assailant jumped him from behind. The man got the wire loop over Tom's head and dragged him back inside the condo just a couple of minutes before Linda arrived. The rest was obvious.

The cops listened intently, grinning as Tom told them about Linda's show of force with the lamp. When Tom finished, one of them picked up the battered and bloody remains of the brass stem and shook his head with admiration.

"Ramsey, you're gonna be a legend."

She tried to smile and secretly had to admit she was pleased with herself, despite the tremors of fear that still rippled through her limbs. After the police left, the two of them sat and held each other for a long time. Tom seemed subdued by it all, she thought; maybe worried, maybe guilty, but not relieved at all.

Her hugged her tightly and said, "You saved my life."

"Or the other way around."

"No, you're the champ, Linda. I was foolish to put you in danger."

"Well, it's over."

"Maybe."

"What now?"

"Well, we leave."

"To go where?"

"I don't know, but we can't stay here. Not while somebody wants to kill me."

CHAPTER 29

They packed a few clothes and left his condo, found a nondescript hotel room near St. Augustine and paid for it in cash. Darden needed a night to clear his head and think about what he should do next. Most of all, he had to figure out a way, a place, to hide Linda where she would be safe.

He thought she would be okay during work hours because she was always around uniforms and first responders. But at night, alone, or anywhere near him, she would be a target when they came back, and he had no doubt they would be back. Whoever wanted him dead had botched the job, hired a clumsy killer, and he had been lucky to survive. He could not count on luck again.

The next morning they woke up early, still tired. The adrenaline rush of the previous day had left them drained of energy. It was not a quality hotel and the maids made a lot of noise out in the hallways, slamming their cleaning carts against walls, knocking loudly on doors. Tom and Linda dressed in shorts and tee shirts and walked to the beach to watch the sunrise over the ocean.

He put his arm around her shoulders, sensing that she had settled down enough to discuss their next move. They walked in silence for a few minutes, enjoying the cool wet sand beneath their bare feet. When the sun broke over the horizon, the glare coming off the water was so strong they wouldn't be able to walk far without sunglasses. He decided to have the discussion right then.

"When do you have to go to work?" he asked.

"Three. Three to midnight, today."

"Do you need to talk more about it?"

She looked up at him, seemed pleased that he asked. "I'm all right. I just wish I'd hit him harder."

"Seriously."

"Well, of course, I'm worried. Ten minutes more, and he'd have killed you."

"We have to find a safe place for you to stay."

"What about you?"

"I'm going to have to stay on the move."

He expected her to protest immediately. When she didn't, it occurred to him she'd been thinking about the seriousness of the danger as well.

"I have a friend," she said. "Nobody would know to find me there. She has a house in a gated golf neighborhood, and a big loud dog. That's about as safe as I can imagine."

"That sounds good, but there's another thing. I can't stay with you until this is over. I'm not going to lead another killer to you."

"I thought you might say something like that."

"You know I'm right," he said.

"But I don't want to be apart. Besides, where can you hide?"

"I'm going to keep moving. Hotels mostly."

"Isn't there some way—"

Her cell phone rang and she removed it from her pocket and checked the caller ID. "I need to take this."

After a brief conversation, she stopped walking and put the phone away. "That was the Chief. He has some new information for us. I think we need to go to Daytona now."

They drove separate cars to Volusia County, with Darden following her down the interstate. They would have to split up later in the day, and he wondered how well he would manage without her at his side. They had become dependent on each other very quickly, and that was a feeling he hadn't known in a long time. It was a welcome feeling, but it would make things harder.

Outside the Fire Services Administration building, he noticed several plain black cars parked in the lot, unmarked government-issue vehicles. Likely, that meant the State Patrol or the FBI was here. Whatever the Inspector wanted, it must be important.

Instead of meeting in the Inspector's office, an assistant led them to a conference room. When they went in, several men in dark suits and very short haircuts looked them over. None of the men introduced themselves. The Inspector gestured for them to sit at the conference table alongside him.

"Miss Ramsey," he nodded to Linda. "Mr. Darden. I'm glad to see you both alive after your adventure in Jacksonville yesterday." The Inspector's serious face rarely wavered, and it didn't now as they nodded in return.

"News travels fast," Darden said.

"Thanks for your concern," Linda said, with more grace.

After the exchange, the anonymous men grouped around the table but said nothing, showed no inclination to sit.

The Inspector got straight to the point. "Our colleagues at the federal level managed to identify the black pickup on the video disc. After a complicated search through a lot of deliberately misleading paperwork, they suspect the man who drove the pickup to the hotel leased it in Texas."

They bumped shoulders and smiled at each other with satisfaction, pleased that their hunch had turned out to be true. The link to the migrants was real.

"So, he was the mastermind behind the bombing," Darden said.

"We don't know that for certain. We do know he followed the U-Haul rental into the hotel parking lot and we know he left the area prior to the detonation."

"How did you find that out?" Linda asked.

"Additional video evidence we recovered near the scene," the Inspector replied.

"What's his name?" Darden asked.

The Inspector paused a moment and looked up at the oldest of the anonymous suits following the conversation, his manner asking for a go-ahead. The older man had the face of a Raptor, sharp lean features with quick, dark eyes. Undoubtedly the senior

FBI man, Darden thought. The Raptor nodded in assent to the Chief.

"We think we know his real name, but we can't be sure. He has a service record in that name, but much of it has been expunged."

Darden leaned forward, astonished. "Expunged? Who can alter a military record?"

The tension in the room held as everyone remained silent. They weren't going to confirm it by answering him, but it wasn't necessary. An instant later, he realized who had altered the record. "An Intelligence Agency." He had practically answered his own question with the question itself. "He's an operative."

"An American spy?" Linda almost shouted. "An American killed all those people?"

"Not exactly a spy," the Chief replied.

Again, Darden suspected he wouldn't get a definite answer, but their silence told him what he needed to know. No one said a word while the suits let them absorb the implications of the unconfirmed information.

"Why did he do it?" Darden asked. "Why kill hundreds of innocent people?"

Finally, the Raptor spoke. "We don't know why. We're telling you this because we hope you can help us find the answer to that question."

Darden looked at each of them, suddenly doubting everything, the whole scenario, this meeting, the conclusion they let him harbor. The FBI asking for his help? It didn't make sense. Was this some kind of set up? He wondered what was going on here.

"I don't get it," he said. "How can we possibly tell you anything about this guy you don't know already?"

"Perhaps quite a bit. After all, you made the connection to the illegals in Jacksonville. You may know more than you think you know. That's why we are willing to share information with you."

Again, Darden felt a surge of suspicion. After what happened yesterday, he wasn't sure if he could trust any of these people. He looked at Linda, and his expression asked her for help to sort out this uncertainty.

She thought a moment before answering him. "I trust the Chief," she said firmly. "Remember, we went to him first, and he has been honest with us from the start."

The Chief looked at her, obviously pleased that she believed in him, even if these other silent, withheld men hardly seemed to be allies. "If you trust me, then I ask you to trust them too," he said. "The point is, you want to catch the people who did it, just like I do, and that means you should tell these men everything."

"I'm a member of the press," Darden said to the Raptor. "You know I don't have to talk to you."

"Of course. That's your right. Whatever you might think, the FBI does not trample the free press. It's your choice to talk to us or not. All we ask is that you not publish anything you learn from us until the investigation is over. Our goal is to get convictions in court, not to see a case ruined by news reports."

Darden sat and thought for a long minute.

"Okay, I'll act in good faith, but you go first to show me you mean it."

The Raptor slid a manila file folder across the table toward them. "The man has several aliases. We don't know who he works for exactly, but he has a nasty resume."

Darden opened the file and saw an official identification photo of a young man with a high-and-tight military haircut. What hair remained on top of his head was bright red, almost orange in color. Despite his youth, the face showed a painful maturity. He had faint scarring about the mouth and his eyes were cruel beyond the depths of hell, dead far beyond his years.

"That photo is him as a young Marine."

Darden slid it aside and the next photo was far less clear. Taken from a distance, it appeared to be a surveillance photograph trained on the entrance to an unmarked building. The man in it was years older than in the first shot, but it was the same man. He had a heavy body, with real weight in his shoulders and chest, built like a wrestler.

"This photo was taken two years ago in the Middle East. The third—"

Darden moved the surveillance photo aside to reveal a close up beneath.

"—is a blow-up of the man's face as he entered a detention center."

When Darden saw the photo, he developed an unpleasant taste in his mouth, the taste of bile coming fast up his throat. He turned and looked at Linda, her face gone pale, her mouth open. Darden put his fingertips to his temples and tried to control the light-headed nausea that threatened to overwhelm him.

Though the quality of the blow-up was poor, there was no doubt in his mind about the identity of the man in the photograph. The contorted features, the vacant eyes, the defiant hostility was there as it had been on the video.

"We have seen this man before."

"Where?"

"Not in person," Linda said.

Darden spoke carefully. "On a digital video disc. It shows him being tortured to death by men speaking Arabic."

The news clearly surprised the FBI people, came like a thunderclap in a library to them. You could almost read their minds by watching their faces. Like him, they wanted to know what the hell this strange revelation meant, each with his own unspoken questions that Darden could easily guess. What video disc? Tortured to death by whom?

"What was his name?" Darden asked.

After the surprise settled, the Raptor answered. "We think his real name is—was—Hoyt Bellows."

The men in suits settled around the table then and several recorders came out of their suit pockets. They turned the machines on while one agent distributed legal pads to each man at the table. The interview began in earnest.

At least a hundred questions and answers later, the FBI people seemed satisfied for the moment that they'd extracted the primary information they wanted. When it was all over, though,

Darden admitted to himself they'd learned much more from him than he had from them. Yes, he had a few extra ideas to pursue, a strong belief that somehow this was bigger than he'd imagined, but mostly he was left with the certainty that he needed more sources, more facts to move ahead. He was a long way from fully understanding this story.

Later, outside, he swapped his thoughts with Linda and they agreed to stay at it no matter how difficult the investigation became. They were already committed and had taken too many risks to give up now. This story had changed their lives and they both knew there was no turning back.

Darden felt weary and already alone, definitely pained that they had to split from each other, at least for a while. Before they got in their cars and drove in separate directions, Linda summed up all the dangling questions perfectly.

"An American kills hundreds of students at the beach," she said. "Then he gets himself killed by a bunch of bloody Arabs. What is the connection?"

His last words to her turned out to be prophetic. "I don't know, but somehow they are connected and I'm going to find out why."

CHAPTER 30

The three men walked across a huge, tilted slab of aging concrete, one of many that covered the site of a former missile installation in South Dakota. They'd left the official helicopter on an old tarmac a few hundred yards back. Secret Service agents walked with them, but out on the flanks at a very discreet distance.

The place had an empty and mournful quality about it, like a deserted home open to the weather. Weeds grew up in the seams between the concrete slabs, seams that had widened and shifted from weather and time. Cracked by decades of freezing snow and browned by blowing dirt and prairie dust, the pitted concrete spoke volumes about the protracted, expensive battle against Communism.

"We really screwed up when we shut these down," The Great Man said, staring off into the distance at the low wind-blown hills, a look of misty sentimentality on his face. "The whole world feared us then."

Baines felt a bit of the same nostalgia himself, standing there in the presence of that era among the remains of talent and energy and dollars that went into the long Cold War. But we won, he thought, and now there was a new war.

He spoke his thoughts aloud. "There is always another enemy for us to fight."

"True, Doctor. There always will be."

Soon, the site would be alive again with workers. Within weeks they would install barbed wire fences, a chain-link compound with barracks, watch towers, the latest in security technology. Yet now that the kick-off was near, he felt apprehension rather than elation, which surprised him. This should be the apex of his success instead of a peak of anxiety. What was he forgetting? Other than the problem with the reporter, everything was on schedule, but still he could not dismiss the feeling that kept twisting tighter in his gastro-intestinal tract. Had he covered their trail sufficiently? Was anyone on to them?

Again, The Great Man spoke. "This will do, Doctor. The site is satisfactory for our first installation." He held a flattened hand above his eyes like the bill of a cap, continued to survey the vast landscape surrounding the facility, seemed to consider the emptiness that would provide its primary security. In this wasteland, no casual onlookers or curious eyes could disrupt its secrecy. "Are you up to speed on the soft side of the operation?"

As usual, Marshall simply listened, rarely adding his own comments.

Baines pondered the question. The soft side? He did not understand the government argot; he presumed the Great Man meant recruitment of personnel. At that very moment, his subcontractors were hard at work locating the talent and manpower they would need.

"We have assembled a formidable team already. Former military guards, interrogators, psychologists, signals specialists, and mostly data analysts."

"So, they're ready to go."

Baines nodded. "Yes."

Already the data was piling up in the huge mainframes of an information technology company in northern California. He had engaged them to compile and sort key profiles, to sift individual files that fit target groups. Soon, they would cast a huge surveillance net across America to record and capture any potential enemies.

"When will I see the first suspect lists?"

"June one, as promised."

"Step up the timetable," the Great Man growled. "I need to know who our opponents are out there."

Baines clenched his eyes shut. Devil, didn't the man

understand how complicated the data processing would be? Just the scanning process involved millions of potential targets, billions of phone calls, retail transactions, credit files and e-mails. The search programming alone was a massive project. How could he possibly make it happen sooner? Simply staying on the original schedule was a Herculean task.

"Of course, sir. The predictive ability of our systems is revolutionary. It researches patterns of behavior; job categories, computer search histories, purchases, acquaintances, political affiliations. Hundreds of factors go into the profiling. At the end of all that, we'll have a very high probability of predicting potential threats and—"

"The details are up to you, Doctor," The Great Man interrupted. "I just want names."

The wind moaned across the prairie, sighing past the bare branches of scrub. With no trace yet of spring here in the northern plains, dead stalks of weeds rattled against each other, playing an empty song.

Baines was cold and flipped up his coat collar, wished the meeting had been back in Virginia, then again, he had not arranged the meeting. The Great Man had called them, insisted on this location, and it wasn't just a site survey to measure their progress. Baines knew by now the man's random conversational style, the aims hidden beneath the banter. In between his comments on the site, he continued to grill them about the failed assassination attempt in Florida, and he was particularly angry that it had made the papers and internet, becoming a story of its own that drew even more attention to the reporter. One minute the conversation was on logistics or weapons, the next it was back to that damned botched murder.

"With so much money and talent available, you could have done the reporter cleanly."

"Yes, sir."

"There was a piece about it in the goddamn *New York Times* this morning."

"Unfortunate, yes."

"The last thing we need is the mainstream press paying attention to this guy."

"Right."

The Great Man had a way of looking at you sidelong while his head was tilted forward. It meant the next line was a serious jab, perhaps worse. "I trusted you guys to handle this without complications."

Neither of them answered as they continued to walk, stepping over the cracks and weeds that grew up through the old concrete, the vegetation running out of control and taking over what had once been solid and seemed indestructible.

Dr. Baines felt the old tic start its dance within his facial muscles. He squirmed as The Great Man's eyes locked onto him, glacial blue behind the rectangular lenses of his glasses. There was nothing Baines could add in his own defense, so he did not reply.

Even Marshall seemed to have difficulty maintaining his dispassionate manner. He looked away and pursed his lips, which was a burst of animation for him. In the overhanging silence, Baines allowed his thoughts to wander for an instant. If only I had that smooth granite face of Marshall's, I could accomplish anything in this world. Marshall had the sort of patrician look that he imagined royalty had possessed since the fall of the Roman Empire. Tall, elegant, proud—all were words he would use to describe Marshall.

The Great Man, by contrast, had a shambling heaviness about him. A bear-like body and likeness that urged you to come closer and look, but there was danger behind that slow pose. Get in close enough and those heavy paws could rip you in two with one swat. Some called him the War Hawk, which Baines hated and thought an inaccurate metaphor. The man was a great patriot, to be sure, but he was also a dangerous man who must remain an ally at all costs.

"Tell me what you are doing to rectify this breach of security."

Marshall finally spoke, trying to smooth the waters. "The police report shows a female was involved, his girlfriend apparently. We are investigating to find out who she is and what she has to do with the reporter's work, if anything." He nodded to Baines to take it from there.

"It, ah, turns out, the reporter is a nobody. He has no connections, no clout in the business. How he got hold of those photos is still a mystery, but we're working on it. We have stories coming out this week to discredit the reporter and his claims, and as Peyton said, we have a surveillance team searching for the girl now."

The Great Man nodded. "But the reporter, himself? Is he covered?"

Baines stomped his feet to shake tension from his body, hoped his voice didn't betray the nerves he felt. "Temporarily off the radar, but that won't last long. We are screening his cell calls and his credit cards."

"Meaning, you lost him."

"Uh, temporarily."

The Great Man stopped walking and turned toward them. "Find out what the reporter knows. If this is wider than him, we need information. Get it straight from him, and this time, make sure he disappears without a trace. No body, no clues."

The wind rose and whipped grit against Baines' face. He understood. No more mistakes allowed.

CHAPTER 31

Darden sensed someone there, waiting in the dark. His footsteps slowed, making only faint echoes off the flat surfaces of the hotel parking deck. Stark and angular, the deck was an empty place of shadows and sleeping machines. Still fifty yards from his car, he stopped walking and looked for the most likely hiding place nearby. At the same moment, his brain accelerated with irrepressible thoughts of another assassination attempt. Was it paranoia or was another killer really hiding there in the darkness, waiting for him?

No, it was not paranoia, he decided. He leaned forward, straining to see if someone was there even though he hadn't seen or heard anything definite. Some sort of mechanism in his primitive brain had been activated by the earlier attempt on his life, and since then he'd felt his body ramping up to a higher metabolism, complete with excess energy and heightened senses. He'd quickly learned to trust this new hyper-acuity, believing it would be more effective than rational thought at keeping him alive.

Even with no sensory evidence to support his suspicion, somehow he knew someone was there, hiding just a few steps away. The parking deck was poorly lit and deep in its interior a concrete pier and an up-ramp met, and there a blot of darkness held. Whoever it was, Darden thought, he or she was hiding in that shadow, waiting for him.

His hand went into his pocket, grasped the small pistol he now carried. It had been his father's gun, an old one from the fifties that he remembered firing in the woods as a teenager.

Darden still thought it a bit dramatic to carry the thing, but after that wire cut into his neck he would not underestimate the danger he sensed or live in denial of it. Serious threats faced him now and he had to admit he felt a bit of relief in the pistol's heavy presence.

He managed as much authority as he could and put it into his voice. "Who's there?"

The shadows moved, a lighter outline shifting within the darker surroundings. It wasn't his imagination.

"Damn you, come out of there!"

A figure stepped into the bare light, his hands raised slightly, palms open in a calming gesture. He was medium sized, about forty, with thick black hair combed back in a sweep to one side. His clothes were casual but expensive looking, with a braided leather belt and matching shoes, a tropical silk shirt.

Darden's fingers tightened on the grip of the pistol, ready to pull it out in a blink. They stared at each other a moment, as if waiting for the other to speak first, but Darden felt he had the initiative and he didn't intend to lose it.

"Who are you? Tell me now or my gun's coming out."

The man took half step back, made the calming gesture again. "Take it easy, Darden. I just want to talk."

"First, who are you?"

"My name is Arvin Webber. I am with the State Department."

"Why are you hiding there, spying on me?"

"I just had to make sure it was you before I showed myself. There is a need for secrecy here."

"How can I be sure you're with State?"

The man came a step closer. He showed his empty palms and relaxed his arms. He didn't appear threatening, but Darden's internal alarms still sounded and he wasn't taking a chance by letting his guard down.

"Let me explain, please."

Darden gave him a halting nod of the head.

"May I lower my hands?"

Again, Darden nodded assent.

"I'm here to help you. I am not armed." Webber patted his

pants pockets to show him. "If you would take your hand off the pistol, please."

"Help me how?"

"I have information for you. A lot of it."

Darden took his hand out of his pocket. "First, prove to me who you are."

Webber smiled. "Okay. Day before yesterday I met an official from the American Embassy in Iraq. He told me he got you out of jail, told me about your photographs, your brief imprisonment. Everything. He said to give you a message."

"What message?

"That he's changing his advice to you. He said to remember it all and report everything you learned over there."

Darden remembered Yates' last words to him. "What was his name?"

"Harrison Yates. Well-dressed. No sense of humor. A career diplomat."

Darden was convinced. He extended his hand. Webber took it and they shook. "Good to meet you, Arvin."

Arvin started walking. "Let's sit in your car while we talk. Less exposed there."

They went to it and got in the Honda.

"Sorry, it's a bit dirty," Darden said.

"You should ditch this car," Webber said. "That's how I tracked you down. They will too, if you keep driving it."

"Who?" Darden cracked the windows for air, let his seat back. "I'm not used to this James Bond stuff."

"That's okay, but you'd better learn quick. Your internet stories have made some people very unhappy."

"Who? I want to know who's after me."

"I'm not entirely sure who it is yet, but I have learned some of what they're doing." Webber pulled a pack of Marlboros from his shirt pocket. "Do you mind?"

"No, I'm reformed, myself."

Webber offered him one and Darden found himself accepting the cigarette. They lit up with the lighter from the console. Darden pulled smoke into his lungs and coughed, but oh, the sweet relief, the heady wash of nicotine through his bloodstream. It was as if he'd never quit. Chemical pathways re-opened in his brain and he felt anxiety drifting away with the exhaled smoke.

"Guess I can always quit again, later."

Webber smiled, understood. "That's what I do every year."

"So, what's the information you've come all the way to Florida to deliver?"

Webber's voice changed, the light tone gone. "That you've walked into a full blown hornet's nest—a political conspiracy."

"Oh, man." The thought of that, or maybe it was the tobacco, made Darden's head buzz. Fear squeezed his insides and he took another pull on the Marlboro, wondered why he'd ever given up such a pleasurable habit. His hand shook as he lowered the cigarette.

Webber continued, "And you've managed to write your way into being a serious threat to them. You might just be their number one target. Since you're already in jeopardy, I want to know if you are willing to go even further."

"In what way?"

"I have proof—not just conjecture—that the wholesale torture you discovered in Iraq was authorized at the highest levels of the Administration."

"I suspected that."

Webber seemed to be holding back. Something bigger was there.

"What else?" Darden asked sharply. "What?"

Webber's face trembled with loathing or anger; Darden couldn't be sure which one. "They are bringing it home to America."

Darden could not quite believe what he'd just heard. "What? Torture?" His heart rate climbed and he felt his own face grow hot with anger.

"Yes, and more." Webber seemed hesitant, perhaps too fearful to speak aloud.

"Tell me, damn it! What else?"

"They are setting up concentration camps. Soon we'll have traffic checkpoints. Electronic surveillance. Wholesale arrests and detention. All in the name of national security."

"A police state."

Darden's head felt full of writhing things, as if it would explode. This was too much to absorb. "You're telling me, someone is going to turn America into a police state, run by some sort of secret army, something like that?"

Webber turned and looked directly at him. His face was stone, as if to assert the point that this was no joke, no exaggeration. This was real.

Darden didn't want to accept it, couldn't believe it was really happening. "Nobody could get away with that. Not even the President."

"Remember how far Nixon went?"

"But—"

"They are getting away with it," Webber said. "It's already underway."

"But people will revolt in the streets. What about the state governments? The news organizations? Congress? Surely, they'll come forward to stop it!"

"Not if they don't know about it."

"Nobody could cover up something like this. It's bound to come out."

"By then it will be too late," Webber said. "Two hundred years of legal precedent and the Bill of Rights will already be dust."

Darden became so agitated he had to move. He climbed out of the car and slammed the door in rage, paced to the front then to the rear, then repeated it. Finally, he beat on the hood with his fists until it hurt.

Webber got out of the car slowly, gave him time to let the pressure out. They stood and faced each other across the roof of the car.

Webber said quietly. "I'll feed you the evidence, if you'll keep writing the truth."

Darden calmed himself enough to speak. "This can't be happening. Not here in America."

"Why not?" Webber said. "It happened in Germany. Argentina.

Happened in Russia. Why not, here?"

"Okay, you say you have proof, but why offer it to me? You could give it to *CNN*, *The New York Times* or *The Post*. Why me?"

"Because you've already shown more courage than most anyone else in reporting the torture story. Besides, huge corporations own the major news services now. I trust you more than them. How deep does the conspiracy go? Why haven't they uncovered it yet? Perhaps corporate interests are suppressing the story."

"Even with proof, who will listen to me?" Darden said, plaintive and unsure, his old weaker self speaking inside.

"People who care will listen to you. They already are."

"I'm just a small timer."

"Not anymore."

"Somebody else will stop them."

"Who?"

"Somebody."

"What if Woodward and Bernstein had said that?"

Suddenly Darden felt ashamed. He felt like a crying child, a weakling who refused to accept the mantle of responsibility and adulthood.

Webber pointed a finger at him, like a judge or perhaps just a fellow human telling him there was no escape from duty. For a moment, the look of Webber's eyes reminded Darden of his father. Eyes deep brown and all seeing, eyes of clarity and purpose as he'd told Darden about standing guard. Whether we ask for it or not, Darden recalled, sometimes it's our turn to stand guard.

"So what's it going to be?" Webber asked. "Do you want my help? If not you, who is going to stop this?"

Darden exhaled a deep breath of resignation, not sure what to say, but saying it anyway as if the answer had always been there, waiting. All his life, he had held back, convincing himself that he wasn't man enough, that he wasn't the one to step forward, but now, he knew that he was the one. For whatever reason, he was enough now, and he was the one.

"I will," he answered. "I'll stop them."

CHAPTER 32

Janice Hill Monroe loved talk radio. As a real estate agent she drove a lot of Florida miles, and when she was in her car alone she always listened to the political guys who proved how stupid most people were, especially the ones who didn't agree with her. Privately, she thought the radio hosts were blessed messengers from God, delivering The Truth to America in their warnings about Democrats, lawyers and foreigners, all those traitors who were out to destroy the nation.

Over time, though, she had learned to turn the radio off when clients were in the car with her. Hard to believe, but some of them didn't agree with her or the talk radio hosts or that one good news network on television. She thought that proved her clients' stupidity, but business came first. She learned to hold her tongue and not talk about politics or religion on the job. In fact, some people were plainly offended by The Truth when she pointed it out, but just because they didn't believe The Truth was no reason for her to lose business.

Today, as she drove to New Smyrna Beach to preview a condo, every talk station was on fire. Something on the internet had really riled up the hosts and callers. One of them—the bald guy—was threatening to emigrate to Australia he was so mad. He said America was no longer American enough for him.

She held her Cadillac on seventy as she kept south on I-95, careful not to drive past her exit. The flat, straight interstate highway was home to her, and she'd spent many hours driving up and down the main corridor to various properties in north Florida, most of them near the beach.

She had missed the first part of the story, wasn't sure what caused them to get so hopping mad, but she knew it had something to do with that reporter who lived up in Jacksonville, the one who wrote those awful stories about torture.

She touched the seek button on her steering wheel and let the tuner find a local NPR station. Maybe she could find out what happened there. She didn't like the NPR stations, but sometimes that was the quickest way to find out why people were mad. You could always count on them to tell it different from the talk shows, to take the wrong side of everything, but at least they didn't drag it out.

Distracted by the radio, she looked up and saw the green sign flash by as she missed her exit. She thought about pulling over and backing up on the emergency lane. Her husband told her never to do that, but she had done it a few times anyway. She hated to go to the next exit and come back, but she couldn't get over to the far right soon enough, so she'd have to keep going ahead for now.

The tuner found an NPR station, and sure enough, they were talking about the same thing, but it was different on there as always. The announcers were so calm and detached they sounded as if they didn't care one way or the other about it. They acted as if they wanted to tell both sides and not tell you what to think, but she doubted it. They always interviewed people who sounded so smart, like they knew everything. Nobody got mad and nobody was accused of treason on those stations. That kind of news just wasn't to her liking, but sometimes it had to do if you needed to know what actually happened.

After listening for a few minutes, she understood what the controversy was about. That reporter had done another one of those torture stories, but this time he said some of it was going on right here in America. No wonder everybody was so mad. He had no business saying that. If the government pressured a few criminals, there must be a good reason for it.

The calm announcer interviewed a man who was some sort of lawyer from a bleeding heart organization—maybe the ACU something or other—and she knew they were always on the wrong side. Always trying to get criminals off, stupid stuff like that. The lawyer said if the story was true about the government detaining people without warrants and forcing confessions from them by torture, then the constitution was as good as dead.

Imagine that, saying America was wrong. She took the next exit and waited at the stop light at the end of the off ramp. She lowered her visor and flipped up the mirror on its backside to check her makeup. Need more lipstick when I stop, she decided, and she'd have to remember to change her hairdresser again; too much blue in the rinse. She poofed it higher in front with her fingers, the way she liked it.

She drove under the bridge and got back on ninety-five, this time going north. Now that she knew what the bald guy was mad about this time, she could listen to him again. She switched the station back and smiled as he called for the reporter's head, said he ought to be hanged for accusing the Administration of torturing real Americans. That reporter had some nerve.

By the time she got off at the correct exit and headed for the beach, she was already late and hoped it wouldn't cost her a sale. Thinking about the commission she would lose, her foot kept pushing harder on the accelerator until she had to slow down for somebody towing a trailer up ahead. The delay made her angry, and as soon as there was a gap in the oncoming traffic, she swung out and passed the trailer. She was doing almost eighty by the time she returned to her own lane.

A quarter mile ahead she heard a siren behind her, looked up and saw blue lights rippling in her rear view mirror. That made her really disgusted, but she had no choice other than to pull off the road. The policeman took his sweet time about it, sitting back there and rapping on the keys of a computer, running a license plate check, she guessed. She watched him in the rear view mirror as he got on his radio and took more time. This yokel was costing her money, no two ways about it.

When he finally came up to her window, she already had her license and registration out, just wanted to get it over with and be on her way. But something in the policeman's face told her this wasn't going to be fast. She buzzed down her window and tried to hand him the paperwork, but he wouldn't even look at it.

"Get out of the car, ma'am." He didn't say it politely either, his right hand resting on the holster at his hip.

"Why? Here is my identification. Write the ticket and we'll be done."

"Get out of the car." He moved the retention strap off the hammer of the pistol with his thumb.

Well, you horse's ass, she thought, as she opened the door and got out. Cars whizzed by on the county road, just a few feet away, their slipstream tugging at her skirt and hair. She felt grit flying up off the roadway, peppering her face. This was really going too far. Why didn't the policeman just give her a ticket and let her go?

"Step behind the car."

"I have an appointment, young man. You are making me—"

He took her by the arm and forced her to the rear, made her stand facing the trunk of her Coupe de Ville.

"Take your hands off me!"

"Keep quiet, lady."

She twisted her head around to watch as the deputy held her wrists with one hand and retrieved his cuffs with the other. She stomped a bit as he snapped them on her. Then he marched her to the cruiser and opened the rear door on the right side, forced her head down and pushed her into the back seat.

"What is this about!" she demanded. In response, he slammed the door shut in her face.

The deputy went around to the driver's side and climbed into the front seat, reported the arrest into his shoulder-mounted radio. Static crackled loudly in the interior of the car. Her skirt was up and she couldn't even reach to pull it down.

"Young man!"

He ignored her as they sat a few minutes while he wrote some sort of report, waiting until a tow truck appeared and hooked up her car.

She started to protest again, but he turned around and glared at her so fiercely she fell quiet. After he exchanged paperwork with the tow truck driver, her car disappeared down the road and suddenly she felt naked, bereft of her independence and her livelihood. Sitting on the sticky vinyl seat of the cruiser with her skirt up, her hands manacled behind her, Janice confronted a new and threatening reality. For the first time in her life, she felt common.

"Sir." This time she managed to moderate her tone. "Would you tell me why I am being treated like a criminal, just because I was driving a bit fast?"

He turned and gave her a hard face. "Ma'am, this is not a traffic arrest, though you will be charged with speeding."

"Then, what?"

"Our computers red-flagged your vehicle registration. Under special provisions of Sedition and Internal Security of the newly revised Patriot Act, you are suspected of domestic criminal activity."

"What exactly does that mean?"

"In short, the government considers you to be a potential terrorist. We're required by law to detain you immediately and hold you without charge."

Janice's mouth opened in alarm, but remarkably she found herself groping for words. What nutty computer would confuse her with a terrorist?

"Young man!"

He ignored her.

"Would you look at me?"

He turned slightly, gave her a sideways glance.

"Do I look like a terrorist to you?"

He didn't answer.

"For God's sake, I'm a real estate agent. I drive a Cadillac. My husband is in insurance. We've lived in Florida for thirty years. Isn't it obvious, I'm not a terrorist?"

He started the cruiser, hit the lights and siren to slow the traffic, made a U-turn back toward the interstate.

"Lady, I don't give a damn who you are. The computer says you're a suspect, so you're going to jail."

CHAPTER 33

"I don't want you to go," Linda said.

With her head resting on his chest, listening to the strong ebb and flow of his heart, she held him close and felt the dread of separation in her stomach. At moments like this, she didn't care about his efforts to rise to greatness. She only wanted him by her side.

"I have to go," Darden answered. "Did you see the news shows last night? The right wing is making me out to be a kook, said I made it all up. I don't even recognize myself or my stories in some of those reports."

"Those were blogs, just somebody's opinion."

"Well, unfortunately, they carry weight in the media. I need more proof to defend myself, and I might find it up there."

The bed shook as she rolled over onto her back and stared at the ceiling. No matter what she said, he was going to put himself in danger again; she knew it. If her willing hands and mouth on his body would not stop him from going, nothing else would.

She was already tired of the motel rooms, the hiding out, the fear she felt for him every minute of every day. She wanted to ask him to give it up, but she held herself in check, knowing it wouldn't work, knowing it would only foster resentment. As much as she wanted to help him, she hated the daily fear and separation that came along with his determination to pursue the story further.

For the first time in his life, he'd told her, he had a sense of himself and why he existed. The personal recognition and public fury generated by his stories gave him a purpose he'd never had before. The national debate over torture and other excesses by the Administration had never been stronger, and the person most responsible for bringing it to the forefront was none other than the Tom Darden lying next to her. She knew that the sense of purpose was changing him, and all for the better. She could see him growing weekly. His resolve, his maturity, his compassion were stronger than ever. Now, he mattered. She couldn't ask him to reverse course when his life had taken such a positive turn.

"Then, how about if I go with you?"

"You know that's out of the question. We can't even be seen with each other. At least here we can get away with it, in a hotel like this, arriving separately and leaving at different times."

"Okay," she said. "I understand why you have to go and why I can't go along, but I don't want you to get killed either. We need to set up a system of some kind to alert me if something is going wrong."

He put his cigarette aside, on the bedside table. She wished he hadn't started smoking again, but that too was something she couldn't alter. There was a new boldness, or perhaps recklessness, about him that she found appealing and frightening at the same time.

A tilted plane of sunlight appeared in the gap at the top of the motel curtains. It fell across his legs, then hers. The light had a buttery, early morning cast to it. He rolled over and kissed her again on the mouth. Despite the taste of burned tobacco on his tongue, she'd never get tired of that kiss. Her future was inextricably bound up in this man and the way he made her feel so full inside.

He pulled back and looked her over head-to-toe. She could see the pleasure in his eyes and she wondered how she'd ever considered herself alive before she met him.

"An alarm system is a good idea," he said. "How about if I call you every three hours, on the hour? No call, you know something is wrong."

"I mean it," she said. "Make it every two hours, on the dot, or I call the Chief Fire Inspector to get the FBI."

"Okay. Every two hours, then."

"Where are you going?"

"It's just a place I have to check out, but it's pretty remote. I don't know exactly where yet, someplace in south Georgia."

He got out of bed and started putting on his clothes. He'd started doing everything faster, as if he was running out of time to get his work done.

"Maybe you want to shave first."

He grinned.

"Maybe a shower too."

"You're starting to sound like a wife."

Hearing him say that, even in joking, made her feel buzzy inside. A wife, huh? Was she becoming just another of those women like the ones she'd always scoffed at, more interested in getting a husband than being themselves? No, she decided, this was different. It wasn't a relationship for the sake of security or status. This was love taking its natural course. She could feel it throughout her mind and body; her very chemistry was changing.

She followed him into the bathroom, washed at the sink while he took a quick shower. "So what do you expect to find up there?"

"I don't know." His voice rang off the tile walls. "My contact said they'd found some sort of paper trail to this place. It might be important. Might not."

"So, the lead is from Deep Throat."

He laughed. "Yes, I suppose so, if that's what you want to call him. But if we find anything there, it might give me some clues how to fight those bastards."

She rinsed her face with cold water. It felt great on her skin, clearing the sleep from her eyes.

She talked as she washed. "It's so obvious something big and strange is happening out there, I don't see how those bloggers can claim otherwise. We're seeing it on the job. More casual arrests every day. The holding cells at the jail are full. Traffic checkpoints for no real reason. It's creepy."

He turned off the water and toweled himself quickly. "It

goes much further than that. Deep Throat says a secret computer system is probing voter registration databases. Someone's mining search engine histories and e-mail systems too."

"Does he know who's doing it?"

"No, that's what makes it so strange. The people who should know won't say a word."

"That's the way cops turn cold when I ask about the increase in arrests. They won't talk about it."

"That's because they've been warned from the top. The local people are just following orders. They're being told this is a top secret national security effort."

"Did Deep Throat tell you that too?"

He laughed and came to the bathroom counter and sink, looked at her nude body in the mirror then stepped behind her and pressed his drying front against the full length of her backside. "You're my deep throat."

She moaned. "Oh, you're going to make me hot again."

"I hope so," he replied in a low voice. "But not now."

He went out to the bedroom and sat down on the bed to get into his shorts. She followed and stood before him in the nude, spreading her feet apart, taunting him to delay his trip. He pulled her onto the bed beside him, but in a sitting position so he wouldn't be tempted by her naked body.

"I need to tell you something," he said. "Not that I think anything is going to happen, but I've taken a precaution."

He went to the dresser where he'd thrown his wallet and keys the night before. He picked up a computer flash drive, about the size of a small pocket knife. He held it up for her to see, then came back and pressed it into her open hand.

She looked up at him. "What's this about?"

"A back-up. Everything I've researched and written is stored on this drive. The unpublished stories. Document scans from the internet. Photos and notes. All my interviews, including names and contact information. Even Deep Throat. It's all here."

She suspected her thoughts were all too obvious. "But why—"

He looked into her eyes, all the confidence in the world

showing on him. He was no longer the uncertain reporter she'd first met, stalled at a gas station and needing her help. She was powerless to say no to him.

"I'm going to write a book," he said with pride. "Most of it is right here, already done." He closed her fingers around the drive. "The book is going to expose everything I've found. It's the most important thing I've ever done in my life. I want you to hide this in a safe place."

"But—"

"Just in case I lose my laptop."

She looked down at the red plastic drive and thought of all the risks he'd taken to collect the information on it. Her guess was he really wanted her to have it in case something happened to him, not his laptop.

He kissed her on the forehead and stood up. "I've got to go." He grabbed his things and went to the door, opened it and took a quick peek outside. "All clear."

"Call me," she said. Then more forcefully, "Every two hours, starting at ten o'clock."

He opened the door, turned back and grinned at her. "I love you, Linda."

The door closed behind him and she shuddered, put her face in her hands, elbows on her knees. The tears started and then she bent double at the waist, seized with a spell of panic and crying so violent she thought she would be ill. Seconds later, she was, retching the contents of her stomach onto the cheap carpet at her feet.

CHAPTER 34

By ten in the morning Darden drove across the state line, called Linda and told her where he was. By two, he was deep in the fields and pine plantations of south Georgia where tree farms dominated the flat countryside, with row upon row of loblolly pines fanning out in all directions from the roadway; the trees uniformly spaced, nearly identical in height and shape, a crop as much as soybeans or corn.

His mind was on the task ahead, so he rarely noticed the farmhouses ticking past on the two-lane highway. Soon he'd need to call Linda again, and most importantly, he had to check in with Arvin and make sure he was ready to go. His destination was a tobacco warehouse in Candler County that Webber thought might be a site used by the Extremist Brotherhood, the name they'd begun to use for the hidden government growing inside the Administration.

Normally he would've been absorbing every detail of back road sights since he hadn't driven these old highways in years. Some things caught his eye nonetheless. Outside Folkston, he saw an ancient moss-covered oak, spreading its huge branches in a wide reach with pale green Spanish moss draping to the ground. He thanked whoever had cared enough to spare the gnarled giant through the decades. To him, such oaks were symbols of a slower and less commercial past, and he was grateful for those few that hadn't been cut up and shipped to a sawmill.

A half hour later he came to a pecan grove on the right and spotted an old store up ahead, set back under the trees. Getting closer, it looked more like an outdoor produce stand that would sell vegetables in the summer and bags of pecans in the fall. A sign out front advertised fresh smoked barbeque. He pulled off the road and saw a pit out back, smelled hickory smoke and pork in the air.

He got out and walked back to the pit.

A very old black man ran the barbeque stand, and he raised the tin cover off the pit to show Darden the meat slow-smoking inside. He was thin and grey-headed, proud of his work. He wore suspenders and kept the collar of his shirt buttoned. The man was a holdover from the past, maybe a preacher on Sunday. Darden wondered if he paid any attention to the news.

"You heard anything about this torture business in Iraq?" he asked the man.

Busy chopping pork and adding his homemade sauce, the old man was slow to answer, perhaps deciding if he should answer at all. "I have."

"What do you think about it?"

"Make me sick inside. Soun' like what they do to folks long time ago."

"Yeah, I suppose it does."

"Tell you one mo' thing," the man added. "Ike or Truman wouldn'a stood fo' it."

Darden bought tea, a pork sandwich and cup of Brunswick stew, walked back and ate it quickly while leaning against the hood of the car. He hadn't tasted slow smoked barbeque in a long time. It was very good and spicy, a sharp contrast to the sweet tea he drank with it.

Finished, he raised the trunk to check his stuff in the back. The car wasn't his; following Webber's advice he'd parked his Honda, began driving his father's car, an aging LeSabre. Why did old guys like Buicks so much? The handling was terrible and it drank gas, but at least it was in someone else's name. Not an ideal replacement, but less traceable than a rental.

He double checked the pistol; it was fully loaded, safety on. He put it back in the binocular case where he kept it stashed. His camera batteries were okay. Laptop charged, as well. Finally, he got out a fresh throw-away phone. He'd bought five new ones before he left home. Webber passed all information to him by phone now, never risking an e-mail or letter. They used either pay phones or disposable cells, never their own numbers.

He had used one of them to check in twice with Linda, precisely on the hour as they'd agreed. She didn't speak of her mood or state of mind, which was okay with him, because he guessed she was as apprehensive as he was about his destination ahead.

Not that today's lead was any more dangerous than others he'd followed up lately, but clouds of trouble seemed to be gathering. Every day he received more hate mail and threats; more of the usual legion of right wing blowhards challenged his stories and his character, calling him a traitor and denouncing his reports as inventions.

In response, he stuck to the back highways, attempting to stay under the radar of whoever might be after him. He zigzagged from town to town, changing highways often, skirting the cities and the interstate. It took much longer, of course, but he thought it far safer. He'd be more difficult to spot traveling on low traffic state highways like 301 and 119 through the likes of Waynesville and Jesup as he worked his way farther north.

But it was slow going, and he never felt completely unwatched. Coming out of the north side of Jesup, a white van got behind him and rode his bumper for more than ten miles. Darden couldn't see who was driving behind the dark tinted windshield, but the van seemed suspicious because it wouldn't pass him, even though there were plenty of straight empty stretches on the highway. He figured the van had to be tailing him, wondered how he could shake the guy off.

Every mile that the van remained in his rear view mirror, he became more convinced it meant trouble. He wished he had the pistol up front where he could reach it quickly. Why wouldn't the guy drop back or just pass him? Instead the van hung on his bumper as if Darden were towing him.

Here and there an abandoned gas station broke the monotony

of the landscape and he wished he could relax and muse about the rusting signs that advertised Pure or Amoco, but all he could think about was the van on his tail.

After a few more miles, he felt heat rising up his neck and into his scalp. Finally his agitation reached the point where he had to do something.

Up ahead he saw another old store, a wooden building close beside the road, its gasoline sign just another forgotten brand from bygone days. Without even planning it, he hit his brakes and yanked the car off the road onto the dirt lot beside the building.

As he slid to a stop, the van shot past him, its horn changing pitch as it moved ahead. He glanced over and saw the driver giving him the finger through the open passenger window, a cell phone jutting from the man's palm.

Darden exhaled, hands shaking, and berated himself mentally. It was nothing but a jackass on his cell phone, yet it took him almost an hour after the incident to completely calm down.

Just north of Ludowici, he watched closely for another abandoned gas station, one that he was expecting. Webber had said the sign out front was a Sinclair, the brand that once had a dinosaur for its logo. Darden kept his eyes sharp and spotted it not long after passing through the town. He pulled off onto the gravel lot surrounding a boarded up building, got out of the car and waited.

Webber appeared from behind the building within a couple of minutes. Gone were the expensive clothes and city manner. Today he was dressed in jeans and work boots, carrying a cheap gym bag. He'd even adjusted his walk for today's role, his gait a bit slower and longer, his shoulders relaxed in a slump.

In a phone conversation two days earlier, Webber had told him the story about the site in Candler County and explained why he thought they should check it out. The tobacco warehouse had turned up on a list of recent land buys routed through a sub-agency of the Forest Service, without standard procurement paperwork. The acquisition bore the hallmarks of a spate of recent property and equipment purchases flowing through obscure federal departments.

Darden could only imagine the legwork Webber and his people at State performed to uncover these shadowy deals, but their efforts bore fruit. A pattern had emerged—the purchases were mainly in rural locations, likely for detention purposes, judging from the equipment delivered to the sites. Other deals with major corporations involved massive electronic espionage of millions of personal phone records, bank accounts, even employee files.

Now as Webber got into his father's car and they accelerated onto the highway, he wanted to learn more. He knew Webber wouldn't tell him everything, and he expected a struggle over the miles ahead to pry more details from him. The man was a diplomatic professional and he only revealed what he needed to reveal.

"Are they spying on everyone?" Darden asked.

"Maybe, but it's too early to say."

"Then, who?"

"Their focus is on potential opponents."

"How do you know that?"

"We ran some obvious names and found recent data searches of their personal records that proved they were targets."

"So, anybody who's supported the other party, or say, attended certain events is a suspect?"

"Afraid so, and the net is widening," Webber said

"The thing that scares me most is the paramilitary stuff."

"It should be. We know the Extremist Brotherhood is uniting and funding vigilante organizations, combining them into a private army of sorts."

"Militia groups?" Darden whistled. "Anti-government? That crowd?"

"The most radical of the radical right wing."

Darden thought for a moment. "Oh, man. An army of skinheads and neo-Nazis. Is it active yet?"

"As of now, best we can tell," Webber said, "The army is being trained, paid, and equipped secretly."

"This is worse than I thought."

"No, it's worse than you ever thought it might be. They might have a deadline to kick it off."

"When?"

"I'm not sure, maybe June first."

"Less than a month away. What happens then?"

"Probably what we've seen overseas. Wholesale detentions. Prison camps. Even torture if they hold true to form."

Darden fell silent at that, thought of his father's story about the concentration camps in Europe. Perhaps it was better the old man had not lived to see this day—prison camps in America itself. Who would have thought it possible? The men behind this were every bit as dangerous as the Nazis.

He'd put a great face of bravado on today's trip, for Linda's benefit, but inside he was becoming much more worried about the dangers of his reporting. He thought back to his days in Journalism School at the University of Georgia, amazed at how naïve they'd all been. Many had gone into reporting in the hope that they'd accomplish great things and become celebrities like the great reporters of the seventies and eighties. Journalists like Halberstam, Hersh, and Woodward were their heroes then; men who exposed the worst misdeeds in the country; men who called bad leaders to accounts and shaped history by great investigative reporting.

None of them as students would have believed an impending national catastrophe would receive so little journalistic attention; none of them would have believed the great news organizations would wither so easily and barely be able to maintain skeleton crews to cover anything. Half-full newsrooms were now the norm. Great daily newspapers had been reduced to a quarter of their former size—thin and empty inside. The whole business of serious journalism had been reduced to rubble by internet technology, corporate takeovers, and a disinterested public.

Yet the sea change in news had also opened a door of opportunity for him personally. He might never have got his stories out without the online news sites. So, here he was, chasing perhaps the greatest story of the past twenty years, and he had to do it mostly alone, bereft of editorial support, legal back up, and basic personal security. He was literally risking his life—and Linda's—to perform the job Jefferson had envisioned as essential to democracy.

He turned to Webber after a few minutes of silence. "You know, this whole thing reminds me of that great quote by Franklin when the Constitutional Convention ended."

"Oh, the one about the republic," Webber said. "How does it go?"

"After all the months of wrangling over the new form of government, somebody outside the convention hall asked him, 'What have we got?'"

"And Franklin said, 'A republic, if you can keep it.'"

They looked at each other, their faces grim, the poignancy of the quote not lost on either of them. Perhaps they and their countrymen had failed to keep it.

CHAPTER 35

Driving the long miles through Tatnall County, Darden learned a lot about Arvin Webber's dislike of extremism. In his career at the State Department, the man had been to a lot of troubled places, and he told Darden that most of the brutality and death he'd seen were the result of extremist groups trying to force their dogma down the throats of the other side.

"So, let them kill each other," Darden said.

"But it spreads, like a disease. Ordinary people are the ones who lose the most."

Darden kept his eyes open for speed limit signs while they talked. "Most ordinary guys just want to stay out of trouble."

"Sure, but they can't avoid it. They're the ones who lose their children to land mines. Their jobs evaporate in the chaos. They're the ones who get blown up in outdoor markets by car bombs."

"You think it'll come to that here?"

"If we don't stop this, I know it will. I've seen it everywhere I've worked. For every extremist militia or violent group that comes along, an opposition develops. They fight each other to the death, and the ordinary guy gets caught between them, hammered by both sides."

"Do you have a family, Arvin?"

"Yes."

"Want to tell me about them?"

"No."

"Why not?"

"If you are captured, it's better you know less about me and my family. That's why I don't ask about your private life."

His last call to Linda before they got to their destination, he gave her a quick update of their location and expected time of arrival at the warehouse, but he knew something was wrong the minute he heard her voice.

"Tell me," he said. "What's up?"

She said everything was good with her, but he persisted, wanting to know more. Finally she opened up. Earlier in the day, while she was at Memorial in Daytona for a drop-off, she went to the burn unit and asked about Jean Hughes.

"What about her?"

"Tom, I'm afraid she's dead."

They stayed silent for the next hour while he fought his way through a hailstorm of emotions. Yes, Jean had not been good for him. Yes, she was a very flawed person. But yes, also, he'd loved her at one time, and he felt the hurt now that she was dead. A beautiful woman who didn't give a damn about politics or fanatical religions or world dominance, or any of the rest of it, but she was dead before her time nonetheless.

When they were almost there, Darden broke the silence. "You're right, Arvin, ordinary people are the ones who get hurt the most."

He forced his mind off Jean and back to the job ahead. Neither of them knew what to expect since they hadn't been to one of these secret sites before, but they both sensed this might be a strong lead. They agreed to look for any useful information at the warehouse then get the hell out of there.

Darden followed Webber's directions and turned off Highway 129 south of the interstate. He drove down a dirt road that ran straight through a succession of plowed fields, most of them sprouting corn or tobacco. They passed a small, white frame Baptist church tucked back among some old oaks, saw a few farmhouses and barns scattered along the way.

The land was flat and the rows of crops ran to the horizon before disappearing against hazy green tree lines in the distance. It was traditional farming country and everything about it seemed so ordinary he could hardly believe what was happening in places just like this all over America. It pained him to know that most of the people tilling this sandy soil were good folks, honest and law abiding. A few were not.

Under cover of secrecy, a tiny number of people from Georgia to Arizona to Michigan felt so strongly about their convictions they lost touch with their own humanity. In their zeal to change or restore something about the country to suit their own vision, they put aside the basic morality taught to them in school and church. They became zealots who were convinced they knew The Truth and The Only Truth to impose on their fellow citizens. Unfortunately, the blind passion of those zealots sometimes led to hatred, then violence which ignited a response of still more violence. Then, as Webber had witnessed in other countries, an entire society teetered on the edge of exploding.

Webber checked a print-out of a satellite map spread across his knees, his right forefinger tracing the line of the dirt road through the fields. "It should be about a mile ahead, on the left."

Darden slowed down and the dust trail following them settled in their wake. He eased forward along the empty road and they watched for the warehouse, finally spotted it ahead.

"So how do you want to go in there?" Webber said.

"Just like we belong."

"What if anything goes wrong?"

"We use our heads and get out."

A single pickup parked in front of the warehouse was the only sign of any people nearby. Darden steered into the parking area and stopped the LeSabre alongside the truck. The tobacco warehouse was a plain building, painted dark green, with corrugated metal walls and a high roofline. He had never been inside one before.

They got out and the quiet was overwhelming. An occasional bird call was the only sound he heard. They went back to the trunk where Darden retrieved the pistol, tucked it inside the waistband at the back of his pants. He pulled his shirt out and let the tail of it cover the grip. Webber got his old gym bag out and unzipped the top. He slung its strap over his left shoulder.

Last thing, Darden picked up his Nikon and decided to carry it in; it might help with the cover story they'd agreed to use if anyone was inside. They went to the front door that stood alongside a giant roll-up truck bay. Both were closed, but the front door was unlocked. Darden opened it and they stepped into the dark interior.

After the sunshine outside, the warehouse seemed dark as a cave. There were no windows or open doors that he could see. It was very hot inside the building and a distinct smell filled the air, rich and organic, like the sweet aroma of pipe tobacco before it has been lit.

"Hello?" he called out. "Anybody here?"

It took a minute or so for his eyes to adjust and Darden could barely make out the shape of the interior. A high peaked roof, wooden uprights and rafters with drying racks hanging from them. A packed dirt floor underfoot and huge bins lining the walls. The only light was a candle burning at the far end of the building. Folding metal chairs surrounded it.

Two young men approached them from the deep gloom and one raised his hand in a half wave. "Hey," he said. "Ya'll here for the meetin'?"

"The new owner sent us," Darden said. "He wants pictures of the property."

The young guys looked at each other. "We didn't hear nothing 'bout that."

Webber spoke quickly. "Yeah, well, he wants some photos of the building just to make sure it's empty and in good condition. Told us to stay for the meeting too, if we wanted."

"That's right," Darden said. "He told us all about you ol' boys. Said you'd treat us like one of your own."

They looked at each other again. "Well, awright then," one of them said. "If he said it's okay."

The two came closer and extended their hands. Everybody shook. The boys' hands were rough and hard. They were barely out of their teens, dressed in jeans and work boots, much like Webber. With beefy arms and shoulders, they seemed like

212 • David Darracott

teammates from high school football. Both wore camouflage tee shirts with a symbol on the front, something Darden had not seen before, a blue lightning bolt surrounded by a red circle.

The talker had a sparse mustache with a shaved head. The quiet, taller one averted his eyes and nodded at them while looking down.

"Glad to meet you," Darden said. "Good to know there's some people up here think the same way we do."

"Ain't it the truth," the mustache said. "Where're ya'll from?"

"Just below the Florida line."

"You got a chapter down there?"

"Sure do," Webber said. "He bought us a building, too. An old airplane hangar about the size of this."

"I ain't met him yet," the mustache said, "But he's got to be a good man to spend all this money on the cause."

"Don't you know it," Darden said.

"What's your names?" the mustache asked.

"We don't use names," Darden said. "We keep pretty tight security."

"Good idea."

Webber managed to remain very casual, spoke in an easy drawl. "You boys mind showing us around the building? Let's get the pictures out of the way."

"Awright." The two kids walked deeper into the black shadows.

Darden and Webber followed. They eyed each other quickly, but it was still hard to see much in there. Darden shrugged and Webber tilted his head toward the two as if to say he wanted to play along and keep working it the same way.

"Course this warehouse ain't been used for tobacco in years," the talker began. "It's just been sittin' out here going to waste." His voice fell flat in the dead air, hardly an echo at all. He droned on, but Darden barely heard a word. It was as if the darkness absorbed sound as well as light.

These kids are so young and dense, he thought, we might be able to learn something before they catch on. And what then, he wondered? Just walk away? Why not? They were only kids, and we are armed. Learn what we can and then drive off. That's the plan. Just like we agreed in the car.

Webber interrupted the talker. "What time is the meeting?"

"'Bout an hour."

"How many you got coming?"

"'Bout twenty. Our chapter's still pretty small. How 'bout yours?"

"We're growing fast."

"Good, the country needs us."

"That's the truth," Darden said.

They stopped walking. The two boys turned and faced them.

"What'd you say was the name of your chapter?"

"Didn't say," Webber answered. "Our security's pretty tight."

Darden raised his Nikon. "Cover your eyes. I'm going to shoot that bunch of rafters up there and the flash'll be pretty bright."

Everyone put a hand over their eyes while he took a couple of shots. They moved on to the far end of the building and he took a couple more. The flash revealed about a dozen wooden crates stacked in one corner of the building.

"What's that over there?" he asked.

"Equipment."

Darden wondered about the vague answer but decided not to push it further.

"That ought to do it," he said. "Unless you ol' boys want me to take one of you two, over by the table there. I'll pass it on to the owner, show him how his money is going to good use."

The two boys led them toward the candle and circle of chairs. The candle sat in the middle of a round makeshift table, a huge wooden spool used for telephone wire. Underneath the candle, a round white table cloth covered the wooden surface. The table cloth had a large design at the center. As they got closer, it was plain the design was the same as that on their tee shirts, a blue lightning bolt inside a red circle. Alongside the candle was the dark rectangular handgrip and squared barrel of an automatic pistol, its magazine removed and lying alongside.

The two boys crouched down, one on each side of the table, both grinning. "Go ahead," the talker said. "Take our picture right here, kneeling at the altar of the New North American Patriots."

Darden felt the skin tighten along his spine and neck. This movement was all too real and happening right here, right in front of them. They were at the epicenter of a sea change in America; a movement of zealous, unquestioning men who believed the country was under threat. Soon the shadow government of the Extremist Brotherhood would unify these men and put them to some ugly work.

Darden closed his eyes and snapped the photo.

"Whoa, man." The talker rubbed his eyes. "You ain't kiddin,' that flash is strong."

For the first time, the quiet one spoke. His voice was soft, almost high pitched, a surprising sound considering his size. "I won't be able to see right for a half-hour."

They sat down in the chairs and one of the boys pulled a package of chewing tobacco out of the hip pocket of his jeans. He opened it and put a wad of leaves between his left cheek and gum, then passed it on to his friend who did the same. They offered the bag to Webber, who kept a straight face as he passed it on to Darden. Thinking it best to accept, Darden took a small pinch and put it in his mouth. He could spit it out soon enough.

They chewed for a minute in silence and watched the flame of the candle. It had an almost hypnotic effect. Before long, Darden felt a bit dizzy from the tobacco and his mind wavered. He felt as if he was taking part in some ancient ritual that bound men together, almost an initiation. They entered the timeless rite of brotherhood, of men sharing their beliefs in a quiet dark place while circled around a unifying flame.

"So, tell me," he said. "Who recruited you boys?"

CHAPTER 36

They talked for thirty minutes or more, and the young men told them about their involvement in the new militia movement. If the boys had been smart, they would have said little or nothing, but instead they were shallow thinkers, young and gullible, who believed too many things too easily and told what they knew too readily. At the risk of staying too long, Darden tried to learn as much from them as possible, asking for as many details as he dared.

"—big feller from out west really got us going," the talker said. "He sent us some special guns and police gear. Told us what was happenin' out at the Mexican border, 'bout the militias organizing there to keep out the illegals."

"We know plenty about illegals in Florida, too," Darden said.

"The government won't keep 'em out, so we have to do it ourselves."

"Damn right," the quiet one said. "Or they're gonna take back Texas."

"California, too." Webber said.

"Don't give a damn what they do with California," the talker said.

They all laughed at that.

"The people in Washington might want to keep California," Darden said seriously.

The talker snorted in derision. "Washington can't do shit. That's why we're gonna have a revolution in this country."

"Well, the military could stop us first," Webber said.

"The military won't do that."

"Why not?"

"They'll join us, 'cause we love the troops."

Webber and Darden nodded in sage agreement.

The boys' convictions were a wild and often contradictory amalgam of anti-government and pro-vigilante ideas, streaked with dislike for anyone different from themselves. They feared a takeover of the country by outsiders, yet most of all they hated and feared the power-hungry federal government insiders. To Darden, little of what they said made sense.

Webber ventured a question. "So, what does your chapter believe we ought to do first?"

The two boys looked at each other and burst out laughing. The quiet one actually spoke up, answering the question. "Well, first thing, we need to destroy the I.R.S."

The talker followed up. "Then, all the lawyers ought to be shot."

"And the politicians," the other one said.

"Yep. Get rid a them foreigners."

"Shut down all that government shit, wasting our money."

To Darden it seemed they mostly hated not being in control of events, as if they ever had been. "Is your chapter in favor of independence from Washington?"

"Don't know about everybody else," the mustache said. "We never voted on that, but I'm all for it. I've heard the Head Man is too."

"Oh, the owner of the warehouse?"

"I guess, since he's the one sending us money and equipment."

Darden tilted his head toward the corner of the building. "Like those crates over there?"

"Yeah."

"What's in them?"

The quiet one cracked his knuckles. "Mostly guns."

"He's a true patriot," Darden said.

"Oh yeah," Arvin said. "He knows plenty of groups all over the country think the same way we do."

"They say he knows when to push back," the talker said.

Something sounded familiar. Darden tried to remember where he'd heard that before. "Yep, it's all about fighting back."

"Is it true what they say about his face?"

"His face," Webber said.

"They say he's the ugliest feller you ever seen."

"Well, I wouldn't say that exactly."

The quiet one looked at him with an ignorant solemnity that was almost innocent. "He says it's time for America to take off the gloves."

Darden definitely remembered that phrase. That was one of the War Hawk's big applause lines. These yahoos would eat up his tough talk about seizing the oil fields and fighting every imaginable threat to national security. But he couldn't be the one behind it all—that business about his face didn't fit the War Hawk at all. Webber would know for sure; he'd ask him later. Even in the dim candlelight Darden could see a gleam of fierce recognition in Webber's eyes.

"Yes, he's a real patriot," Webber said.

Darden thought about the implications of what they were hearing. If the pieces truly fit, some renegade was well into the process of trying to overthrow the Constitution. Failing that, he might try to orchestrate some sort of break-up of the federal system with a few states withdrawing from the union. God, what a nightmare this was becoming.

His heart notched up a few more beats. He dropped his head to shield his face from them as he thought it through.

In earlier times, boys such as these would have been easy converts to the Klan or even one of the violent left wing groups of the sixties, like the Weather Underground. Left or right didn't matter much to them; they just welcomed a call to violent action. Out to bring down what they considered an oppressive government, these kids were ripe targets for most any radical message. They were so impressionable that revolution and secession sounded like good ideas to them, though they'd never considered the consequences of such actions. No, they saw themselves as the new patriots who would save America from her own weakness.

He coughed and spit the plug of tobacco on the dirt floor. His mouth tasted awful from it.

The Extremist Brotherhood was already arming this chapter and others like it. If these groups ever unified and became organized, the country would pay an enormous price. Violent confrontation between enraged radicals from opposite sides would be inevitable. The nation could well descend into the worst period of bloodshed and chaos since the Civil War.

He looked over at Webber and could almost detect the same wheels spinning inside the man's mind. Webber looked back at him, and without saying a word, they both understood they'd learned enough. It was time to get out of there.

Webber stood and stretched. "Well, it's getting pretty late. Sure has been good meeting you ol' boys."

"That it has," Darden said, "But we better be gettin' on."

The young guys stood with them and offered their hands again. Everybody shook and all four moved through the hot gloom toward the front door.

"Ya'll sure you don't want to stay for the meeting?"

"Nope, we better be hittin' the road."

The one with the mustache spat a big wad of tobacco juice on the dirt floor. "Before you leave, suppose you tell us what you're really doing here."

"What do you mean?" Darden replied, as he kept moving ahead.

The boy snorted in reply.

Just before they reached the door, the tall quiet one put his hand on Darden's shoulder. "You don't really think you're leavin' here, do you?"

They stopped walking. Darden and Webber glanced at each other.

"What did you say?"

"I mean you ain't going nowhere, Mister."

The mustache stepped closer. "You think we're pretty stupid, don't you?"

Neither of them answered. Darden saw Webber's right hand sliding toward the open top of the gym bag hanging under his left shoulder.

The quiet one remained behind Darden.

The mustache spoke again. "Think we're a couple of dumb country boys you can fool with."

Darden raised his camera slightly with one hand and covered his eyes with the other. He tapped the shutter and the flash went off like a bomb; he could see the explosion of white light even through his closed fingers.

The talker staggered back and put his hands over his eyes. "Damn!"

The tall one behind Darden had to be half-blind too, but he'd managed to get an arm around Darden's neck. Darden bent, tried to throw him over his head, but the kid was too heavy.

"Get him off me, Arvin!"

The boy used his free hand to throw a punch into Darden's back, but he missed the left kidney and his fist landed on Darden's hip bone.

"I can't see," Webber said. "Move this way."

Darden managed to work the boy closer to Webber. The kid was big, but Darden had strong legs and he whirled the kid's weight toward the sound of Webber's voice. A second later he felt the boy's arm come off his neck as Webber hit him on the head with a gun from his bag. It sounded like the rap of a big spoon on a watermelon.

"Got him," Webber said.

The talker heard it too and lunged for them. This time, Darden got the first blow in as he sidestepped the kid's rush and smashed him on the head with his Nikon. The kid went down groaning but continued to flail outward with his arms, trying to get a hand on one of them.

Darden stepped forward and kicked the talker in the stomach, heard the rush of air burst from the boy's mouth. Okay, that ought to give them time to make it to the car. He went to Webber and grabbed his arm.

"Come on, I'll get us to the door."

They walked fast the rest of the way.

"Keep your gun out," he said to Webber.

"Got it."

Darden pushed them through the front door and instantly they were both paralyzed by the brightness outside. The late afternoon sun was in their face and it forced its way into their darkness-conditioned pupils. Their eyelids clenched shut involuntarily.

They both stopped, wishing for a moment to let their eyes adjust.

"That was close," Darden said.

"No kidding."

By the time they could crack open their eyes, they had managed to stagger a few steps in the direction of the car. Still half-blind, Darden could just make out the outline of the LeSabre off to their right, a halo of blue within a field of yellow white glare. Webber still couldn't see and wandered off line. Darden grabbed his sleeve again.

"This way," he said.

They had stumbled halfway to the car when Darden realized there were several other vehicles in the parking area. They sat at a distance, but definitely were grouped around the Buick. He saw men positioned behind one truck, then another, black rods of gun barrels pointed up, silhouettes of menace against the red sky.

A strong voice came from a pickup on their left. "Stop!"

Darden kept moving.

"I said, stop!"

Darden heard the sounds of weapons; the mechanical meshing of pump loaders on shotguns and pistol hammers cocking. They stopped.

"Drop your weapons!"

Darden tried to think, but it was all happening too fast. "Who are you?" he yelled.

"We are hellfire and damnation descending upon you. Drop your weapons, now!"

They stood still, Darden trying to get a take on the situation. "What do you want to do?" he said quietly to Webber.

"I can't let them capture me," Webber replied in a flat voice. "I know too much."

Before Darden could say another word, Webber raised his pistol and got off two quick shots in the general direction of the voice. In response, several shotguns and pistols opened up, the shots loud and overlapping.

Darden heard bullets snapping through the air. A couple caught Webber's body like a kick. He went down quickly, but more bullets punctured him on the ground. Blood flowered grotesquely on his shirt and jeans as his torso convulsed, hands twitching, then he went still.

Darden could not make himself move. He could not have run, sat, or fired his own pistol even if he'd thought of it. He could only stand and watch the blood seeping through Webber's clothes, small puddles of it clotting on the hard-packed earth beneath his lifeless form.

CHAPTER 37

Linda kept trying Tom's cell phone, but there was no answer. She'd already left four messages since his last scheduled call-in at six o'clock. By seven o'clock she was seriously worried. By eight she was frantic. Never should have let him go, she told herself. She had to save him; she'd saved his life once before; she could do it again.

She picked up the phone again, dialed the Chief Inspector over at Fire Services.

He answered on the second ring. "This is Chief Ins—"

Linda started crying before he could finish the sentence. Even though she wanted to explain things clearly, her voice was out of control and none of her thoughts came out in sequence.

"Slow down, Miss Ramsey."

After a few moments of broken phrases she forced herself to go slower and tried to order her words coherently.

"I'm sorry, Chief. I need your help."

His voice was slow and calm as ever. "Tell me what's happened."

"It's Tom," she cried. "They've got him, I know it!"

The Chief was a methodical man, and his professionalism took over from there, just as she'd hoped. He pressed her for details, tried to keep her answers on track. Step by step he asked her to explain where Darden was, who was with him, information about his car, and who she thought had kidnapped him.

"He was supposed to call me every two hours. That was our signal. And he did, but then the calls stopped. He's in trouble. I know it."

The Chief broke in quietly, "Easy, Miss Ramsey. Try to slow down."

His patient approach worked. By the time she told him about Tom's plan to meet Deep Throat at a location in south Georgia, she was almost calm enough to think clearly. She wasn't sure exactly where he was, but she knew where he'd intended to go, a sort of farm warehouse near I-16. She explained that Deep Throat was a contact out of Washington who was a government employee, but she didn't know his name.

Finally after telling him everything, she stopped. Then, "One last thing, Chief. Please call me, Linda."

"Okay, Linda," he said. "Let me get hold of the FBI men that we met here. See what I can find out."

"When? How long before I know something?"

"I'll get back to you as soon as I can."

She was focused now, knew what she had to do. "Chief, if you don't call me within a half hour, I'm going after him myself."

He paused at that, seemed to consider. "Don't do anything foolish. It would take hours just to get up there. I'll call you within thirty minutes."

She went into the guest bedroom of her friend's house, her temporary home. No, her hideout, and she was tired of hiding. Even though she trusted the Chief, she refused to count on anyone else. She grabbed her suitcase out of the closet, threw in a few random clothes. FBI or not, she was going to find her man.

Twenty minutes later, she was in her Jeep heading north on the interstate when the Chief called her back. She saw his name on the caller ID read-out and wasted no time with a greeting.

"What do you know, Chief?"

"More than I did before, but not as much as you want."

"Where is he?"

"We don't know yet. The FBI's just started to search. They'll canvas every warehouse in the county along the I-16 corridor. The best bet to find him quickly is the car. Do you know the license number?"

"It's still in the name of his father. Thomas Watts Darden,

deceased. Florida plates."

"That'll help."

"What about Deep Throat? That's a lead."

The Chief didn't respond immediately. She sensed meaning behind his hesitation.

"So far, he's our best possibility. The FBI knows of contact between the two of them."

"You mean they've been spying on Tom?"

"Well, yes," the Chief said. "Mainly trying to keep him alive."

She doubted if that was their primary motive, but if it helped, it was okay with her. "What else?"

"The contact works for the State Department. Name is Arvin Webber. An Under Secretary who has a long standing relationship with the FBI asked them to keep an eye on him, said Webber was doing some confidential and dangerous work for State."

"What work?"

"I can't answer that, Linda."

She almost exploded, but managed to control her voice. "Chief, I have to know."

He was slow to answer, apparently decided she had the right to know. "He and Tom were tracking down some secret funding, money that was going to some sort of domestic terrorist group. It seems State and the FBI both suspect some of the same things as Tom. They take his reports about torture and illegal imprisonment seriously."

Visions of torture cells and the Daytona bloodshed swam in her mind. The bodies she'd helped recover from the ashes of the hotel. The video of the man dangling from a hook. Who were all these lunatic people? Didn't they have any real lives to keep them busy? Did they have some sort of grudge against ordinary people who wanted to work and laugh and have babies?

"Damn it," she said. "Why didn't Tom tell me any of this?"

"He wanted to protect you. The less you know, the better."

"Can they find him, this guy Webber?"

Her cell phone crackled. She glanced at the speedometer; she was doing well over eighty. She slowed down to listen closely.

"They'll find him. And when they do, I think they'll find Tom."

"Just one more question, Chief."

He waited on the other end, the connection mostly static and the call breaking apart. Dark thoughts also stressed her voice to the limit of audibility.

"When they find him, will he still be alive?"

CHAPTER 38

"More time?" The War Hawk did that thing where he tilted his head forward then looked at you sideways.

Baines nodded.

"You want more time." Though his tone varied little, the question actually carried a hint of incredulity. "Surely you realize that's the one thing we can't afford."

Icy waves came off the Great Man as Baines stumbled for words to explain that the June first launch date was unrealistic.

"But, sir—"

"No, no more time."

The Great Man silenced him with a glare, removed three twelve gauge shells from the pocket of his field coat, one shell wedged in each V between his fingers, then he fed them into the hinged chamber on the bottom side of the shotgun. Reloaded, the shotgun went back to the ready position in the crook of his right elbow, left hand under the wooden handguard on the barrel. "I'm starting to notice something, Doctor," the Great Man said as he started to walk again. "You never bring me good news. And you and I were only supposed to meet once that first time in Washington."

A few quail flushed ahead and to their right, the wing beats sounding like a fast drum roll as the birds darted upwards then sideways, briefly visible in their erratic flight. The Great Man swung his shotgun up and over, the barrel no more than two feet in front of Baines' face. He fired two quick shots, and the doctor felt hot gasses from the gunshots push against his exposed face.

"That was a bit close, sir."

"Hell if it was. I missed both of them."

Baines suppressed his irritation and opened his mouth to make his ears pop; they were ringing from the blast.

Baines thought quickly about the next thing he was going to say. He understood fully at this moment why they called him the War Hawk; this man was an expert at intimidation. All his life, Baines had been able to back anyone down—his face was useful in that respect—but around the Great Man he realized there was more to dominance than mere appearance. It took absolute confidence and ruthlessness as well. Baines sometimes wondered, at those times when his thoughts became scattered and random, if he possessed those qualities in sufficient amounts or if he simply deceived himself.

"Well, sir, it so happens I have good news."

They stepped through the weeds at the edge of the field, headed toward a brush pile near the pines and Baines made sure he lagged a couple of paces behind. He didn't want to get shot, accidentally or otherwise. Perhaps that was why the Secret Service men stayed at such a distance. They knew the Great Man was a danger with a weapon in his hand. Maybe this quail plantation was empty of other guests for more reason than one.

"Good, let's hear it."

"We have captured the reporter at one of our yellow sites and managed to kill a second intruder who was with him. Turned out to be someone who worked for State."

The Great Man stopped dead still and whirled on Baines. "You what?"

"You wanted us to get the reporter, so we got him."

"You killed a State Department man?"

"He was collateral damage, sir."

The Great Man pulled himself up straight and looked as if he wanted to turn the gun on Baines. "Have you asked yourself exactly what a State Department operative was doing snooping around our facility with that lousy reporter?"

Baines thought it better not to answer. He took two steps back as the other man edged toward him, malice twisting his mouth, a vein of stress appearing on the high, tanned forehead. Baines had heard the War Hawk's rage was volcanic; he was about to find out firsthand.

"You idiot," the Great Man hissed. "That means someone at State, and probably other agencies, too, are tracking the money and getting close to uncovering our operations. The last thing we need is them looking closer. A dead man makes it certain they will."

"He fired on our—"

"I don't want excuses, Doctor. I want results. Do you think I piped you millions of dollars just to bring State down on our heads? Those assholes are always against us, and they're too close to the FBI. Don't you know anything? I'm starting to think my trust in you and Marshall was misplaced."

Baines felt scolded, just like a child. It was a feeling he did not appreciate, but long ago he'd learned not to argue with the paying client. Better to let them rant until the anger dissipated. This was still his Master Plan and he would maintain control of it, despite what the Great Man implied.

"We just need more time, sir. Our militia people are not fully armed and organized. They're not ready yet to launch. Every phase of the operation must start at the same time to ferret out our enemies here at home. To arrest, detain and interrogate these traitors, we must have the personnel in place to activate our black sites."

The Great Man lowered his shotgun, giving Baines no small amount of relief. The man's anger had passed quickly and he was back to his usual frigid temperament.

"No, Doctor," he said. "Delay is not possible. Instead, we must accelerate the plan. This intrusion means the opposition is aware of us and growing in strength. We need boots on the ground, right now. Start rounding up opponents and open the detention centers."

Doesn't the man hear anything I say, Baines thought. I have no troops yet to round up anyone. WE ARE NOT READY, he wanted to scream. His head felt overheated and he sensed the return of a mental state that had been flickering inside him lately, a sort of dark pain screaming within. He did not like the racing thoughts that came with it, the cracks widening in his self control. Just a stress reaction, he assured himself. It will pass.

"Doctor? Did you hear me?"

Baines squeezed his eyes shut, then opened them. "Ah, of course."

The Great Man started walking quickly, back in the direction of the lodge. Baines caught up with him, still intent on repairing the damage, but his benefactor seemed to have turned inside to think, started talking, yet it seemed to be more to himself rather than to Baines.

"We must act quickly. If they are that close, we haven't a day to waste. I must take other steps. We need the military on our side."

"What do you mean?"

"I mean, this whole damn thing is unraveling thanks to your sloppy security."

"But—"

The Great Man gave him that sideways glare again. "I'm taking over."

"You, what?"

"We can't risk exposure at this stage. Not until we are firmly in control. I must take charge. Now."

Baines almost shouted. "This is my plan! You can't ... just take it."

The Great Man paused, lowered his voice until it was a soft growl. Baines had to strain to hear him.

"I can do this with you," the Great Man said. Again the sidelong stare, but this time with a hostile seriousness. "Or without you. What will it be, Doctor? We can go back and hunt longer if you wish."

Baines had never had someone threaten him so directly. He could become a hunting accident in a matter of minutes if he said the wrong words. Thing was, when he looked at those steady eyes, he had no doubt the man would do it, would decide right here on the spot and make it happen. Baines realized he had no choice. Just like that, he'd lost control of his Master Plan. Years of effort and planning gone in a wisp of a moment. His bravado collapsed. Perhaps if he played it smart, he could at least keep the millions he'd stolen.

"What can I do to help, sir?"

"That's much better."

They started walking again, picked up the pace.

"Get to that damned reporter. How close is he to the full picture? How much does he know? Since he's been in contact with State, how much do they know? Find out everything you can from him."

"Yes, sir."

"And, need I say it?"

"Of course not. No more bad news, sir."

CHAPTER 39

A blazing pain in his legs brought Darden to consciousness. He lurched awake reflexively but found himself unable to move his body. Doubled over at the waist, a stick or bar, maybe something like a metal broom stick, ran behind his knees. A rope around his neck secured him tightly and held his upper body forward. His arms were wrapped around his shins below the stick, tied and pulled tight behind him by the other end of the rope around his neck.

Together, the stick and ropes bound his body into a tight ball, chest against thighs, with no room for movement or shifting of limbs. The restricted position had set off cramps in his hamstrings, the resulting pain forcing him awake. The muscles of his legs knotted like fists against the lack of motion, his entire body throbbing in response.

A groan came out of his mouth against his will. The leg muscles clenched again and locked violently, stayed contracted despite his efforts to keep them relaxed. Unable to stretch his legs out straight, the pain was unceasing and convulsive.

He must have been tied in this position a long time to set off such cramps, but he didn't know how long. Ever since the fight outside the warehouse, he'd been knocked out by an injection they gave him. It took many men to hold him down and keep him still enough for the needle, but eventually they won. Of course, they did, he recalled; one against many always had the same outcome, it seemed.

Now, here he was in purgatory, though he didn't know where. The pain was so great he could not even clear his mind enough to take stock of his surroundings. Wherever he was, whoever was holding him, it did not matter. The pain overwhelmed everything.

He had only one aim—escape.

He groaned, even screamed for a long time, but he heard nothing. He saw nothing. He was in a pitch dark space, his butt sitting on what felt like a concrete floor. No smells or sounds provided any clues. He was trapped in a void; a timeless, shapeless void.

Had his body not been in such pain, he would have suspected he was dead, perhaps in a real purgatory, though he'd never been convinced of its existence. To his mind, a good and righteous God would never commit humans to eternal torment, but what if he had been wrong about that?

Later, the muscles in his back began to cramp too. His back arched against the restraints, convulsions wracking his entire body which caused the noose to tighten about his neck. He felt something give way in his lower extremities, then smelled waste emptying from his bowels.

The smell convinced him he was still alive. He must be alive to perceive such stink and torment.

Images and memories shot through his mind at lightning speed. It seemed that millions of bits of information stored over an entire lifetime in the deep recesses of his brain had been set loose. Most of them were horrifying. Nightmares from childhood. A dental drill whining into enamel and pulp. A knife accident, when a sharp pinpoint of blade opened the skin of his thigh. A broken collarbone, fragments grating on fragments. The distorted face of a monster in a horror film. The raging fever of flu. Vomit burning its way up his throat. The car accident as an infant. His forehead cracking against the dashboard. His mother's face, her head lolling behind the wheel, blood pouring from her mouth.

Darden knew he was going mad. Like the crazy Iraqi prisoner, Khalid, in the Baghdad jail, he'd never have a sane thought again.

How long it went on, he did not know. At some point, one thing saved him. Despite the intensity of the pain, exhaustion set in, his mind went blank and darkness enveloped his mind.

When he woke up, his body was no longer bound, but the cramps had left his body contorted. He could hardly move his limbs. Lying on the concrete floor, his legs were still clenched, heels pressing tight against the back of his thighs. Arms a bit better, he was able to straighten them and flex his hands.

Why were they doing this? What were they after? Surely, they had nothing to gain from him. Punishment, he decided. It must simply be punishment, because he had opposed them.

So, was he to pay the ultimate price for his actions, for telling the world the truth? Most likely. Had it been worth it? Had he achieved anything by exposing this sort of abuse of human beings? He would probably never know. Success was a misty thing.

He struggled to remember how he got here, but his brain was not functioning well. Too many images and thoughts ran rapid-fire through his neural pathways for him to lock onto a single one. But he remembered the warehouse. Oh, yes, Arvin was dead, he remembered that. Then, perhaps a dozen men wrestling him to the ground. The militia, that was it. They held him down, drugged him and then must have brought him here. But where? He might be in Alaska or eastern Europe, for all he knew. The space was still soundless, lightless, without shape or definition.

The only solution—escape.

For hours, his thoughts tumbled along, a rockslide inside his head. Slowly, very slowly, the muscles in his legs and back began to loosen. The simple reduction in pain became an enormous pleasure. Maybe they would decide to let him go. Should he dare to hope? He tried to stand, but couldn't. Wait. Be patient.

A long time later, he slept again. At some point, a rush of bodies surrounded him in the dark, pinned him down. Then a blinding light seared the retinas of his eyes, the wasp sting of a needle penetrated his left bicep.

When he woke up, he was in a completely new place. It was brightly lit and hummed with equipment, but again he was immobilized, this time strapped to a table. Heavy restraints on his ankles and wrists, across his chest; a strap across his forehead too. All he could see was the acoustical tile ceiling above him with its perforations, also several recessed light fixtures.

A dark figure came into his field of view, a silhouette in profile against the bright lights of the ceiling, an outline of horror descending upon him. Then the man turned, revealing himself fully. He was the ugliest human being Darden had ever seen.

"I am Doctor Josiah Baines."

"So?"

"You are going to talk to me."

Baines leaned in close to him, so close Darden could see the details of his mangled face: missing muscles, the raw tissue exposed by lack of skin cover, the fault line running through the left cheekbone and eye socket. It looked like an earthquake had occurred there, with a lateral fault separating one part of his face from the other. A hole where his left jaw should be, molars leering through it. Nothing fit in its proper place. This man was a walking, breathing jigsaw puzzle from a Picasso nightmare.

"I'll tell you anything you want to know, if you'll just go away so I don't have to look at you."

"Interesting. You still have some fight left."

He seemed to be inspecting Darden, touched an eyelid and raised it for a closer look at the pupil beneath, glimpsed inside Darden's mouth, ears, even nostrils. Clinical. Detached.

"So, what do you want to know?"

"Everything."

"Then we'll be here a few years."

Dr. Baines leaned back and straightened up, almost smiled, but his broken face would not allow it.

"Very interesting. You still have a sense of humor and resistance," Baines said. "The stress positions should have removed those from you."

"Maybe the 'stress positions' made me stronger."

At that, Baines actually laughed, though it came out as a grunt. "No, no, Mr. Darden, they did not. What I have planned for you does not make you stronger. It turns you into a whimpering child."

CHAPTER 40

After driving all day, Linda stopped at a convenience store near I-16 for gas when she learned by phone that her trip had been pointless. She was filling her tank when the Chief rang her cell and told her Darden's Buick had been found on a lucky tip.

A man and his son came on the LeSabre while hunting rabbits and found it ditched and burned in a pine thicket. When they reported their discovery, the police from Vidalia searched the surrounding area, including nearby farm buildings where they turned up shell casings outside an empty tobacco warehouse.

A weight came down on her head when he mentioned gun shells. She tried to interrupt but couldn't get a word out as the Chief went on about how they eventually discovered human bloodstains there as well.

"But—"

He'd said nothing about finding Tom or the other man who'd been with him.

"But what about, Tom?"

"He could be anywhere at this point," the Chief finally answered. "It's an interstate case now, so the FBI is all over it. They're treating it as a kidnapping."

The FBI soon learned the warehouse had been under suspicion for several weeks due to rumors in the community that a group of self-styled militia had been meeting there. The FBI assured him those involved in the militia would be found and questioned. After talking to the police herself, she spent the night in Vidalia and admitted there was nowhere else to look for him, nothing more she could do there, so she had no choice but to drive back to Florida. Exhausted, she turned south and thought about the situation all the way home. She felt sure Tom was still alive even though she had no proof of it, and she decided the best thing to do was bring pressure on the law enforcement community to find him as quickly as possible. The best way to do that, she determined, was to go public. That would expose her to a certain amount of risk, perhaps him as well, but she felt there was no other choice.

Back in Daytona, the first thing she did was call the local newspapers, television news stations, and *CNN*. They all wanted to interview her when she mentioned her knowledge of Tom's disappearance, so she decided to meet with them all at once. Tom had become something of a minor celebrity among reporters, though his controversial stories produced wildly different reactions among them.

In just one afternoon her offer to speak publicly turned into a press conference of sorts, because she refused to grant any single outlet an exclusive. The idea of going on television made her uneasy, but she thought the publicity might save Tom's life. By going public, she thought whoever took Tom might be less inclined to harm him.

The news people set up everything quickly, because they were so eager to talk to her. The story of a missing reporter was red hot, especially since he'd been writing such explosive stories. From Tom, she had learned a bit about the ways of the news business and she intended to use their headline mentality any way she could.

A television studio at the local *NBC* affiliate became the site for the press conference the next day. She had never been in a studio, never even been on camera before. Certain she would appear ill at ease, she wore her E.M.T. uniform in the hope of gaining more attention, perhaps even sympathy, from viewers.

At ten in the morning the next day, a production assistant led her through the chilly blackness of a high-ceiling studio to a small stage that glowed with white lights. They seated her across a table from four newscasters, each of them dressed in bright stylish clothes, their hair sprayed, their faces wearing heavy make-up for the cameras. They were strikingly thin and acted self-important, checking and re-checking their appearance in off-line monitors.

Several other reporters sat in a second row of chairs wrapped in a semi-circle behind the ones seated at the table. By now, she knew about the hierarchies at work in the business; the high status and salaries that went to the few and the low pay and backseat rank reserved for the many.

The ones up front were television faces; the ones in back were real journalists dressed in everyday business clothes, probably all print reporters. One was overweight, another gray; most wore glasses. They were the ones like Tom who had to scrape for stories to make a living. They were the dying breed of news people he talked about so often, underpaid and unheralded, they were the ones who dug for facts and sifted out lies simply because they loved bringing the truth into daylight.

The technical people wearing headsets went through sound checks and light level readings while she tried to stop blinking and squinting from the brightness of the stage lights. Just be yourself, she said in her mind, and sincerity will show through in everything you say.

Shortly, the production assistant touched his headphones and signaled to Linda with a nod. "Ready, Miss Ramsey?"

"Yeah, sure."

A red light went on above a camera lens and stared at her. She cleared her throat and the interview began. It went well for the first few minutes as the television people asked questions and gave her enough time to answer them. She explained the whole background of Tom's investigation into the events leading up to the present, how he had been imprisoned briefly in Iraq, and how he wrote story after story about torture over there despite resistance from a lot of people.

"Why did he do that?"

"Because he thinks torture is wrong. He thinks it's the job of the press to report wrongdoing."

"Who opposed him?"

"Who?" Incredulous, she looked at the questioner sharply. He was young, with perfect dark hair combed back, thin lips. Didn't these guys know anything? "The military, the Administration in Washington, even his own employer, that's who."

The young broadcaster turned hostile. "He wasn't a national figure. Why did he feel he should be the one to question the government's security decisions?"

"Because, hardly anybody else would even touch it. Where were all of you when he challenged the nation's conscience?"

"Did he fear for his life?" a bleached blonde asked.

"Of course, ever since the attempt to kill him last month. You all remember that attack in Jacksonville."

"Why did he continue the investigation even after a murder attempt?"

"He thought it was his responsibility to keep reporting wrongdoing, even when it's unpopular." She couldn't keep the accusatory tone out of her voice entirely. "He thought somebody in the news business ought to do it."

A couple of the showy television people squirmed at that.

She went on and told them about the death threats and false accusations directed at him, the attempts to discredit his work. They asked about Tom's disappearance and where his car had been found, about the lead he was following, about the federal employee who'd possibly been with him. She said she suspected they had been kidnapped by the same people who tried to kill him before.

"Do you think he is still alive?" a doe-eyed newscaster asked her, oblivious to Linda's struggle to control her emotions.

It was the worst possible question to be asked. Linda couldn't respond verbally, so she simply hung her head and nodded.

They gave her a moment to compose herself, even though she suspected they wanted her to break down on camera. What a juicy six o'clock lead her tears would make. She refused to cry, cleared her throat and sat up straight, though she was sure her eyes had a sheen on them.

She answered more questions about the research he'd done

and the gruesome photographs he'd published with his stories, how he came by them. She held back very little, only steered away from the things they'd promised the FBI to keep secret. She simply said that some of the material had arrived anonymously once he started investigating and reporting torture.

"Was Tom a good reporter?" someone asked.

She wanted to fire back and say that was a stupid question. Instead, she kept her cool.

"He is a great reporter." She stared right back at the idiot. "Don't forget, he helped the FBI identify the primary suspect for the Daytona bombing."

"Did he learn any more about that terrorist?"

"Yes, he knows what happened to him."

"What was the Daytona bomber's name?" one of them shouted.

"The FBI will have to tell you that."

"Tell us what happened to him," another interrupted.

"He died in an Iraqi prison," she said. "He was tortured to death."

That was new information to them. Everyone in the room started talking at once. Order broke down and they threw loud overlapping questions at her, the volume of their voices rising. The print guys in back stood and shouted to get her attention.

"Who tortured him?"

"Why didn't Tom reveal the terrorist's name?"

"What else did he know about Daytona?"

"Why release this information, now?"

She ignored them for a minute to let the chaos settle. When she refused to answer any more questions, they finally backed off and stopped shouting. The set gradually became quiet as they waited for her to speak again.

"I'd like to say one more thing." She reached into her shirt pocket and removed a plastic flash drive. "The answers to all your questions, and more, are on a drive just like this. Tom is writing a book that tells everything—it's almost finished. The officials involved, names, bank accounts—all on a drive. His files have been saved and stored securely."

She paused and let that sink in. She could see the envy in their eyes, what they would give for that flash drive.

"So, whoever kidnapped Tom, I want you to know that you can't kill this story by killing him. There are several copies, and all of it will be released immediately if anything happens to him or to me."

She looked directly into the camera with the red light. Her voice rose with emotion she couldn't restrain.

"If you see or hear this message, please help me find Tom Darden. He risked his life because he loves his country and believes in every citizen's right to know. If you have any information about where he is, please call the FBI. I love him and I want him back alive."

CHAPTER 41

Exhausted but frazzled, Linda slept poorly that night and awoke tired when her phone rang early the next morning. It was the Chief, and he asked her to come to his office at eleven, because a man was flying down from Washington who wished to speak with her.

"Who is he?"

"I don't know, but he's very high up the chain. He has a lot of clout with the FBI."

"I'll be there."

On her way to Fire Services, she tried to plan what she would say to the man, wondered how she could persuade him to do more than was already being done. But, she thought, what if he's not coming down to help at all? What if he isn't even on our side? What if he's part of the crowd who wants to keep everything secret? The more scenarios she considered, the more uncertain she became about meeting him.

Then the thought came to her to stay focused on the most important thing—to find Tom before he got hurt or killed. That was her goal, her only goal.

In the parking lot outside Fire Services headquarters, she saw three of those big, black Suburbans with tinted windows. That probably meant more FBI people. They must have escorted the bigwig from the airport.

She took a deep, slow breath and went inside where the Chief came to the lobby to get her. He looked more tired than ever, the creases at the corners of his eyes deeper and darker. To her surprise, he walked up and put his arm on her shoulders, a fatherly act for such an undemonstrative man. She wasn't sure why she had this effect on him, but she was glad of it. He'd definitely taken her into his orbit, and she resolved then and there that she would have to pay him back in double favors someday.

They sat down in the same conference room where she and Tom had met the FBI people before. As before, it was crowded with men in dark suits and rigid faces, some of them the same ones, such as the Raptor, the one in charge who had told them the bomber's name.

Most important though, her eyes stopped on a new person in the room. A large, older man sat in a corner, his head down, everything about him stooped and heavy. When the movement of chairs and random talk settled, he stood and walked over to her. His grooming and clothes were impeccable, out of place among the workaday world of law enforcement people. Had he not been so old, his appearance would be considered elegant, she thought. His great head was bent forward, his face lined by a thousand worries. He carried himself with dignity and looked straight into her eyes as he extended his hand.

"Hello, Miss Ramsey. I am so pleased to meet you."

She shook his hand and it felt like an old baseball glove enclosing hers. He held onto her hand just long enough to make an extra impression of warmth. She did not know him, but his manner made her feel they were on the same team, that they had been friends for a lifetime.

He sat down carefully across the table from her and put his manicured fingertips together on the tabletop.

"Thank you for coming to see me," he said. "My name is Roger Hoffman, and I represent the Department of State."

She nodded. "Good to meet you, sir."

"We could begin at many places and expend many words, but instead, I want to advance straight to the point of my visit. Your friend, Mr. Thomas Darden, is still missing and I want to express my empathy for your situation. I will do everything in my power to help find him safe and healthy."

"Thank you, Mr.—"

"Hoffman. And it is I who should thank you, for the facts you and Mr. Darden brought to the nation's attention. I watched your interview on television last night, and it made me feel good to know that we have such citizens."

"Thanks, but Tom is the real hero. I've just been tagging along."

"Hardly. You risked your life to do right, and that is no small thing."

She couldn't say much to that, but it unquestionably made her feel proud.

"Mr. Hoffman, thank you very much, but I don't think you came all the way down here just to praise Tom and me. Can you find him?"

He looked quickly at the Chief and over at the Raptor, smiled imperceptibly.

"Indeed," he said. "We must find him. Much depends on it."

"I don't understand."

"A man you don't know, a man who works for me, is with your friend. I sent him to help Tom uncover the truth, on an unofficial basis. Now, both are missing."

"What's his name?"

"Arvin Webber."

"Tom wouldn't tell me that, but I knew they were working together."

"Arvin is almost a son to me. I promised his wife and children I would bring him back. Now, I must deliver on that promise."

"Then, we—"

The door opened and yet another FBI agent entered. She was younger than the others, but her conservative clothes and brusque manner left no doubt she was with the task force. She wore her hair pulled back tight and secured behind her head. Vertical creases showed between her eyebrows.

Everyone looked up as she entered the room. The Chief and Hoffman showed a trace of annoyance at the intrusion.

"Pardon me," she said.

She had a cell phone to her ear, addressed the Raptor in an

urgent tone. "Sorry, to interrupt, sir, but Quantico just called. You'll all want to see this."

They watched as she went to a television sitting on a table at the end of the room. She flicked it on and found a news station in less than twenty seconds, adjusted the volume and stepped back so they all could see it.

The War Hawk was on the screen, speaking in mid-sentence, somehow maintaining his insider smirk even as he spoke to millions. He stood behind a lectern in a White House briefing room that was full of reporters who were restless and waved their hands for attention. Several Pentagon officials in uniform backed him up, their faces grim as undertakers.

The War Hawk looked into the camera, his measured voice droning without emotion.

"—increased terrorist activities in the President's absence. To meet this threat, we have elevated the country's security readiness to Level Red. All border activity ceases as of now and non-military air traffic is hereby grounded. Military and police units in every state are on the highest alert. Under authority of the latest provisions of the New Patriot Act, I hereby declare a national state of emergency and the United States of America to be under Martial Law."

The room erupted with dozens of voices shouting at once. A hundred questions flew at the War Hawk in seconds. It was impossible to separate a single coherent voice from the chaos of noise bouncing off the walls. The pandemonium grew as reporters jumped to their feet, yelling over each other. Several newscasters ran from the room, presumably to report the bombshell he had just dropped.

In the conference room at Fire Services even the FBI men showed emotion, mainly astonishment, their expressions of shock breaking through the usual stern mask. A couple of them looked at each other in dismay. The Raptor put an unsteady hand to his forehead.

Linda felt as if she could not breathe.

Mr. Hoffman looked as if he might have a heart attack at

any moment, she thought. "Oh, my word," he said quietly. "It has happened."

On the television, the War Hawk held up his hands for quiet in the briefing room. Most of the people present ignored him and continued talking loudly into their cell phones and shouting questions at him.

"Is the President aware of your action?"

"Who authorized you to—"

"What about the Attorney Gen—"

"—the Pentagon agree that—"

Again, the War Hawk raised his hands and motioned for silence. "Please, if you will allow me to finish."

"Where is the President—"

"—tell us why the threat requires—"

"Is the cabinet—"

"Please!" the War Hawk bellowed into the microphone. The word was an order, not a request. "Quiet!" he shouted.

The stunned crowd settled down and watched the hunch-shouldered figure glaring down at them from the podium. His face burned scarlet, his eyes blinking furiously behind the rectangular glasses. A general standing behind him seemed embarrassed and placed a hand on the War Hawk's shoulder to steady him.

Not sure what they were witnessing, the unsettled reporters and staff took their seats, becoming observers rather than hostile questioners.

He lowered his voice, but the mike was still open, "Damned unruly press. That's going to end."

They grew quiet and watched him closely. He calmed himself and returned to his written statement, read it as if the outburst had never occurred.

"—consider these steps necessary to maintain national security. The classified report we spoke of earlier clearly shows the bombing in Daytona Beach, Florida to be the work of Islamic factions from the Middle East. I will not allow further terrorist activity to undermine our way of life. While the President is absent, I will be in command of the armed forces to implement the rule of Martial Law here at home."

He gestured toward the Generals flanking him to step forward.

"Now, for additional details," he continued. "You may direct your questions to these brave men from the Pentagon. Tonight, I plan to address the nation on live television with further developments. Thank you, and God bless the United States of America."

As the War Hawk stepped down from the podium, the briefing room erupted again in a torrent of questions and shouts. A door opened to the left of the small briefing stage and he marched through the exit without any further word of explanation, an aide closing the door behind him.

Television coverage shifted instantly to the headquarters of the network. A news anchor appeared on the screen and began to summarize the briefing they had just witnessed. Even the seasoned newsman seemed rattled, his impassive face and voice cracking with a rare show of agitation.

A collective exhalation of tension ran through the conference room at Fire Services in Daytona Beach. The FBI men looked to the Raptor for direction; the announcement had clearly caught them too by surprise.

Linda felt limp, wrung out by the swiftness and gravity of the moment. Martial Law. It didn't make sense. The Daytona bombing was committed by an American agent, not Iraqi terrorists.

"What just happened?" she asked no one in particular.

Hoffman turned to her, his face a paler shade than she would have thought possible among the living. "Miss Ramsey, we have just witnessed a *coup d'etat* in the late, great United States of America."

CHAPTER 42

Hamed knelt in the cool dimness of the mosque and considered his options. His knees ached as they did every time he kneeled to pray and the arches of his feet often cramped in that position, but as always he maintained his outward show of faith even as he forced his mind to the task at hand.

It was time to make a decision about the American problem. Now that the reporter had disappeared, who would tell of the infidels' torture of Iraqis? Who would expose the lying ways of the Americans?

Most Muslims would consider it sacrilege to think of worldly problems during prayer. Certainly the Imam droning on at the front of the prayer hall would think it wrong, but Hamed had long ago abandoned such piety.

"*Allahu Akbar ...* "

Indeed, he no longer considered his own participation in prayers to be a sacred duty, for Allah no longer spoke to him in the same way as he once had. Over time, an understanding had come to him that destruction of human bodies—even westerners—was not a dictate of his religion. Fealty to Allah did not command torture and death. The need to commit those acts was instead a weakness inside his heart. Other than avenging his father, nothing he did to the Americans seemed pure any longer. Instead, it all seemed born of an unclean need to spill blood.

The price of his work on the battlefield had been high. Inside, his soul was black. Though he had done many wretched things and said they were done in the name of Allah, he could not maintain that illusion any longer, at least within himself. Publicly, he was still a believer, a warrior for the one true faith. Yet in his zeal for violence and retribution, he had lost that faith, and now he only felt crippled inside.

But again, what of the American problem? Weeks ago his men had collected evidence of American brutality from the man called Texas, beaten and burned the location of his files from the big American. Once the photos and videos were in his possession he knew exactly what to do with them. He sent copies to the reporter after he learned from his spies of the man's actions in the Green Zone. His spies inside the American compound were excellent; translators who had won the trust of naïve Americans. Americans who thought they could change his land. Who were they to say how Muslims should live? Stupid infidels.

He bent forward as ritual prescribed, touched his forehead to the carpet. The Imam chanted the prayers dutifully and all the faithful followed his lead.

" ... *Wa taba rakas muka wataʾala Jadduk ...* "

His spies learned that the reporter had been caught stealing photos from his fellow Americans then had been jailed for the act. The half-mad Khalid confirmed this, said they had shared the same cell for a time. According to Khalid, the American was a crusader, one who hated his own government's conduct of the war. That made the reporter useful to his plans. He wanted the world to know what Americans did to Iraqis.

Hamed then fed the reporter photographic evidence that would certainly be published in America. Those fools in the west allowed anything to appear on television and newspapers. By sending the evidence anonymously, he was confident the reporter would use it. Hamed wanted him to think the photos and videos were from some peace-loving fellow American, not a desert snake who hated them all, and it had worked just as he planned. The world was outraged. The Americans were shown in their true form. Jackals.

But now, just as Hamed prepared to send a final video, one that surely would enrage the American people to new heights, the reporter was no longer available. Perhaps some operatives inside the American government had dropped their guise of freedom and seized the reporter to shut him up. Regardless, the reporter was gone, so how could he best complete his aim to expose the true nature of the American occupation?

" … *Alhamdu lillahi* … "

After prayers, Hamed rose on his aching knees and feet, straightened his legs to loosen the muscles. Outside the prayer hall, he and his assistant retrieved their sandals and moved toward the exit. A few worshippers lingered in the mosque though it was time to return to work. We spend too much time and energy on ritual, he thought. More effort should go to action.

As he stepped outside and the hot afternoon sunlight hit his face, a thought occurred to him. Surely the idea must be straight from Allah; to have a thought coincide exactly with the light of the sun was a sign from on high.

Hamed turned to his assistant. "Did our latest reports from America not say a whore lives with the reporter?"

"Yes, a slut sleeps in his bed without the blessing of Allah."

"And we know her location?"

"Of course."

Hamed stroked his long gray beard and looked up at the sky in thanks. He knew now where to send the remaining video; she would release it just as the reporter would have done, thinking she honored him by imitation.

"Allah always provides for the true believer." Even when his faith grows weak, Hamed thought privately. Withholding his doubts, always resolute among subordinates, he spoke with his usual tone of conviction.

"Now, let us go kill more infidels."

CHAPTER 43

Linda stood in the lobby of the Roosevelt Hotel near the revolving doors and waited for the limousine to arrive at the curb outside. The car was late, which was no surprise with the streets as bogged down as they were. She had gladly accepted Mr. Hoffman's offer to escort her to the *CBS* studios. New York seethed with danger today and she welcomed the extra security his presence offered.

Dressed in her best business suit and unfamiliar heels, she felt apprehensive, yet charged with an energy that was familiar to her. It was much like the tense alertness she felt when arriving at an emergency scene with the siren wailing, knowing people were injured and that her actions might determine whether someone lived or died.

As she watched yellow cabs stop and pick up passengers outside the doors, her mind replayed the events that had brought her here. Since they first met in Daytona Beach two days earlier, the Under Secretary had used his best connections to arrange a live interview in New York with Manley Wells on *Sixty Minutes*. Hoffman even got her to New York on a government jet since commercial flights were grounded. A *Sixty Minutes* interview would offer the widest possible audience to her plea for Tom's safe return, so she agreed instantly to do it. She wanted to do anything that might help Tom survive.

Then it had all happened very fast, and now she found herself in New York on Sunday afternoon, watching and waiting as the streets erupted around her hotel, the riots starting the night before. All day it seemed as if the America she knew was shifting under her feet, morphing into a country she did not recognize.

Sixty Minutes readily agreed to the interview because they had broken the Abu Ghraib story four years earlier, and Tom's reporting so closely reflected that blockbuster revelation, they viewed this almost as a follow up piece. His mysterious disappearance also became a flashpoint in the national crisis over Martial Law. Both the left and the right equated his kidnapping as the work of an out-of-control government.

The War Hawk's unprecedented attempt to take over the nation's military and law enforcement apparatus had pushed the entire country to the brink of Civil War almost overnight. Anger quickly spilled into the streets and dominated the news as nothing had since anti-war demonstrators clashed with police over Vietnam. For those like her, too young to have experienced the sixties, it seemed as if the country was splitting apart along every possible dividing line—rich against poor, right against left, and north against south.

Everyone blamed everyone else for the trouble stalking the American landscape. Few agreed on a way to stop it.

To those old enough who had lived through earlier national turmoil, the events were tragic but seemed reparable nonetheless. That was one reason the Under Secretary arranged her *Sixty Minutes* appearance. He said if Linda could put a human face on the nightmare facing them all, it might pull moderate Americans together to oppose and defeat the War Hawk.

Her reverie broke when the doorman spoke to her and gestured with his hand, "Your car is here, ma'am."

The limo arrived at the curb and she stepped out of the hotel onto 45th and quickly took in the turmoil raging on the streets and sidewalks. Rioting had erupted periodically since last night, leaving overturned trash cans and glass from smashed windows littering the pavement. A car burned on the next block, dark smoke billowing from its charred body. Young people ran in every direction, some carrying weapons, many of them shouting slogans and threats.

Closer to the hotel, a small band of demonstrators had formed a line across 45th Street, blocking traffic in both directions. Their signs and costumes proclaimed them to be pro-constitution and anti-Martial Law. They sang the Star-Spangled Banner and wore Old Glory tee-shirts. A few had American flags draped over their shoulders.

They joined hands and chanted over and over with all the volume they could muster. "NO MORE TORTURE, NO MORE KILLING, DOWN WITH THE WAR HAWK, GOD BE WILLING!"

She hurried toward the car, then stopped, mesmerized as mounted New York City police emerged from alleyways to confront the marchers. The police walked their horses through gaps in the stalled traffic and formed a line opposing the demonstrators. Blood would be shed when those two lines met.

The driver opened the rear door of the limo, and Mr. Hoffman beckoned her from inside. She slid onto the seat next to him and settled back with an exhalation of relief.

"Whew, it's scary out there."

He took her hand and patted it. "You are brave young lady to come outside at a time like this."

She removed a thick satchel from her shoulder and placed it on the leather seat beside her, unconsciously kept one hand on it. The car pulled away from the curb and took a U-turn to avoid the line of demonstrators blocking traffic down the street.

"I couldn't do this without your help, sir."

His massive head turned toward her and all those folds of flesh around his eyes and mouth warmed into a faint smile. He was more reassuring than anyone she'd ever met. If only the leaders of the country had such calm confidence. The President had not spoken to the nation or even returned to Washington, for unknown reasons. Congress was in as much upheaval as the city streets, with members physically assaulting one another in hallways of the Capitol.

She would put her money on men like Hoffman, those who worked diligently behind the scenes to revoke the declaration of Martial Law and get the country back on track. She knew there were others out there like him, but were there enough?

He stayed on his cell phone constantly, taking reports from allies and calling other contacts to round up support for a counter-offensive against the War Hawk. According to his contacts, legal actions were being filed in every state to defy military takeover, he told her between calls.

"It is always touch and go, trying to avoid armed conflict."

She wondered if it would come to outright war.

The limo crawled along as traffic bogged down where debris and abandoned cars partially blocked the streets. On Park Avenue they detoured west to avoid a barricade of overturned trucks, burning tires, and barrels that rioters had erected overnight. They threw rocks from behind the barricade to keep a mob of stalled drivers and police from rushing the obstruction.

The barricade stood for the time being, but she saw military bulldozers backing off transports two blocks short of it. Tonight, the violence might be even worse as National Guard reinforcements poured into the city to suppress the rioters and clear the streets.

She grasped Hoffman's arm as a pair of wild-eyed teenagers ran up to their barely rolling limo and tried to smash the windows with baseball bats. Starbursts appeared where they struck, but the glass held.

"This is a State Department car designed to withstand attack," the driver explained.

The teenagers soon moved on to easier targets, but she had flinched when the blows landed. This was all crazy, pointless.

"It's hard to believe this is America," she said.

The Under Secretary nodded. "I know how you feel. So many times we've witnessed this chaos elsewhere in the world, but here it seems a bit unreal."

"How did everything get so out of control?"

"We'll have to leave that question to the historians."

A shiver of fear ran through her when she thought about the days ahead. From the television news, she knew violence was rampant in most every city. If she had been on duty in Florida, their orange and white would be working around the clock picking up casualties from fights and riots.

"I'm nervous," she said.

"You'll be fine. Just remember you are doing your best to rescue Tom and Arvin."

At the mention of his name, a touch of anger and frustration flared inside her. "Why hasn't the FBI found them yet?"

"I don't know, but just be glad the Bureau is on our side. They oppose the madman who started all this. Most of the state governments are still with us as well. I suspect your boyfriend is a key to our success in ending this lunacy."

"What about the military?"

"The military is teetering, could go either way, depending on which branch wins the argument. So far, the chain of command has not agreed to the invocation of Martial Law. The courts are firmly on our side, but intelligence agencies support the War Hawk."

"This is all so big. How can my interview help?"

He nodded easily. "Anything that puts more pressure on the captors might shake them up enough to release Arvin and Tom."

"Or kill them," she replied in an uncertain voice.

"My dear, if the kidnappers' intent were to kill them, I suspect it has already happened, and we could not affect the outcome regardless. But if they are still alive, your television appearance may help. Think of it that way."

His cell phone rang yet again. He answered it, listened for a minute, replied tersely. "Call me back as soon as you know more."

Mr. Hoffman turned and looked at her, his face so grave she went silent. She wanted to ask him what the call was about, wondered if he'd learned anything about Tom, but she held back the questions.

"Sir," the driver said. "The street's blocked ahead."

They looked up and saw the traffic stack into a snarl, then stop altogether. There was no way to see past the stopped cars to determine when they might move again.

"Check it out," Hoffman said.

The driver got out and jogged up the sidewalk, oblivious

to the chaos. He returned within three minutes and rapped on Hoffman's window. The Under Secretary buzzed it down.

"What is it?"

"A barricade of trucks blocking the street, with rioters manning it. No emergency vehicles are in sight to remove them. It could take hours."

Hoffman checked his watch. "We can't be late. Linda, would you be up for a jaunt through Rockefeller Center?"

She grinned to hide her doubts. "Whatever it takes."

They got out of the car and the driver pushed a path through the hostile crowd swarming on the sidewalk. Most of them appeared to be street punks, dangerous in the best of times. A few of the bigger ones shoved the driver back, but he knew his business and flattened two of them as Linda and Hoffman jogged through the opening. They picked up the pace and ran between two skyscrapers as several rioters screamed obscenities at them.

"Pigs!"

"Fascist bastards!"

Insanity, she thought. They don't even know who we are.

Ahead, she saw the plaza where the ice skating rink stood in winter, then almost stumbled as they sprang up two steps to an open area. Her feet were already killing her. Why did I ever wear heels, she thought, today of all days? The shoes won't even show on television.

They hurried toward the plaza, and she saw much of it had been vandalized. The Prometheus statue was missing an arm. A crowd clambered over it, hammering at the bronze with heavy pieces of pipe, trying to break off more parts. The driver steered them wide of the area, heading to the northwest.

Mr. Hoffman was surprisingly nimble, but his breath came in ragged jerks. He held on to her arm with a large, firm hand. She felt awkward jogging in her heels, the leather satchel flopping against her ribs. They emerged onto 6th Avenue and turned right, the wide street shooting straight north toward the black *CBS* building on the corner of 52nd—Black Rock, New Yorkers called it.

A line of marchers refused to give way on the sidewalk, and the driver steered them past the shouting group and out into the street which seethed with stalled traffic and angry drivers. Gangs of young men wandered among the cars, trying to break into them to rob the occupants. Curses and shrieks rose from the confrontations.

Still, the driver led the way north, pushing aside anyone who challenged them.

The black building grew larger, rising straight ahead as they ran, then Linda caught a heel in a grate and broke it off. She quickly abandoned her shoes without stopping. Barefooted, now huddling against Mr. Hoffman as they wedged their way between stalled cars, the three of them pressed forward. The driver slammed a car door blocking their way and they broke into the open intersection at 52nd, scrambling past wrecked taxis and brawlers swarming together like packs of dogs.

Finally, onto the sidewalk, then the entrance where two guards at the entrance of Black Rock saw the seriousness of their clothes and opened the doors to let them in. They plunged inside, wheezing and coughing from the exertion of the run, sweat and relief showing on their faces.

Safety.

CHAPTER 44

Even though Darden felt himself at the edge of an endless fall into darkness, the water kept pouring into his mouth. Darden tried to hold it back, but with his sinuses, throat and nasal passages overflowing, the reflexive muscles of his throat could not withstand the pressure any longer. He gagged and water flooded into his lungs. Convulsive coughing tore at his insides as he tried to disgorge the liquid.

Baines leering face hovered over him, watching as if drowning was an experiment of vast scientific import.

Gasping, Darden fought to raise his head, but found it impossible. He was strapped to a board with his head tilted lower than his body, and the restraints on his forehead and torso allowed little movement. With his lungs still trying to suck in air, the water went deeper and explosive heaving and simultaneous inhalations wracked his abdomen. No matter how hard he tried to clear the airways, his lungs continued to draw water inward.

Unable to obtain fresh oxygen, his breathing stopped and his vision went dark again.

"Whoops, almost too much that time," Baines said, raising the pitcher. It was a distant voice, heard through a heavy fog.

Several times since Baines first started drowning him, water had filled Darden's lungs and prevented oxygen from flowing to his brain. Early on, Darden guessed that Baines was keeping him under too long, likely in the mistaken thought that the technique would be more effective if pushed to the limit. But that was a long time ago, back when Darden could still think.

Each time Baines went too far and deprived him of oxygen,

Darden's vision started to fail and his breathing stopped. Then he felt life itself draining from his mind.

Yet the miraculous human body would not stop trying, even as the darkness came, he fought back. Shortly after the water stopped, his senses returned, his breathing restarted, then more coughing tore at his lungs and throat, his involuntary reflexes trying to expel water and suck in air simultaneously.

Each time Baines repeated the process, the drowning induced panic and an overwhelming fear of death that Darden found impossible to control. His heart rate shot up to deadly heights, became a jackhammer inside his chest, and then it climbed still more.

As the process went on, his mind, emotions and body converged and he became a struggling animal that knew the end was near but struggled all the harder because of that certainty. He was surprised he could think at all, but consciousness returned just when he felt he would die, as his lung passages cleared enough to take in a few gasps of restorative air, then his brain began to function again and he comprehended where he was and what was happening.

Every time he opened his eyes and realized he was still alive, Baines leaned over him and repeated the same tired questions.

"What do you know of our plans?"

Darden looked up at the grotesque face and glared in hatred.

"Tell me who else knows about us."

Darden refused him with a shake of his head.

"My, my, you are a stubborn man." Baines clucked his tongue. "You must have been mistreated as a boy."

Darden moved his chin to indicate he wished to speak. Baines removed the cloth covering Darden's mouth and allowed him a moment to recoup his voice.

"Go ahead," Baines urged.

Darden managed to choke out a few words despite his damaged vocal cords. "You are the ugliest fucking monster on this planet."

Baines frowned and lifted the watering pitcher with an

almost weary motion. He replaced the cloth over Darden's mouth and poured water through it again. He continued as the cloth became soaked and heavy, as the nasal passages and sinuses became clogged, and when the mouth and throat filled, he kept on pouring until Darden could not stop the accumulating force of the liquid by tightening his throat.

Once again, Darden's heart rate climbed to a level he'd never experienced before, the stressed organ ramming inside his chest like a piston.

Baines kept pouring until water overflowed onto Darden's face and hair and shoulders, his eyes blurred with it. Finally, the throat muscles gave way and he gagged again, inhaling still more liquid. The water flooded into his lungs as before and he inhaled desperately for air. This time his intake was so desperate, he sucked the cloth halfway down his throat while Baines held onto the protruding end. The wracking coughs and gasping for air grew, then Baines yanked out the cloth, tearing the lining of Darden's throat. More violent coughing followed, bringing up blood.

Then the water stopped and a few moments of respite began.

Baines shook a finger at him like a schoolteacher. "For that last remark, we will repeat this sequence three times before I give you a chance to speak again."

The man was stranger than strange, no doubt about that.

Even in his reduced state of consciousness, Darden could see the man took perverse pleasure in inflicting pain even though he maintained a pose of clinical distance. An occasional giggle of excitement and a quivering of the lips gave him away. He was so perverted, he enjoyed the suffering of his victim in an uncomprehending, childlike way. All that ugliness, Darden imagined, a lifetime of humiliation and despair had congealed in the man, making him a lover of torment. Inflicting pain was an elixir to the man, sweet relief from a life of numb disengagement.

Then the water again.

Darden knew what to expect and understood the effects of waterboarding, because he had researched it as he wrote about the resurgence of torture over the previous weeks. His mental notes were extensive, covering the long history of drowning torture and its infamous resurrection by the American intelligence community.

As Baines continued the process, Darden recalled everything he knew about it, reciting facts to himself in an attempt to counteract the physical torment and fear. Perhaps he would remember something that might help him survive longer. Since escape was no longer a possibility, only his survival offered hope of a small victory.

It was an ancient form of torture, he recalled, but a dangerous way to acquire information for it kept the victim on the cusp of death. More than a few men had died when the victim was kept under long enough to stop their breathing as Baines had him. Sometimes victims suffered brain damage; others drowned beyond the point of resuscitation; sometimes the heart simply stopped from prolonged tachycardia.

Drowning torture had been around for centuries, a relic of the most brutal governments of the past. Used by the Gestapo, the Khmer Rouge, and most infamously the Spanish Inquisition, drowning torture was a clumsy method of eliciting confessions even though the confessions were known to be tainted. Anyone undergoing drowning torture would eventually break down and say anything to make it stop. Most people broke within seconds and said whatever the torturer wished to hear.

Most recently, in one of the most advanced and humane nations in history it had been resurrected and renamed a bureaucratic euphemism—waterboarding. The War Hawk and his ilk further whitewashed the practice, calling it "simulated drowning." So much for the progress of humanity, Darden thought grimly.

He remembered reading the CIA's own definition of waterboarding, which he found in a depressing account of his nation's lapse into condoning torture as a useful and legal instrument of the state. From a memo leaked by the Justice Department, he had unconsciously memorized the definition by reading it many times as he attempted to unravel the mentality behind the practice.

The words from the memo had been burned into his brain from the very first time he scanned them on the internet weeks earlier: "*In this procedure, the individual is bound securely to an inclined bench, which is approximately four feet by seven feet. The individual's feet are generally elevated. A cloth is placed over the forehead and eyes. Water is then applied to the cloth in a controlled manner. As this is done, the cloth is lowered until it covers both the nose and mouth. Once the cloth is saturated and completely covers the mouth and nose, air flow is slightly restricted for 20 to 40 seconds due to the presence of the cloth ... During those 20 to 40 seconds, water is continuously applied from a height of twelve to twenty-four inches. After this period, the cloth is lifted, and the individual is allowed to breathe unimpeded for three or four full breaths ... The procedure may then be repeated. The water is usually applied from a canteen cup or small watering can with a spout ... it is likely that this procedure would not last more than twenty minutes in any one application.*"

What precise instructional detail, he thought, what sanitized language to describe the torment of a human being. The word itself—waterboarding—was a silly and useless term, one only the military establishment or some intelligence community ghoul would use. The act was drowning pure and simple, as anyone involved with it would attest, drowning slowed down to induce maximum pain and terror, but drowning nonetheless.

All these thoughts streaked through his mind in seconds as Baines pushed him once more toward a blackout. He felt sure one of these drops into the abyss of darkness would be so deep he would not return from it.

Then he deliberately pushed the details of water torture from his mind, trying to deny the pain. While he was still lucid, he made a decision. He would give torture, and depraved men like Baines, no more of his dwindling moments in this world.

He decided to die thinking about the people who mattered to him most.

He pulled up images of Linda walking on the beach, the soft look of affection on her face, the feel of her warm skin against his. He envisioned his father behind the wheel of his Buick, the backhanded wave he always used to say goodbye. Then Darden smiled inside and resigned himself to the inevitable outcome he could not control.

CHAPTER 45

His first words were gentle, calming, the issuance of a practiced voice. "Quite a roller coaster you've been on, Miss Ramsey."

The bright lights of the television studio had shut off her ability to speak and he was trying to help. The staring faces and waiting looks forced her to struggle for composure just as they had at the press conference in Florida.

"Yes," she said, barely managing to get the words out. "A roller coaster."

Manley Wells looked directly into her then, his large sad face seeming to know everything about her thoughts and past. His red-rimmed eyes seemed huge and brown, brimming with empathy, the whites showing a yellow tinge of age. She saw all the deep wrinkles beneath the make-up, imagined the lifetime of experiences that made them.

He waited a beat, probably allowing her to adjust a bit more to the tension of live national television.

"Tell us about Tom Darden."

She swallowed, stared back at him, frozen. Then somewhere inside her, Tom's presence made itself known. A warm confidence spread through her center and she began to speak. She could weather anything if it would help him survive.

"He is the best man I've ever known."

"What makes him tick?"

"The need to do right. He reported those things because he knows they are wrong. He hated the fact that his country had stooped to the level of thugs and terrorists."

"Why do you think he was kidnapped?"

"To shut him up. To stop him from writing more stories."

"Who do you think wanted to silence him?"

She wondered if she should speak her mind, just come out and say what she really thought, but would that help him or hurt? What was the smart thing to do? Then again, Tom's voice seemed to speak inside her. Don't think about the smart thing, it said. Just do the right thing. Tell the truth.

"I think it was the White House."

"The President?" Wells leaned closer, his voice heightened a notch. "You think the President of the United States had him kidnapped?"

"No, the other one—the one who really runs things—the one who declared Martial Law."

Wells was visibly surprised, didn't expect such a direct response. This pleased her; she knew he was accustomed to interviewees evading or bending the truth rather than telling it.

"That's an extraordinary accusation, Miss Ramsey."

His doubtful tone perked her up. "The War Hawk declared Martial Law to take over the country. The streets outside this building are filled with demonstrators and riots. Why would it surprise you that he had Tom kidnapped?"

Wells bent forward and rubbed his hands together; a glimmer of respect showed on his face as if he hadn't expected her to be so bold in her responses. He took his time now, formulated his next question carefully, she guessed. She could almost hear the wheels turning behind those all-seeing eyes.

"Some say Martial Law is justified, that it is a sensible response to terrorist acts in the absence of the President. Most legal experts are divided."

"What he is doing is not about national security."

"Then, what?"

"I can't answer that until Tom is found."

Dead silence fell on the studio, not a whisper, not a movement.

"You are saying the Administration is covering up something else?"

"Yes, that's exactly what I'm saying."

Wells appeared stunned, the wind knocked out of him, if that was possible with such a veteran. She guessed at what he was thinking now. Is she just a kook making a wild charge or is this really the biggest story in the history of American government?

"Why would they do that?"

"To hide the true reason for the takeover."

"Which is?"

"He wants control of the police and military for his own purposes."

Wells began to look distinctly uncomfortable. "What purposes?"

"Profit. Pure profit. He wants to privatize national security, turn it over to corporations."

Wells looked up at the control room, momentarily looking for direction on how to handle this astounding turn. His voice dropped again, conciliatory, coaxing. "I have to ask, Miss Ramsey, do you have proof?"

She picked up the leather satchel she'd lugged across Rockefeller Center and opened it. "I certainly do."

She began to remove pages of notes and discs and photos.

"This is Tom's research and a rough draft of the book he's almost completed. It proves the crimes of the Administration, including murder and torture committed by men working for the War Hawk."

Wells straightened in his seat, his eyes changing, now becoming the veteran reporter who smelled a larger story and could not help but push ahead. She sensed the change in him, the realization that the interview was far bigger than what he'd been promised. He wouldn't waste an opportunity for more revelations.

"If what you say is true, the whole case for Martial Law is a sham. The entire Administration is a disgrace."

The floor director signaled Wells to go to commercial. Wells turned his chair toward a second camera and the red light went on above the rectangular lens. He gathered himself and regained his on-camera voice and authority.

"We're talking with Linda Ramsey, the girlfriend of

266   •   David Darracott

presumed kidnapped reporter, Tom Darden. In my thirty plus years with *Sixty Minutes*, I've never heard a more electrifying set of allegations. After this station break, we will continue with our live interview. Please stay tuned."

He turned back to Linda and smiled. "This is quite a story to share with—"

Wells stopped talking and reached for his earpiece, listened closely to a message coming from the control room. Alarm, perhaps astonishment, appeared on his face.

"What? Are you sure?"

Everyone in the studio stopped and watched him.

"Now?"

He listened a second more.

"Yes, of course. I go as soon as—"

The floor director used his fingers again to signal a return to live cameras in four, three, two, then a forefinger pointed at Wells. The red light went on above camera two and the veteran was set, looking wise and steady as ever at the big lens. Even handling an ad lib on a major news development, he never wavered.

"We interrupt our live interview with Linda Ramsey for a remarkable announcement. Though unconfirmed, inside sources tell us Tom Darden may have been found. The missing reporter who took the Administration to task over the issue of torture is possibly being held at a location not yet disclosed. We now go live to our man in Washington for this update."

Linda was out of her seat, tearing off her mike before the red light on the camera went dark.

CHAPTER 46

The Bell Ranger banked steeply above the Virginia countryside, taking a sharp turn to the south, tilting the passenger window toward the earth where Linda saw green pastures with tree lines running along the creeks, even though it was almost dark below. The watercourses twisted their way between the hills and down the slopes toward the larger streams and rivers that lay farther east. To the west, the last rays of orange sunlight shot over the horizon.

She fought her jumpy stomach and clutched the handholds available to her as the pilot maneuvered the helicopter in a random series of dips and climbs combined with quick moves to the left and right. She heard the intercom crackle with static in her headphones. The pilot must have read the nausea on her face.

"Sorry," he said, his voice breaking apart electronically. "But I have no intention of swallowing an anti-aircraft missile. You can't be too sure about security the last few days."

She nodded and tried to swallow back the bitter taste rising in her throat. The only other helicopter ride she'd ever taken was during her E.M.T. training on an air rescue unit, but it had been nothing like this. This was a violent and wildly fast roller coaster ride, but she really didn't mind. She was grateful for it. Every minute in the air put her closer to Tom.

Oh Lord, let him be okay, she repeated to herself.

Only at this moment had she realized the full extent of Mr. Hoffman's clout. Within minutes of leaving the *CBS* studio, he'd arranged an FBI flight to meet her on top of the old Pan Am building. They called it the Met Life building now, he told her, and its helipad hadn't been used in years, but for this flight they would make an exception.

His limo was waiting at the curb outside Black Rock by the time they reached the lobby.

Inside the car was the same tough driver who had helped them reach the building on foot earlier, but this time he steered the car back around Rockefeller Center with no problems. There was still sporadic fighting and chaos on the sidewalks, but the National Guard had begun to take over the streets, directing traffic through intersections and clearing barricades which allowed traffic to flow again.

The limo dropped her at the curb beside the MetLife building and Mr. Hoffman sent her off with a nod and a wave of good luck, a cell phone still pressed against his left ear. A security guard met her at the main entrance and escorted her to an express elevator that shot straight up seventy-seven floors where it opened onto a flight of metal stairs that led to the roof. When the guard unlocked the door at the top of the stairs, she saw the helicopter waiting outside on the helipad, its rotors whirring at idle speed.

As she ran toward it, wind tore at her hair and clothes, a cool ocean wind coming up the Hudson like a rough thief, pulling at her possessions. She held onto the leather satchel with all her might. Thank the Lord she'd had the presence of mind to snatch it up when she ran off the *Sixty Minutes* set.

And thank you Mr. Hoffman, she thought. Thank you for your connections and for this helicopter, and most of all, for your sense of duty. Without your humanity and your power, they might never have found Tom.

The pilot's voice sounded through the headset. "That's it, straight ahead. Those are assault units arriving."

It was dark now, and all she could see of the FBI teams were the headlights of cars converging on a dark building. There was also a spot where a tarp had been set up, with lights glowing beneath it. Perhaps it was an outdoor command post of some sort. As they got closer, she realized the cars and people were gathering in a parking lot outside the building which was old and completely dark, apparently abandoned.

Still closer, she saw what it once was. With its guard towers and high fences positioned around the perimeter, it reminded her of an empty carcass. Cell blocks and barred windows formed the dead body, stark remains of what had once been a dangerous living thing, a hive seething with an endless ferocity.

Why an old prison, she thought? Who would use such a place?

The helicopter landed in a storm of rotor wash, kicking pine needles and dust up from the ground. The pilot powered down and reminded her to exit to the front of the machine. "Don't go near the tail rotor." Then he gave her a thumbs-up and she removed the headset, climbed out of the seat and jumped to the ground.

She bent over instinctively and duck walked toward the lit-up area underneath the tarp. The first person she recognized made her heart jump.

"Chief!"

She ran to him and lost all restraint. He almost smiled as she threw her arms around his neck and hugged him in relief. He patted her back while she clung to him, her nerves clanging with a mixture of tension and relief.

"Oh, Chief. I'm so glad you're here." She pulled back and looked into his bloodshot eyes. "Where's Tom?"

"We're not sure yet, Linda, but the FBI thinks he may be in there," he said. He turned his head toward the dark building and lifted his chin. "This place has been under surveillance for days and our directional listening devices tell us that a number of people are being held prisoner inside by a renegade group that's somehow tied to the War Hawk."

Her eyes followed his and she saw the rusting wire, the concrete block walls, the wire mesh and bars on the windows. She felt another tremor of dread—the worst one yet—cascade through her body. She started walking toward the building, but the Chief took her arm gently and drew her back.

"Not yet. Try to be patient. And remember, he might not be

in there."

All around them, men in black jumpsuits and helmets started to gather. Dozens of them fell into place and gave their weapons a final check and assembled into teams. Ready now, they fell quiet and waited, stood at attention until a trio of men emerged from beneath the tarpaulin, headsets on and radios in their hands. The three of them appeared to be in charge and didn't carry rifles, but she saw black pistols at their waists.

The tallest stepped forward and began to speak. She recognized him as the Raptor from Daytona Beach. As commander of the assault team, he was higher ranked than she ever guessed; perhaps a Deputy Director. From the looks on the faces surrounding him, he carried a lot of respect with the team.

"Men," he said quietly. "And ladies. Remember first and foremost, this is a rescue mission. Our first job is to protect the lives of any captives. Secondly, we are to capture anyone else alive, if at all possible. Keep the perimeter secured. No escapes. They undoubtedly know we are here. Fire only if a captive or you yourselves are under immediate threat. I do not have to restate the importance of this mission. The future of our nation may be at stake. Assume your positions and wait for the go signal. Do your jobs well. That's all."

They nodded in assent and moved off quickly to their respective locations. The urgency in the air was palpable. The Chief escorted Linda to a safe position behind a van with heavy gauge wire screens over the windows, built for carrying prisoners.

A second later, immense floodlights came to life around the perimeter and illuminated the building, the grounds, and the surrounding wall as if it were high daylight outside. Most of the lights sat on top of the building and its watchtowers.

An authoritative voice blasted from a loudspeaker system inside the compound.

"Do not enter! In the name of the Executive Branch of the United States, do not enter this facility. It is protected by the forces of Martial Law and national security. If you try to enter this facility, your lives will be in jeopardy! I repeat—"

Before the voice could finish the warning, a dozen radios sounded the same word. "Go!"

Boots scraped against the earth and a quiet sense of movement emanated from the darkness as barely seen figures rushed toward the compound. At the same time a dozen or more rifles opened up and the floodlights inside the compound shattered. The loudspeaker emitted a screeching whine, then died altogether. Darkness returned, darker than ever.

Standing behind the van, watching through its thick windows, Linda saw a glass-distorted movie of the FBI at work. A team of three rushed the main gate located between a pair of guard towers. Two of the men went at the task of securing a charge on the gate's locking mechanism, then another on the hinges to one side. The third kept an assault rifle pointed up at the towers to protect the team.

A silhouette appeared on the catwalk of the tower to the right, but rifle fire from three directions stopped the figure instantly. The silhouette melted into the deck of the catwalk and disappeared from her field of view.

Dead, just like that, she thought. This assault unit knows its business. If anybody can get Tom out alive, it's them.

The demolition team withdrew from the gate and a second later a compact explosion ripped the gate from its mounting posts. Before the smoke and dust cleared, she saw the team leader signal a second unit of three men who waited near their van. They assumed a one-knee down position in the shadows and fired grenade launchers at a high arcing angle into the compound.

The grenades landed with a loud thumping sound rather than explosions, and smoke began to spew from the point where they landed. Within seconds, thick roiling clouds of smoke filled the compound and enveloped the gate and guard towers.

She could hardly see a thing except members of the assault team charging the downed gate and disappearing into the smokescreen beyond. She heard shots inside the compound and men shouting. Radios crackled with static. More FBI men moved into place alongside the van, wearing gas masks and carrying short barreled automatic rifles. They had some sort of grenades hooked to their waists on a special belt.

She looked at the fat grenades and couldn't help but think they were too much firepower, turned to the Chief who saw the worry on her face. She couldn't conceal it from him, didn't even try.

"Those are just stun grenades," he said. "This team will work the hallways and rooms inside the building as soon as it's secured."

"But—"

"The grenades aren't high explosives. They're designed to disable anyone who might be a threat inside—without killing them."

A radio squawked a command to the team and they moved out at a run and disappeared into the smoke ahead. More automatic rifle fire sounded from within the building. Shouts and commands echoed somewhere inside. The smell of gunpowder and smoke reached them and stung the inside of her nose. This all seemed like a movie, but it wasn't; it was real and deadly.

Linda felt as if insects were crawling on her skin. She couldn't stand any more of the waiting. She had to know.

"Sorry Chief—" she said, tearing her arm from his grasp.

Then she was free, running toward the gate as fast as she could go despite the warning shouts and orders to stop that came from behind her. In seconds, nothing but smoke all around her.

CHAPTER 47

She groped through the darkness, trying to keep away from the flashlight beams that slashed through the gloom. They were FBI flashlights, but if one of them saw her she knew they'd drag her back outside in a second. Holding her breath as long as she could, her eyes had to remain open and they began to pour tears.

Needing a breath, she dropped to the ground and pulled her skirt up over her mouth and nose, breathing through the fabric. It helped a little but the air smelled like chemicals and burned her throat and lungs. Still she moved ahead, sometimes on her hands and knees, and reached the main wall of the old prison, saw double metal doors blown open and flashlight beams guiding more agents through the opening.

Crawling toward the dim glow of the doorway, Linda wondered if she would make it, though the opening was only ten yards away. She had never coughed so hard or felt such difficulty breathing in her life. Whatever the smoke was, it disabled people by causing respiratory lockdown.

"There!" she heard someone yell inside. "Three o'clock!"

A burst of gunfire followed and more voices shouting, "This way!"

Her throat constricted and her lungs rebelled when she tried to draw in air; the coughing grew worse, expelling what little amount of air she managed to inhale. She focused on breathing slowly, but it did not help. No oxygen seemed to reach her lungs and she knew she was close to passing out. She coughed and wretched with the violence of a dying person, struggling against a heaving involuntary response that would not stop.

What a foolish thing to do, she realized, as if reaching Tom in her condition would somehow help, but she hadn't thought about the impulse to get inside. She had simply reacted, driven by her fear for him, by her need to be near him.

A few feet closer to the opening, she could barely make it out. Heavy tears distorted her vision of the wavy rectangle to the point she could hardly see anything, but she continued to crawl forward, not knowing what else to do. Flashlight beams inside the doorway seemed to promise rescue of some sort, though she couldn't have said why. Perhaps her survival instincts simply chose light over darkness.

She was almost to the doorway when someone tripped over her.

A pair of hard legs connected with her right side and knocked her all the way down. An agent fell over her body and onto the pavement as one boot caught against her ribs.

"What the—" he yelled, turning to see what he'd run into.

She was flat, almost out. The collision had taken what remaining strength and self awareness she had left. Her body hurt all over.

"What the hell are you doing here?" the agent demanded.

She could only cough in reply. His flashlight blinded her for a moment as she tried to speak again, but she could not stop coughing. Next thing she knew he put a breathing unit over her face and she felt the sweet relieving presence of oxygenated air swirl into her mouth and nose.

A second later, another man knelt beside her, and she could just make out his face through the distorting Plexiglas of the visor. It was the Chief. He pressed the mask to her face for a tighter seal and bobbed his head with reassurance.

He patted the agent on the shoulder. "I'll take care of her from here."

The agent nodded, stood, and ran off into the doorway.

She looked up at the Chief weakly and tried to say thanks, but it took too much effort. As least the coughing began to subside a bit as she felt the restorative power of oxygen in her throat and lungs. Only now, with the return of breath, she noted the pain in her ribs and a burning sensation on her bare legs. Oh Lord, she thought, what was the stuff they used in the smoke?

A couple of minutes later she sat up, though aching and shaky.

"You crazy, crazy girl," the Chief said finally. "You must love this Darden guy so much it hurts."

She nodded and started to cry again.

"That's okay," he said. "I remember what that's like, even though it was a long time ago. Can you stand up yet?"

She nodded and got to her feet with his help. She felt beat up, but solid on her bare feet. Still, no shoes.

"Let's go find him," she said. "Okay?"

"Okay, Linda."

By now the smoke was thinning and the commotion had died down. An occasional pair of agents walked back out of the main doors of the prison, moving slowly with the drained look of men coming down after a firefight. A medical team passed them at a jog and hurried inside with their gurney.

Linda and the Chief followed the medics, unsure where else to go.

Inside the building they saw prisoners lined up, facing one wall of a corridor where the FBI agents had them down on their knees, fingers locked behind their heads, plastic tie-down handcuffs on their wrists, shirts stripped down to the waist. The prisoners were quiet and had the look of defeat about them.

But her main question remained unanswered. Where was Tom?

They went farther down the corridor and saw the Raptor on the radio, two agents waiting for instructions alongside him. The Raptor looked up, saw the Chief and Linda, motioned for them to follow. He started walking, put away the radio and turned a corner to the right.

"There, up ahead," he said to them. "Prepare yourselves before you go inside the room."

A cluster of agents stood outside a set of double doors. At

that moment, the power came on inside the building and bright lights flickered overhead, buzzing to full intensity. From the room, a wash of illumination poured out and lit up the agents in the hallway where they milled about in their assault gear and jump suits, helmets and weapons in their hands, eyes fixed on the room as if they were watching some sort of exotic animal in a cage.

Linda's knees felt weak as the Chief held her arm and guided her toward the doorway. The agents parted like guests at a funeral. She took a deep breath and they stepped into the fluorescent glow of what had once been the prison infirmary. The room was crowded with medical rescue teams and forensic people already at work with their evidence-gathering equipment.

At first glance the room looked like a massive crime scene. Blood pooled on the floor near several bodies that had been shot to death by the assaulting agents. The dead men wore military camos, but no insignia or unit patches. The room must have been their last stand where they tried to fend off the FBI raid. Splatters of blood and fragments of human tissue stuck to the white tile walls and ceiling. Already the place smelled of death.

Had she not been accustomed to seeing crime victims and the human damage caused by car accidents, she surely would have fainted. This was the way she imagined a battlefront hospital would look: bodies and blood, rudimentary lifesaving equipment, and piles of stained bandages. She could not see over the taller people.

"Where is he, Chief?"

He answered by tilting his forehead toward a gurney parked at the far side of the room, but her view of it was obstructed by a crowd of agents struggling to subdue someone in a corner. Screams and hoots, rants of lunacy sounded from somewhere among the crowd, noises like those of a baboon or perhaps a hyena.

They moved through the shifting bodies and reached the gurney where four medics performed CPR and rigged IV lines to a prone body. She broke through them and exploded into screams of her own, all in a single rush.

To her experienced eyes, Tom looked dead already. His color was wrong; no pink beneath the surface of the skin at all, pallid and motionless, except for the shudders that ran through his torso on every compression of his chest. One medic had inserted a tube down Tom's throat and squeezed the air bag on its upper end in a careful cadence, timed to alternate with the chest compressions. Something else was wrong, too. His nose and mouth looked raw and bloody as if the flesh had been torn from them.

Her mind instantly assessed the team as professionals. They moved with cool efficiency about the body, checking and probing, taking careful steps to revive someone whose heart and lungs have failed, but they weren't moving fast enough for her.

She moved closer and slid between two of them, put her hands on Tom's bare leg. The flesh was cold, much too cold for a living person. The feel of him was so deathly cold it seemed to transfer up her hands and arms then spread throughout her own body, a deep chill that wrapped around her spine and made her shudder.

One of the medics had dug some hot packs out of his kit, activated them, and he placed the packs strategically around Tom's core, trying the keep the body temperature up. But Linda was more concerned with his respiration and lack of oxygen to the brain.

"How long has he been under?"

"We don't know," one of them answered. "We've only been in here about a minute, maybe less."

"Any pulse?" she asked with a tremor.

"Not that we can detect by touch. We need electrodes to know more."

She pushed forward and pressed her head to his chest. Nothing.

"Stand back, please." A medic pushed her away from the body.

She shook him off violently, her anger taking over, anger that her lover might not come back. Ever. His brain might already be ruined. She took the medic by the front of his shirt and held him in a clench to get his attention.

"Do you have a de-fib unit?" she demanded.

He looked her up and down.

"Do you?" she screamed.

"Of course."

"Then boost him. Right now."

"First we—"

"Now!"

She sobbed and screamed at the same time, but only a shattered thought came out. "Or there won't be anything left to save."

CHAPTER 48

He came to consciousness with a lurch, then a moan, and felt himself breathing heavily, a wet rattle rising from deep in his chest. He wondered for an instant if he was alive or dead, because he saw bright lights above, so bright they burned through his closed eyelids, causing him to see the red arteries lining the insides of them. He remembered reading that people saw bright lights ahead as they were dying, lights that beckoned them to the next world.

Then he felt—or was it that he recalled—the sensation of fire exploding through his body, jolting his limbs and organs, a massive stiffening of muscles that released and became movement and then brought the return of feeling in his nerves. From his chest, that was it! The fire came from his chest, triggering some movement, yet he felt incredibly heavy, weighed down with torpor so deep that he could not raise a hand if he tried.

His eyelids were red from the bright lights; he tried to open them but they were too heavy to move. Then pain came, mostly in his throat and abdomen, a pain so profound he knew he was not dead. No pain such as this could survive death.

A high, wrenching sound hit his ears, clanging in his head, a sound that had a bestial quality to it. Where was he to hear such a thing? Then many voices overlapped each other, shouting and giving orders, coming from the same place. He sensed struggle, and movement, plenty of bodies working together and muscling against something that was wild and wrestling against them.

Then the sound again, a screeching sound, mixed with some words or perhaps only syllables pouring from an uncontrolled mouth. The sound bounced off the walls and ceiling and raised his thought processes a notch higher until something like recognition registered in his brain.

It was the monster, the ugly monster whose demented yowl of a face was the last image he had seen before the blackness enclosed him. Yes, that was the sound the monster made during the progress of torturing him, the same monster who had fallen, or regressed, toward some interior nightmare, babbling insults and curses as he fell inward, and finally mouthing fears so deep and terrifying that his monstrous face and essence became even more distorted with self-loathing.

That was the sound he remembered hearing during the choking and gagging of his own body, the sound that had risen higher and higher with each pour of the water until it became a beast screaming in a dark jungle. It came from the warped, vindictive, raging monster who had tried to kill him.

With enormous effort, Darden raised an eyelid open a fraction and saw the monster squatting on top of a table, ranting and screaming at the men surrounding him. As they attempted to grab and restrain his limbs, the men shouted orders and warnings to each other while the monster whirled, stood, and danced on the table with his hands swishing down toward one, then again toward another.

A metallic object flashed momentarily in one of the monster's hands, a hand covered with blood and gore. One of the men reaching for him grunted with pain. The monster squealed in delight and stepped sideways, then the flash of metal appeared against his own face, and Darden saw that the ghastly face was a bloody mask covered with criss-crossing slashes where the monster had used the scalpel on himself.

The monster had gone fully insane, perhaps from the threat of death or capture, and tried to remove the badge of ugliness that had warped his entire existence. Finally taking control of all the rejection and fear and self-disgust that had marred his life, he attempted to destroy the source of it by complete disfigurement. His hatred of his own horrific appearance had finally exploded in an orgy of self destruction.

On command the men backed away and let the monster rant and slash himself at will. The blade rose again and slashed across his nose and cheek, gouged the eye above it, blood spraying profusely from the wound.

Then another group of men appeared. They unfurled a large plastic sheet and tossed it accurately over the monster, pulled down the corners. The job was over in seconds as they subdued and disarmed the raving maniac then carried him from the room.

Darden fought to keep his eyelid open and realized he'd been brought back from the dead. Somehow he was still alive. Rescued.

Then he felt her—Linda's hands on him—it could only be her. The fine, strong hands with a lightly calloused touch, the back of them grooved by raised, slender tendons. He managed to keep his eyelid cracked just long enough to see her face moving close to his then he felt her warm breath on his skin, her lips pressing against the raw surface of his face.

Rescued. She'd saved him yet again.

CHAPTER 49

Darden wasn't sure exactly why he had been summoned to the place known among military personnel as Naval Support Facility Thurmont, but he intended to make the most of it. Few people ever got a chance to meet with the President privately and he saw it as a one-time opportunity to ask questions—a reporter's questions. Even if he did not get many of the answers he wanted, the President's lack of response would provide answers in itself.

Most of all he wanted to know if the Administration was responsible for his kidnapping and torture. If so, the crowning story in his months' long effort of reporting on the misdeeds of the Administration would also be the biggest. To his thinking, this meeting would provide the opportunity to complete his investigation.

The public knew of the presidential facility as Camp David, and Darden had always known it as the President's weekend retreat in the Maryland mountains, but from the seat facing Darden, Undersecretary Hoffman said it was much more than that, always had been. Far away from the prying and scrutiny of Washington, it was actually an ultra-secure location where the President could do serious business privately. Guarded by specially selected Marines who were trained solely to protect the President and his guests, it was a place where many Chief Executives chose to meet with world leaders in seclusion.

Driving through the forests of the Catoctin Mountains in a State Department limo, Hoffman told them that the President had remained secluded at Camp David ever since the Martial Law crisis erupted. No one was sure if he was hiding out from the public or staying here due to genuine security concerns. Perhaps an assassination attempt had been part of the whole plan behind the declaration of Martial Law.

"Why doesn't he address the country, at least?" Darden asked in a raspy voice. "Just to let us know he opposed the War Hawk's takeover. He could have stopped this Martial Law thing in its tracks with one statement to the press."

Hoffman smiled cryptically. "With this President, who knows?"

The words held in the air as Darden sifted his own thoughts about the man who had served so uncertainly and recklessly. In too many ways, even on the most drastic decisions ranging from the Iraq invasion to allowing torture of suspects, he had abdicated decision-making again and again to subordinates in an apparent attempt to keep himself above the controversy of those acts. But it was impossible to be sure about the man's motives, because he seemed unable to acknowledge or even understand the import of his actions. Was he indifferent to the consequences of his decisions? Or was he playing crafty by allowing blindly loyal staff to act as lightning rods and ultimately to serve as culprits? Or perhaps, Darden thought, it was as so many feared; the Chief Executive just wasn't up to the job, was not able to perceive the outcome of the policies he'd put in motion. It was almost as if the President's mind was so simplistic he had no ability to see where his decisions might lead or even to consider future results when he rushed to action. Perhaps he just wasn't smart enough or reflective enough to think things through before he did them.

Linda patted him on the thigh and broke his introspection.

He turned his head painfully to look at her. The smile on her face was the most radiant thing he'd ever seen, full of warmth, a sunburst of life. She sat close to him, her body tucked up against his on the leather seat, and her breasts felt full and soft against his arm. At last, it seemed luck had found him in life. Since his rescue, she wouldn't leave his side, would hardly even let him go into another room by himself as if somehow he would disappear and never return.

He looked into her eyes to reassure her that he was back for good and squeezed her hand as he thought how grateful he was to be alive. Then he wondered what sort of country they would live in for the rest of their days. Would it be free from the grip of national police and surveillance or would it descend into the sort of state where its citizens lived in perpetual fear?

Perhaps he would get answers to that question today.

The limo stopped at three separate checkpoints for identification and passes, each stop more thorough than the previous one. Before the guards allowed them to proceed up the hill toward the collection of rustic lodges that made up Camp David, they searched the leather satchel he carried and scanned it with electronic devices, but after a thorough inventory of the papers and discs inside they finally let him keep it. At each stop they did the same with the Undersecretary's brief case and with Linda's purse.

A half hour later they sat down in the Laurel Lodge conference room, he and Linda side by side at the big table. Undersecretary Hoffman joined the Senate Majority Leader on the other side of the table; between them sat the Speaker of the House and the Director of the FBI who had been waiting in the room when they arrived. There were no formal introductions or small talk, only a couple of grim nods exchanged in greeting.

Other than the Secret Service men who stood silently in the corners, no one else appeared until the President came into the room wearing jeans and a hunting shirt, the kind with padded shoulder patches to cushion recoil from a shotgun. He closed the door himself and sat down at the head of the table very casually, looking as if this was to be an ordinary briefing. He rolled his eyes and rocked his head from side to side to stretch his neck muscles or perhaps to dissipate nervous tension.

"Well," he said. "You got your meetin', gentlemen. What's it gonna be?"

Then he looked at each of them quickly, avoiding eye contact. His own narrowly spaced eyes gave him the appearance of stupidity, but he seemed serious enough until he adopted his usual smirk, not quite a laugh or smile, just a childish smirk as if he wanted to show he was one of them, cool and relaxed in a crisis.

No one returned a smile or offered a greeting.

"Here we are," he said. "Imagine this. A little ol' constitutional crisis and just the handful of us to sort it out." He let loose the peculiar small laugh he frequently made under his breath, as if laughing to himself. "Life can be funny that way."

The FBI Director spoke first, his voice hard and flat, his bald head bristling with a few short gray hairs. "Mr. President, there is no humor in this. The country is on the verge of Civil War."

"We have insurrection in the streets," the Senator added.

"Congress is divided," the House Leader said loudly. "Completely paralyzed. "

Finally, Under Secretary Hoffman spoke. "You must speak to the nation to restore order."

The President laughed lightly. "Well, I don't know if it's all that bad out there."

The Under Secretary frowned in dismay and lowered his eyes to the table. The others looked at each other, baffled, as if to say, who wants to try next?

The FBI Director tossed a pile of newsmagazines on the table. The covers all had photos of rioting on them, with burning cars and mobs battling in the streets.

"Look at these, Mr. President. Chicago. Atlanta. Los Angeles. Riots everywhere," he said.

The President hardly glanced at the magazines.

"The government is split along the lines of Martial Law," said the FBI Director. "The Joint Chiefs cannot decide which way to go. With each branch of service unsure whether to cooperate or not, their commanders won't budge. Most Federal agencies are opposed to the declaration, but some are wavering. The Supreme Court refuses to decide the issue quickly."

The President kept his eyes on a window.

"Some states are talking about defying Federal authority altogether," the Senator said. "Actually seceding!" His pink face glowed with emotion, his eyes bugging out. "You must act."

The President leaned back and put one leg up on the table; the bottom of his boot was caked with mud and manure. He'd been riding before they got here. His eyes wandered the room when they finished; none of the bad news registered on his face which maintained a blank expression.

"Well," he said, examining a fingernail. "I figgered this thing would just blow over if I stayed out of it."

The others looked at one another with incredulity. This man was the leader of the free world? He really did not get it. It was a wonder he had not blown everyone up by now.

"Sir," Mr. Hoffman said calmly, "I have served in the State Department under five Presidents, and I have never seen the nation in such a state of crisis. You must denounce the declaration of Martial Law and hold the War Hawk to accounts for his actions."

The President's eyebrows shot up, the first sign any of this had dented his thoughts. "I know he's a bit headstrong when it comes to fighting the bad boys, but we need him on our side."

Darden had heard enough. He had nothing to lose; this idiot had damn near cost him his life.

"Mr. President," he said. "He is not on our side or yours. He is acting on his own, trying to take over the country by force while you hide out here riding horses. That is treason."

"Who the hell are you?" the President shot back with contempt. "What do you know about anything?"

"He is the reporter I told you about, Mr. President," said the FBI Director. "He brought some painful facts to light."

At last, Darden's frustration got the best of him. President or not, somebody had to get through to this mountain of density.

"Listen to me," Darden said harshly, his damaged voice hissing with outrage. "I believe he gave the order to torture me and then have me killed."

The President glared at him and said nothing. The others watched as Darden kept his eyes locked on the President, demanding an answer.

"Didn't he, Mr. President?"

"I don't believe it." The President brought his hand down on the table with a loud slap. No one moved. "Why would he want to do that?"

Linda spoke up, her voice steady but heated. "He did it because Tom knows something terrible about him."

The smirk appeared again, his way of discrediting her before she even said anything. "And what might that be, young lady?"

"Tom knows he ordered the hotel bombing in Daytona Beach."

CHAPTER 50

"That crazy bastard!" the Senator screamed.

The revelation about Daytona set off a loud argument, and the furor raged back and forth across the conference table for twenty minutes as the men from Congress hurled accusations and insults at the President, and he responded with threats of retaliation. Even Linda got into it, denouncing the President as an unethical rube who was destroying the country. Darden did not have enough of a voice left to join the fight.

The Secret Service stood on edge, their eyes darting uncertainly, each of them ready to pounce if any violence broke out. Mr. Hoffman and the FBI Director remained fairly calm as the noise gradually subsided. Eventually, the outraged men exhausted themselves and settled back into their seats.

"I still don't believe it," the President concluded.

Darden opened the leather satchel and removed a digital video disc. Placing it on the conference table, he said with his weak voice, "I have proof."

At that, the President lost all his bravado and the expression on his face fell to abject defeat. It was easy to read his thoughts; he knew the game was up. There would be no squirming out of this crime; a bombing that killed hundreds was no ordinary political scandal that would blow over. This was mass murder, committed by his right hand man.

The President eyed the disc. "Is that the only copy?"

Darden shook his head no, grinned without humor at the President's pathetic attempt to grasp for straws.

"Then you have been withholding evidence," he tried.

⋅   The FBI Director shook his head as if he were watching a guilty child. "No, Mr. President. He made the contents of the disc available to us weeks ago."

"Charlie," the President said to one of the Secret Service men. "Put this disc in that player over there, and let's just find us out what sort of cards this reporter is holdin'."

As they watched the video recording of Hoyt Bellows' torture, the President flinched repeatedly. Even though Darden had edited it for time, the recording still conveyed the terrifying reality of the man's painful death. The members of Congress appeared horrified at the brutality of it. These were men who routinely ordered others to their deaths, he thought, but they couldn't stand it when faced with actual suffering.

When the disc came to the point where Bellows confessed that the War Hawk had hired him to bomb the hotel in Florida, the President sank back in his chair and sat slumped through the remainder of it.

Darden thought about the chain of events the President had set in motion, trumping up the threat to the nation from terrorists, shamelessly playing on the fears of the public, and finally making the case for unchecked aggression against anyone suspected to be a threat. Now it all came home to roost. Had it never occurred to the man it would eventually lead to this?

When the grisly show was over, Darden said, "I didn't release it immediately because the FBI asked me to keep it secret."

The President's voice was low. "And why would these good servants of the people do that?"

The Undersecretary straightened in his chair, leaned forward. His face took on a look of composure and resolution that had been a lifetime in the making, and it occurred to Darden that he had been engineering this moment for weeks. Mr. Hoffman lacked a major office, but in all ways he was vastly more presidential than the man who held the title. He was a center of power because of who he was, not what he gave people. How different, Darden wondered—and how much better—the country would be if it elected men like him as President rather than men of such low ability and hollow moral conviction.

Hoffman spoke. "I asked Mr. Darden to keep the information secret because I thought it might help us defuse this national crisis."

"That is why we insisted on meeting with you privately," the FBI Director said.

The President squirmed in his chair and cleared his throat, at last gave in. "Okay, what do you want?"

Hoffman spoke again. "The country might never recover if this information ever got out."

"I doubt it, but go on."

"A sitting official—your closest confidant—blows up a hotel to incite national fear and anger and blames it on foreign terrorists. Then he uses that fear to justify his takeover of the country by declaring Martial Law. Think about it."

Slowly, dimly, the President seemed to get the idea. His face began to heat up and turn a darker shade of tan. Had it ever occurred to him that he had been duped? Or had he simply looked the other way out of weakness?

"And what do you want me to do?"

Mr. Hoffman continued, patient as a prosecutor leading a defendant to a predetermined and inevitable plea bargain.

"We want you to demand his immediate resignation and to announce that you have referred his actions to the Attorney General for criminal charges."

"Hah!"

The President yanked his manure covered boot from the table and rose halfway out of his seat. "I won't do it."

"And then, Mr. President, you will—yourself—resign from office."

The President leaned toward Hoffman with an enraged snarl on his face.

"I tell you, I won't do it! You State Department bluebloods— you snots! Always think you know better'n us, don't you? With your fancy manners and foreign tongues, you mock us behind our backs, don't you? Well, this is one ol' cowhand you can't just kick out the back door. Trying to make me look like a fool."

The President kicked a chair across the room where it bounced off the wall and spun awkwardly in the air. The sound of its spinning seat was surreal in the quiet conference room.

"I tell you, I won't do it!"

"Yes, you will," the FBI Director said firmly. "Call him now."

The men from Congress nodded their heads vigorously. Veterans of power politics, they smelled blood in the water and already were calculating how to get their share of the spoils.

The President's eyes narrowed, became dark lesions between the heavy folds of wrinkles.

"And just how can you be so sure I will?"

Mr. Hoffman replied, "If you don't, we release all the information about your secret war of torture and you can take your chances with the public and the courts."

"In which case, you will stand trial for war crimes alongside him," said the FBI Director.

"But I had nothing to do with it."

"Perhaps," said Darden. "But I doubt it."

"He acted on his own."

Darden spoke again, "Do you think anyone will believe you? The public is outraged, as they should be. After all your evasions and lies, how could they believe you?"

"So y'all want to throw me under the stampede."

"No," said the Undersecretary, as he pushed the phone across the table toward the Chief Executive. His voice became almost soft. "Just for once, we want you to act like a President."

CHAPTER 51

"Twelve months to the day," Linda said.

"Seems like years," he answered. "I woke up again last night dreaming about it."

"I know. I felt you struggling in your sleep."

Darden fumbled with his tie, trying to get the length of it just right, where the tip would cover his belt buckle. He hardly ever wore a tie anymore so he was out of practice and couldn't get it to come out right. Watching himself in the mirror, he noticed once again how much his fingers trembled, saw that he was almost gray-headed now, his hair and beard flecked with new color.

"Admiring your distinguished self again?"

She shuffled over on wide-spread feet and drew the bright blue silk print from his fingers, stood before him and re-tied the knot, got it right the first time then snugged it up to his collar button.

"Not so tight," he said crossly. "You know I don't like that feeling around my neck."

She gave him her cool look, the one he'd come to recognize as mildly scolding.

"Sorry," he said.

He had trouble holding his temper lately, which occasionally brought on that look from her. He was grateful that the scolding look was usually her strongest response, because he often deserved much worse due to his unpredictable anger. No matter how hard he tried to dampen it, his temper flared up at even the smallest things.

He did not sleep well anymore either; most every night was

filled with a cycle of restless hours when his limbs twitched of their own accord, and he woke up shivering between damp sheets, his heart loping inside his ribcage. Ever since the medics brought him back to life in the prison infirmary he'd known something was wrong inside his head, and he knew it would probably always be wrong. At times, he was jumpy as a bird; most always he was irritable; every night he woke from awful nightmares. The psychiatrist he consulted said it was Post Traumatic Stress Disorder and that it would take a long time to recover. Anti-depressants helped, but he suspected his brain would not ever fully return to normal, just as his lungs and throat would never fully heal. Some scars are permanent, he thought.

"No need to be nervous," she said. "Think of it as the end of your ordeal. After today, you have closure."

"Not if he gets away with it."

"He won't. Not after you tell them the truth."

The calmness of her touch and voice soothed his ragged nerves a bit. Twelve months, he thought, twelve months since the day he met her and she made his life worth living, but it was also the first anniversary of the Spring Break Bombing in Daytona, as it had come to be known. The day his life changed. Since then he had become famous; soon he would even be rich. The last year had been filled with television appearances and speaking engagements at universities. He had done countless interviews and published several major pieces in national news magazines that paralleled the long-running trial of the War Hawk.

After Darden testified today, everyone would also know his face. His book would hit the stores within a few weeks and his agent said it would sell millions of copies.

At this point he was an unqualified success with an endless string of opportunities ahead, and he was supremely grateful to be alive. He loved his new wife and they would be wealthy by the end of the year. Best of all, her swollen belly promised a new life ahead for them to share, and already he had learned the hopeful feelings that a future child produced in his mind, feelings of fatherhood that were beyond understanding.

Still there was unease deep inside him. Had it all been worth it?

She kissed him on the cheek and they put on their coats and left the suite to catch their ride downstairs. Provided by the prosecution, their car would be high security with a plainclothes guard on board.

One way Darden knew he had made it to the top was the amount of hate mail he received, much of it fueled by talk radio. His agent said a reaction from the lunatic fringe was inevitable now that he was a national figure, and he couldn't dispute that the laudatory mail sent to him outnumbered the haters by more than three to one. Still, notoriety made him uneasy. Even with an unlisted address and phone, the memory of being kidnapped and imprisoned would not go away, and he felt like a target much of the time.

They arrived at the United States District Courthouse on Constitution Avenue amidst a surging storm of reporters, media trucks, and thousands of protestors lining the street. Metal barricades and National Guardsmen held back the Red Sea of people and kept the street open to allow courthouse traffic to make it through the horde.

From inside the security of the car, they watched demonstrators chanting and waving signs on the sidewalks. Some of them damned the trial and others praised it, but unending protests between the left and right had become a permanent fixture in Washington. Each new revelation about the previous Administration brought the crowds of demonstrators out onto the streets again to throw insults at one another.

Linda turned to him. "This is the way New York felt the night I was on *Sixty Minutes*."

"Except the nation is functioning now."

"Well, better anyway."

As soon as the new President took office, he had announced that his Administration would scrupulously maintain all civil liberties. That drew a clear line between him and his predecessor and it calmed the nation, but it also meant that radicals fought each other constantly, with their battles usually playing out in public places. The protestors were a nuisance and made governing difficult to the point that business leaders called for more order, but the President steadfastly refused to crack down on the protests. He reasoned that Civil War had barely been averted and it would take time for tensions to dissipate. If the federal government suppressed those tensions, they might develop into underground warfare. Better to let people of excessive passion scream it out in the streets and keep the conflict in the open, he insisted.

The war crimes trial of the War Hawk was in its ninth week and the nation talked of little else. Viewers collected around computer screens and televisions everywhere to see what would happen next. Cabbies kept their radios blaring with it, all day, every day. Students tracked the proceedings on their cell phones. Arguments broke out in barbershops. Fights in bars were commonplace, but no one turned off the news. It was the biggest story since Kennedy's assassination and everyone knew history was taking shape before their eyes, and everybody had an opinion about it.

When Darden entered the courtroom, a collective buzz rose from the spectators. They knew he was the key witness for the prosecution because he could corroborate so much of the earlier testimony against the defendant. Already the evidence was overwhelming because the War Hawk's aides had caved in as soon as they faced charges of treason and conspiracy. No amount of loyalty to the man would induce a single one of them to risk a potential sentence of execution.

Prior to Darden, the most damning witness had been Peyton Marshall, the wealthy kingmaker from Virginia. To avoid murder charges, he explained in great detail how he had taken Baines' plan to privatize surveillance, detention and interrogation of potential terrorists to the War Hawk. The plan had not been his, of course. It was all Doctor Josiah Baines' idea. How unfortunate that Baines was confined in a hospital for the criminally insane and unable to refute this point. The broad outline and details of the plan had strictly originated with Baines, the plan's creator. He,

Marshall, only served as a conduit, a way to pose the plan to the War Hawk.

Once the plan was underway and the War Hawk had financial control, everything changed, according to Marshall's testimony. The War Hawk expanded its scope and rationale. It became a means to eliminate all political opposition to his true aim, which was to take over the country and install a military dictatorship; of course, with the War Hawk himself at the top. Marshall testified he knew nothing about the Spring Break Bombing or the War Hawk's intention to declare Martial Law.

Even though it was obvious Marshall was only interested in saving his own skin, his testimony was damning nonetheless. The pieces of Marshall's story fit the evidence and chain of events so neatly that they confirmed the War Hawk's guilt.

At eighteen minutes after ten, Darden took the stand and found himself shaking, unable to keep his hands still, not with fear but with the portent of the moment. He was helping to convict the War Hawk of the crimes of treason, torture, and murder, and he was glad of it. The man deserved the worst sentence the court could give him. His official legacy was dead citizens; lives ruined; some like Darden himself permanently damaged. No official had ever served his country worse.

As Darden took the stand, a distant sound of thunder shook the walls of the building, vibrating the room as if it were a movie theater. The spring storm that had threatened all morning arrived and rain pounded on the roof as the thunderstorm descended on them like artillery fire.

Darden looked out at the silent, bleached faces in the courtroom and remembered how shocked he and Linda had been the first time they saw the video of Texas' torture. Now the spectators in the court wore the same shock on their faces, because they had watched the torture video shortly before he took the stand.

In that moment, he realized he had at least accomplished one thing with his efforts. The public, too, would eventually see the video, and the American people would witness the true horror of torture and they would be repulsed by what they saw, by the pointlessness of it, and they would reject it for what it really was—cruel and unusual punishment without benefit of charge, trial, or jury—expressly prohibited by the Constitution. He hoped they would also come to agree that is was a barbaric act unworthy of a civilized nation.

CHAPTER 52

The second video shown to the court was far different from the first. It had been delivered to Linda's office by mail while Darden was imprisoned in Virginia. The FBI had held a copy for almost a year, but Darden had not released it to the public at the request of the prosecutors.

Though it was also a homemade recording of poor quality, the setting was not the same. The camera pointed at a plain kitchen table with a background of newspapers stuck on the wall behind to confirm the date. A healthy and strong version of Texas appeared in the frame and grinned for the camera, though it was not a grin of humor. It was more a mocking grimace, an expression of the emotionless void inside him.

He tested the sound level. "My name is Hoyt Bellows."

Angry freckles and moles covered his permanently sunburned face, the scars about his mouth spoke of many fights in the past. His eyes were flat and empty as the deserts of the Mideast. Darden had never seen such a maw of a face—the man behind it was long bereft of human feelings, perhaps even human thought.

His face reminded Darden of an animal he had once seen in a zoo, a bear who had been caged in a tiny cell so long he had gone insane and in response to his imprisonment paced back and forth, rubbing against the bars incessantly with the same motion; rubbing the same spot on the same bars, scratching the same point on his furry rump hour after hour until the skin was exposed and raw, then continued rubbing until the bare spot was a dangerous sore. The bear's eyes had a wild madness in them, a mindless boredom or perhaps displacement that drove it toward self-destruction.

Texas sat at the kitchen table, reached forward and adjusted the camera a bit, drew the microphone closer before he began.

"My name is Hoyt Bellows, former United States Marine, and I am the man who bombed the Tropical Vista Hotel in Daytona Beach Florida in spring of 2008."

He paused and waited for the confession to sink in to anyone viewing the disc. His admission that he had killed hundreds of innocent vacationers had an earthshaking effect on the courtroom and sucked all normal stability from the space. Every head craned forward, every face rapt; they all were locked on the screen by the blunt, cold confession of this mass murderer.

"I bombed the hotel because the War Hawk paid me four-million-eight-hundred-thousand dollars to do it. He said it was for the ultimate good of the country and it would make us stronger. I didn't believe him then, and I don't believe him now. I think he had his own reasons.

"But you can believe this—I know when someone is lying and he is a liar. You see, I know about liars because I am paid by the government of the United States to torture people until I get some version of their lies to pass as truth. You heard me right, I torture human beings in the name of the American people, so I know all about lying. How's that for a joke?"

He shifted in the chair, put his hard fists on the table, shook his head like a great beast as if to clear some annoying bugs from his face.

"By the way—"

He paused, looked down at the table, seemingly to get his voice right.

"If you see this video, I am already dead."

Again he shook his head to jolt something inside. Darden wondered how many indelible images of pain and terror must be contained in the man's mind, how crowded it must be with the unthinkable acts he had committed.

"I am making this video now to hold the War Hawk at bay,

to keep him from sending a hired gun to kill me, but it might not work. If he gets to me, I've arranged for this disc to be sent to someone who knows how to use it."

He stopped speaking for a moment, dropped his head forward and rubbed the reddish buzz cut on his scalp with a heavy hand. Once stopped, he seemed not to know how to start again. He appeared uncomfortable with words, a man who could only explain himself through action.

Like everyone in the courtroom, Darden watched the display without moving a muscle, his breathing shallow. No matter how many times he saw the video his reaction was the same. He felt loathing and pity for the man at the same time.

Texas finally raised his head and stared at the camera lens. The expression on his face was mixed; he seemed to want to explain himself, but he was so far removed from his innate humanity that he could not reach that part of himself anymore, could not find the thoughts and feelings that added up to the sum total of him, that he was a man without remorse, without regard for other human beings or their lives.

"I—" he started again, then stopped. "I just want you to know one thing. I kill and maim human beings, but it doesn't accomplish anything. No one wins, but your leaders want it done, so I do it. I am a product of this country, of you, of your complacence and your acceptance of the idea that we should rule the world."

His face turned hard again, the jaw clenched, harder than Darden would have thought possible. Cords of muscle popped out on his neck as a wind of rage swept through him.

"You think that's not true? Our forces are in every country in the world, manipulating, interfering, using force and violence to control events. You allow your government to do it, and in my way of thinking that's the same thing as you doing it yourself. I am nothing but your instrument. Your government turned me into a hard blade to kill in your name. How do you like that? Somebody like me, working for you."

He shrugged, paused, seemed suddenly to want to get it done. No patience for explaining things.

"Hell, what's the point? You won't believe me."

He reached out of the camera frame and retrieved a fat manila envelope, slid it in front of the mike. "Then, believe this— it's all in here."

He put his big hand on top of the envelope.

"Dates. Locations. Bank transfers. It's all here. Follow the money trail and you'll find I was paid to do the bombing through a private corporation controlled by a Virginian named Peyton Marshall. The money was funneled to his corporation by an intelligence unit operating directly under the orders of the War Hawk.

"So there you have it. All those people burned to a crisp in a hotel because one of your high-assed officials wanted more power. And I was paid to do it with your tax money. So the world turns. Some must die, that others may live."

Then, his eyes again looked directly into the lens, eyes so cold they might have been distant stars in a winter sky.

"And what do I care? I'm dead already."

CHAPTER 53

So now there would be justice after all, and justice was the only outcome that could bring a note of virtue to this whole ugly episode. This time, at least, the brutes had not won, because the War Hawk and his ilk would pay for their crimes in the end. Perhaps the desire for justice was humanity's gift from God, Darden thought, the one thing that truly sets us apart, an understanding that despite the terrible wrongs human beings commit, most of us still retain the impulse to right those wrongs, often failing in the attempt but nonetheless striving to bring the unjust to accounts.

He looked out over the courtroom and saw the source of justice in all those human faces, flawed, yet yearning to be better. He took a deep breath and suddenly felt good inside for the first time in a long while. Months of trepidation left him and his mind steadied. The nation was still alive and its hurts would mend eventually.

He looked at Linda sitting in the first row and smiled at her, mouthing the words, "You were right."

She smiled back and gave him the thumbs up sign with her right hand, her left resting on her enormous belly. She was pregnant with his healthy child and her face emanated admiration and joy, her eyes filled with great expectations for their future.

At this moment he knew for sure—yes—it had all been worth it. He stood guard when few others would, and his father would have been immensely proud of him for standing up to the brutes. Just as his father had helped in a small way to make the world a bit better, he had done the same. Soon, his own son would enter this world and it might be a better place for him to grow up, at least it would be more open.

Darden had made sure of that earlier in the morning when he sent out copies of the discs and documents to a dozen internet news sites, all the evidence he had accumulated throughout his investigation, including the contents of the envelope Texas had revealed on the second video. Oh, he had long ago given copies to the Undersecretary and to the FBI to help in the prosecution of the War Hawk, but none of them knew he had planned all along to release the evidence to the public as well.

He'd never agreed with their view that the most damning evidence against the President and other administration officials be kept secret. No, he had never accepted that idea. Unlike them, he believed secrecy was a major part of the mindset that led to the whole catastrophe. To his way of thinking, most secrecy was not about protecting people in service of the country; it was about covering up the warts and mistakes of leaders, hiding all the poor decisions made out of greed or incompetence or revenge that eventually grew into bigger lies and complacency.

That dirt would not be withheld, not on his watch. Everyone would find out about it and let the facts be known, sown into the jet stream of human knowledge. In the end, he trusted the public to handle the truth as much or more than those determined to keep it secret.

Let the public serve as the decision-makers, he believed, not a handful of self-serving officials. For all the uncomfortable facts he'd released and the many groups he had angered, he felt most sure of that, felt sure he had done the right thing in reporting the entire story.

Afterward, on the wet steps outside the courthouse, the shoving mass of reporters made it impossible to flee to the waiting car. The crowd gathered around them so closely he had to push men and microphones away from Linda's pregnant belly. He held up his hands and asked for their consideration, but they ignored his request. They shouted questions non-stop and pushed their microphones ever closer. He would have to stop and talk to them;

he couldn't risk someone jostling her dangerously in the free-for-all.

The news people had been waiting in the rain all morning; their hair dripped with water, their clothes soaked into limp rags; they could have been street people for all he knew, but they were on his side for the most part, members of the same team. He felt an affinity for their bedraggled persistence. He pulled Linda close and they stood side by side on the concrete steps, looking out over the drenched bodies, listening to the chants of protestors and the steady roar of agitated citizens who hooted and yelled in the background.

"Their passion is still up," he said to her. "Someone could get hurt here today."

Perhaps he could help calm them. He waited for the news people to give him a chance to speak, held up his hands to indicate he would make a statement.

The rain had stopped and he looked up and saw a break in the sky where a few roiling clouds tore apart on a high wind. A sharp jet of sunlight pierced the opening and flared through as it set the whole area alight. Suddenly the quivering raindrops on the trees turned to diamonds, and the crowd calmed briefly as sunlight transformed the gray world with brilliant spring colors. It was an extraordinary new day, alight with promise.

He turned to Linda. "I feel so good that—"

He sensed more than saw the arm that jutted between two reporters and pointed at him; he didn't even hear the shot. All that registered was the look of horror on Linda's face as the bullet struck him in the chest, a white hot saber point of sensation that burned its way deep into his core. Then he felt a wet heat at his center as the impact jerked his legs out from under him. Down, he closed his eyes and wondered why the wet pavement felt so cold against his cheek on such a bright spring day

EPILOGUE

Hamed heard the news about the American reporter after prayers at the mosque. Later, he walked through the streets of Baghdad with a heavy slowness, hardly aware of the turns he made on his way home. Home? What home, he thought momentarily? I have no home, only safe houses to which I go hide, houses which change at a moment's notice.

He had not been to his true home, the home of his father, in years. He dared not, for fear of capture or death. He lived with that fear constantly, and it weighed on him more each day. In recent weeks the fear grew so large, an understanding came to him that Allah no longer blessed his life. He had become nothing more than a hunted animal—a rabid dog that drove everyone indoors.

Even his success against the Americans brought him no self-contentment, certainly no joy. He had accomplished everything he wanted with them, and more. The discs he'd captured from the big Texan proved useful beyond his greatest hopes, and sending them to the hungry reporter had been his masterstroke, the best decision he had made in years, so why did news of the reporter's shooting disturb him? Why did the reporter's life matter more than the thousands of others who had died in the struggle?

The videos proved every ruthless thing the Americans had done, which united *jihadist* fighters everywhere. The crazy War Hawk was out of office, though another of the same stripe might well replace him soon. American pressure on his forces had eased, because their generals had to deal with the crisis back in their own homeland.

But most important, the Americans had been disgraced. Their credibility as liberators and lovers of freedom was broken.

306 • David Darracott

Not a sane man in the world of Islam would believe them now. No matter the dollars they spent or how many bombs they dropped, the Americans would lose here, because no country using such wretched methods to win could keep the respect of those who loved God.

At least, he could go to his end knowing that. He revealed the Americans as they truly were and they could never overcome that blow. Muslims would not accept their ways or their word. Some day the Americans would run out of patience, or money, or men and they would go home, but we will still be here with our own religion and our own laws.

He had won. He knew it. It was just a matter of time before the Americans admitted it. Yet, still no serenity came to him from Allah.

He turned a corner and looked for the familiar building that should be there, but it was not. Where had it gone? He must have lost his way again. After so many safe houses he had lost track of everything. He did not recognize anyone or anything on the street where he stood. He turned back to try again, continued walking, though he did not know where.

For all his victories in the name of Islam, Allah still would not grant him peace. He puzzled over this many nights while trying to sleep and still he received no answer. Finally he concluded he would get no answer because Allah no longer talked to him. His victories in war had cut him off from the one and true God.

Early in life he had only wanted wisdom and true understanding of Allah. Then he put off that quest to fight the Iranians and later the Americans. Now an old man, he found that so much killing crowded out his search for understanding. There was not enough room inside him, perhaps in anyone, for both wisdom and war.

He had chosen war, so to him, Allah no longer listened.

About The Author

David Darracott is the author of *Wasted* and other fiction available at amazon.com. He holds a Masters degree in English and is the recipient of writing awards for fiction and nonfiction, including a Hambidge Fellowship in 2009-2010. A graduate of Emory University, he lives in north Atlanta.

Visit his web site at www.David-Darracott.com

Made in the USA
Charleston, SC
17 February 2015